Mia's
IRISHMAN

THE WOMEN OF WORTHY SERIES - BOOK 2
A STRANDED TOGETHER ROMANCE

SERALYNN LEWIS

MIA'S IRISHMAN WAS THE MANUSCRIPT SUBMITTED
FOR THE SERIOUS WRITER'S WRITER OF THE YEAR CONTEST.

Copyright © 2020 by TimiDio Press, LLC

First paperback edition November 2020

Edited by Carla Rossi
Book cover & Formatting by Qamber Designs & Media

ISBN 978-1-952953-03-3 (paperback)
ISBN 978-1-952953-02-6 (ebook)

ACKNOWLEDGMENTS

My writing partners have been invaluable in reading and critiquing my stories during the draft stages. My sincere thanks to Cheryl Krmarczyk who has been with me since almost the beginning of this journey.

My partners at the Durham HCRW critique group who read and critiqued the beginning chapters of this book: Susan, LaVerne, Matto, and Mara. Thank you for your encouragement, comments, and support.

To my beta readers who gave me great feedback. Thanks goes to Debbie, Jan, Betty, Nancy, Rhonda, and April.

To my editor, Carla Rossi, who encouraged, inspired, and helped with the publishing aspect of being an author. Thank you.

"To forgive is to set a person free and discover that person was you."
— *Lewis B. Smedes*

Chapter 1

A deer shot out from nowhere and Mia Nardelli slammed on the brakes, but the Honda skidded on wet leaves and pitched down the steep ravine. Her muscles stiffened when she gripped the steering wheel and fought for control. Her terrified scream died in her throat.

The car plowed through saplings and grasses and bounced over rocks. Her arm jammed against the window and her head jerked and hit the headrest as a large branch shattered the windshield before the Honda hit a massive boulder.

Mia's body slammed forward, and she gasped for breath. Rough material smothered her face and knocked the wind out of her. Dazed and disoriented, her head throbbed, and the dust from the deflated airbag clogged her throat, making her cough. When she caught her breath, an eerie silence stretched around her.

With her wrist burning, she pressed her bloody sleeve against the wetness on her face. The metallic taste on her lips made her shiver. Taking deep breaths to calm herself, she shook her head. *How did this happen?*

With blurred vision and wooziness, she fumbled for the door handle. Loud creaking pierced her ears as she grunted and pushed the door open. Struggling, she stepped out, wincing at the throbbing pain in her ankle. Leaning on the side of the car, she cradled her wrist and stumbled to the car's trunk. A wavering creek flowed beyond the car's crumpled front end. The car hadn't rolled—a miracle that no doubt saved her life.

Blinking several times until her vision cleared, she surveyed the path the car took. She shook her head and peered at the steep ravine. *I have to get to the road and get help.* Tears gathered. She'd never be able to climb those soaring walls with the pain in her ankle and wrist.

Maybe if she sat in the car and waited. Maybe she'd be rescued. She took deep breaths to clear her mind. No one would look for her in this remote area. The tall pines stood sentry overlooking moss-covered rocks and hid her car from view.

Not a sign of life. When darkness came, the late summer air would turn cooler. Even in this isolated West Virginia wilderness, it wasn't uncommon for houses to be built near rivers and creeks.

She checked her cell phone, but it yielded no bars and the battery was getting low. Hopefully, a cell tower could be found nearby. Agonizing wrist pain made carrying camera equipment impossible. Everything went into the trunk along with her bulky purse. With her good hand, she shoved her useless phone into the jacket pocket.

Pain shot from her ankle to her heel and she limped along the creek's edge. She'd been eager to shoot more nature shots for her updated portfolio, and she stressed over having enough time to return home to pick up her nieces on the last day of gym camp.

Thankfully, she'd told her friend to take her nieces home with her in case she'd be late returning and hadn't anticipated an accident that would leave her stranded in the wilds of West Virginia. And worse, her brother was out of the country until Monday. She'd told him the housekeeper would be in town all week, but his housekeeper had been called out of town last night. Getting to civilization was her top priority now. She'd do whatever it took to get herself home, despite whatever injuries she has.

When her sister-in-law died, Mia returned to her hometown of Worthy, Ohio to care for her brother's two children. Her own tragedy buried deep, she dove headlong into caring for the two solemn toddlers while her brother attended to the family business. She dismissed returning to New York and high fashion photography and instead focused on her two nieces—a welcome relief from fashion divas and the pain of loss. The trauma of losing her husband and the realization she'd never have children had gutted her.

For the past five years, she took photos of her family on special occasions. She enjoyed being a doting aunt. Seeing her nieces' animated faces in her mind's eye gave her a reprieve from the intense pain.

The dappled sun dipped behind the hills. The cracked face on her watch read five P.M. Worry about the girls crowded her thoughts and caused her heart to ache. She had mentioned to her friend she might occasionally be out of cell range, but knew her friend would have collected the girls from camp. As each step became more and more difficult, she focused on moving toward her goal of getting home.

Excruciating pain in her wrist pushed her beyond her limits and the sting in her face kept her jaw still. Her ankle ached with every step. She wouldn't be able to go any further when the suffering proved too much. What would happen then? With God's help and her sheer force of will, she plodded along.

She trudged along the creek's edge until it ran into a gully and found a shallow section where she could cross. Focusing on the other side would keep her from thinking about her fear of water. Her mind concentrated on getting across the wide creek rather than on the gurgling water that splashed with every step. Stopping every few steps to maintain her balance on her bum ankle, the chilly water eased the throbbing in her ankle. Her lips trembled and sweat beaded on her forehead as she waded across the broad creek.

The gully narrowed, and she slumped against a rock. A dead end. No ground on either side of the creek for her to continue on and she couldn't walk in the creek. Not happening. Shrubs and trees spilled from the rocky ridge in front of her and the musky scent of wet earth filled her nostrils.

Climbing to the road sounded easier now. No use whining over it. She'd come too far and she couldn't go back now. She'd climb the cliff and hoped to find a house.

A skinny branch dangled overhead. Everything ached as she stretched too far and too fast and then slipped. Her injured hand flew up on impulse, but it wouldn't hold. Sudden pain ripped a scream from her throat. The sound bounced off the walls of the ravine as she lost her balance. The phone flew from her pocket and bounced on the rocks with her tumbling after it as it hit the water and sank before she landed with a thud on the rock-strewn creek bed.

Lord, keep me. Protect me and send an angel to find me.

Then darkness swept over her.

Sean McDermott sipped fragrant coffee as he leaned on the

rustic cabin's porch railing and stared at the ominous early evening clouds. He sniffed the air. Fierce weather headed his way. Rain. It suited his mood.

He'd spent the last five days unwinding after a grueling year of treating a multitude of sick animals. He found solace in the remote West Virginia hills. Getting away from his life as a veterinarian to write the animal husbandry manual might be easier than facing his lonely life. *Maybe.*

His Irish setter raced to the steps, barked, then ran to the trail and back again. Something was wrong.

"What is it, boy?"

Sean stuffed his feet in boots, leaped from the steps and followed Rusty, who barked and ran in circles waiting for him to follow, then raced ahead.

"Better not be leading me on a wild goose chase. Weather could turn any minute."

After a fifteen-minute walk, the dog disappeared over the edge. Sean shook his head. He slid down the steep incline and spotted a bloody hand peeking out from the rocks below. He crouched as Rusty sat, tongue lolling, next to the body.

A woman. Dead or unconscious? *Lord, let her be alive.* He checked her pulse. Weak. Dried blood on her hands, severe cuts on her face and a swollen wrist. She was chilled to the bone.

Even with the bruises and cuts, her beauty showed through. Blood, dirt, and grime covered her blond hair and porcelain white skin. Who was she? Why was she in the middle of nowhere?

He pushed open her eyelids. When the pupils reacted to light, her incredible blue irises made him breathe deep. No concussion.

He couldn't carry her and go the same way he came. He'd have to take the long way around and it would take some time. Cradling her, he stumbled toward the trail to the cabin and hoped to make it before the heavens opened. Hopefully, the landline still worked, but if it wasn't…

Unhitching the horse trailer from his pickup in the rain and mud was out of the question. He'd already tried that a time or two and got stuck, even though he'd had several tons of gravel delivered to the cabin last year. The weight of the fifth-wheel truck sank even with the additional layer of rocks. Historically, that rickety county bridge washed out, making it dangerous to even try.

Sean shifted the woman in his arms. The closest farm was twenty miles away. Riding through the meadows and creeks on Thunder would cut the trip short, but wasn't an option with night falling. If he waited until morning, the horse's fear of storms would kick in. He hoped the landline worked because this woman needed it.

Out of breath, he reached the cabin steps, but not before the clouds dropped their load. Rivulets of water cascaded down his cheeks like a waterfall. He protected her from the rain with his chest and arms, and she groaned but didn't awaken. Rusty frolicked at his feet, shook his body, and hurled water everywhere.

Sean flung his hair from his eyes, shouldered his way into the cabin and laid the woman on the double bed in the small, spare room. One wet leather boot hung off the side. Removing it revealed an ankle swollen to double its size. He examined it and determined it wasn't broken, but severely sprained.

Her wrist was another matter. It appeared to be broken, but without an x-ray, he couldn't determine how severe of a break it was.

Grabbing a towel, he dried her hair as best he could before he filled a bowl with warm water and squirted mild soap on a washcloth. With a gentle touch, he washed her face and hands.

The wounds near her hairline and chin needed stitches, but he had taken his medical kit out of the truck. He hadn't expected to need it here. The other cuts and scratches weren't deep. Despite the wounds, her face carried a model's bone structure. Her injuries pricked his heart. He applied antibiotics and butterflied the cuts.

Sean inhaled. "You reek, Rusty. No sleeping on the bed tonight."

The dog whimpered.

"Sorry, pal. The lady won't want dog smell on her."

She moaned and shivered.

He covered her with a blanket and retrieved a cotton shirt and a small pair of drawstring shorts that might fit. Well, somewhat.

Removing her zippered nylon jacket proved futile. Cutting it off was his only option. Her swollen wrist would have to be set, but he needed to warm her first.

He kept his eyes on her face in case she awoke as he dressed her. Sean pulled down the covers on the other side of the bed and placed her between the sheets. He drew the wet comforter off the bed and replaced it with another blanket.

"Keep an eye on her, buddy."

Quickstepping to the ancient black desk phone in the kitchen, he picked up the receiver. Dead. How soon the phone would work again was anyone's guess. The driving rain pummeled him as he ran to the truck and jumped in and turned on the radio. Good reception depended on the weather and the radio wasn't cooperating either. He pinched the bridge of his nose between his thumb and forefinger, then closed his eyes and stroked his beard. The only solution he had was to wait out the storm and then get help.

Running back into the cabin, he stowed his boots in the kitchen and dried his hair. After he dressed in fresh clothes, he went in search of leftover shims in the storage room to serve as splints. He'd elevate the swollen ankle he believed was an acute sprain. Now if she would wake up, he'd talk to her.

With a light touch, he set the wrist as best he could, placed the shims, and wrapped ace bandages from the first aid kit he kept at the cabin.

"You can wake up now, young lady." To his own ears, he sounded like a stuffy doctor with an awful bedside manner.

Sean checked his medicine cabinet for pain medication and then made a cup of tea. He positioned the reading chair near the bed to monitor her. She'd be in pain and afraid when she woke up. Time to pray. For her and for himself.

He settled into the chair, grabbed his Bible, and read Psalm 91. The words reassured him and he contemplated yet again how she came to be in this remote area. Then resigned himself to work on the manual while the wind howled and the rain and tree branches pelted against the windows. No way to know how bad the storm would be since no television, internet or cell service reached this far out.

After giving Rusty treats for having saved the woman, his dog raced to the bedroom to maintain his vigil over her. Sean eased himself into his reading chair and began the arduous process of organizing his notes. His eyes grew heavy and his hands slipped from the keyboard.

His laptop slid off his lap to the floor with a thump.

The woman moaned, but didn't open her eyes. The storm raged on. The generator hummed outside the bedroom window and made him thankful they wouldn't be in a darkened room.

He moved to the bed, rubbed her arm, and hoped she'd awaken, but she didn't. He sighed. Who was she? His colleagues pressed him to finish the manual, but he'd take on her care until he got her to a hospital.

He washed up, fixed breakfast, and hoped the smell of bacon and eggs roused his guest. It didn't. He fed Rusty and let the dog out while he ate his own breakfast.

Sean sat near the woman's bed and worked. He checked her from time to time and dreaded what he'd do when she awoke. He wasn't comfortable around women. Not since his accident.

Keeping an injured woman in his cabin was impossible. He didn't have the wherewithal to care for an invalid. He'd have to take the day off, ride over to Grogan's farm and call an ambulance. Then he'd be free to work and get back to his practice.

He drew his hands through his hair, paced the room and squinted at the guest room. Forget it. The weather wasn't cooperating, and neither was the woman. He slumped into the chair and knew he'd make her care top priority regardless of what he wanted, what happened outside, or if he worked on the manual.

He rubbed his dog's ears. "We better feed Thunder. I'm sure you want a break from your vigil. I don't think she'll wake up soon."

Rusty followed at his heels, through the gusting wind and sideways rain.

Dropping food into Thunder's trough, Sean then brushed

the horse. "I don't know what I'll do about the lady in there. She's hurt, and the storm isn't letting up. We're stuck here until the creek recedes and she needs more medical care than I can supply."

He leaned his head against the wall as the rain and wind battered the small barn, spooked Thunder, and made him prance in the tiny enclosure.

"Whoa, boy." He moved to pat the horse and ease his fear. He whispered in the horse's ear. After a while, the horse settled and Sean replenished the horse's water.

When he returned to the cabin, Rusty raced past. Sean stepped into the room and checked the woman's pulse and touched her forehead. She had no fever. He checked her eyes again. "She sure has beautiful eyes," he whispered.

But when she sees my face, she'll scream.

Hours flew by and the storm continued. Sean tapped the woman's good hand. "She should be awake by now, Rusty. I'm worried."

He adjusted the pillow, examined her foot and moved to sit next to her. Sean drew her hair from her face. "Won't you please wake up?" His voice was soft and he took a gentle hold of her shoulder and a slight groan escaped her lips.

Over twenty-four hours and she hadn't woken. She'd be dehydrated soon. He washed her face again, and with a soft touch replaced the band-aids. Pacing in the living room, he threw his hands in the air.

I'm not a medical doctor, Lord. Please wake her up so she can tell me who she is and what happened to her. There's a reason you brought her here, but I'm at a loss as to know why. Please help.

A drawn-out groan pierced the silence. Rusty whimpered. She thrashed about until he stepped closer and touched her arm. "It's OK. You're OK." The same soft tone he used with terrified animals calmed her and she drew a deep breath. "Please wake up. I want to help you."

She didn't move for more than an hour, and he knew he'd spend the night in the chair again. It damaged his neck and back, but he'd stay the course until she woke up.

The wind howled and the rain pounded with relentless force. He settled into the chair to work on the book's outline and hoped it distracted him from the woman in the bed.

He nodded off instead.

Later, he woke with a start, rolled his shoulders and opened his eyes to find the woman staring at him.

The intense crystal-blue gaze he'd waited for pinned him to the chair. "Who are you? And where am I?"

Chapter 2

The woman hadn't screamed. *Thank you, Lord.* Sean rose from the chair with slow precision and moved closer to the bed. Her eyes widened as he approached and she leaned into the pillows.

Sean stopped in his tracks at her indrawn breath. "How are you feeling?"

"Who are you?" Her voice rasped.

He couldn't be sure if she was in trouble and if it would visit his home and business. "Can you tell me what happened to you?"

Tension filled her face. "I don't know." She squinted as if she grasped at memories. "I remember nothing." She drew her hand to her forehead, and a startled look crossed her face. "What happened to my wrist?" She moaned and touched the bandages on her face.

"I think you had an accident. Rusty found you and I brought you here. You've been unconscious for over twenty-four hours."

"Rusty?"

"Aye. My dog." Rusty laid his head on the edge of the bed. His tail thumped and her uninjured hand moved to scratch the dog's ears while she stared at Sean.

"Where am I?" Her eyes narrowed. "Did you hurt me?"

His face must have shown his angst because the tension in her body faded. "I wouldn't hurt you, Lass. I found you injured near the creek, set your wrist, cleaned and dressed your cuts, and elevated your ankle."

"Are you a doctor?"

"I'm a veterinarian."

Her loveliness and angelic voice moved him, but her injuries prevented him from thinking along those lines. With his full beard and the monstrous scar, she probably thought him a mountain man with an evil streak.

"We're in a remote area of West Virginia." Sean paused and followed her gaze to the plaque on the wall with his twin's name on it.

She lifted her good hand and pointed. "Shannon's place. You must be Shannon." Her head cocked and her gaze was clear. "But you're not from around here, are you? That's an Irish name, isn't it?"

"That it is." He breathed an inner sigh of relief. He didn't like misleading her, but for the time being, it was the safest bet. He didn't need any further difficulties in his already complicated life. What was the harm in letting her believe he was his twin? Besides, she could be real trouble. He leaned in. "And you are?"

She scrunched her brow. "I don't know who I am. There's a big, black hole where my brain used to be. Nothingness." Her eyes filled and the overflow dripped onto her damaged cheeks.

Memories of the buckets of tears shed by his family members pierced his brain. Sean froze and swallowed the ping pong ball in his throat. "There now, don't cry. You've probably had a knock to your head. Your memory will return. Give it time."

She didn't utter a sound, but the trail of tears covered her face. The eeriness of how she cried made his insides turn to mush, and he stood glued to the spot. Rusty whimpered and nuzzled his snout near her forearm. The dog reassured her better than he did. What was he supposed to do with an emotional female in his small cabin?

She drew in a breath and smiled at the dog. "Hey there, Rusty. Thank you for finding me." She scratched the dog's ears with her good hand and chanced a glance in his direction.

Sean moved near her. "I'm so sorry. I'll give you pain medication."

"He won't hurt me, will he, Rusty?"

He cringed as he heard her whisper to the dog. Thank goodness Rusty was with him.

He couldn't seem to put one foot in front of the other. The glass in his hand shook as he lifted it from the nightstand. "I'll help you so you can take the pills."

She lowered her voice to a whisper and glanced at the tablets. "What are they?"

He showed her the bottle. "Extra strength aspirin. They're the only pain meds I have."

When he moved to give her water, her wariness made him clumsy and awkward. Her eyes captured his and he couldn't look away. He bent to lift her shoulders to place the cup to her lips. Her hair, despite the dirt and grime, had a fresh aroma like spring time. His lips curved as she drank and shifted into the pillows. Her stomach grumbled. Rusty barked and eased the tension in the room.

His heart beat like horses galloping on a race track. "Where are my manners? You must be starved after sleeping for over a day, and I don't know how long you were unconscious in that ravine."

"I've been here for two days?"

"More like eighteen hours. Ever since the storm. And it hasn't let up."

Her stomach protested again.

"Let me make you food. I don't have a wide variety, but I can make oatmeal or eggs and toast."

"Eggs and toast, please."

Perhaps she wasn't one of those women who chattered on and on. He hoped she enjoyed silence.

She was stunning. Her delicate features, marred though they were with her injuries, soothed his battered soul. He shook his head. She could be a criminal. What was he thinking?

He brought her a tray and plumped extra pillows behind her shoulders.

Her eyes darted around the room and her cheeks flushed. "I need to use the bathroom."

"Sorry." He helped her move her legs to the floor. "Can you stand?"

"I think so."

When she wobbled, he caught her around the waist and half carried her to the bathroom. She fit nicely in the crook of his arm. It'd been years since he held a woman that way. The church ladies hugged him every chance they got, but that didn't count. He couldn't even think of his patient along those lines. And with her injuries, she needed his help, not a drooling fool.

"I think I can take it from here," she said.

"Are you sure?" Her safety concerned him more than her modesty.

Her face turned a delightful shade of pink, and she nodded. He backed out and closed the door.

When she opened the door, she leaned on the door jamb.

He caught her watching him fluff her pillows and fixing the blankets. She limped and winced. He strode to her and put his arm around her waist. "Do you need me to carry you?"

"I can walk. Thanks for the offer, though." As she settled onto the bed and he arranged the covers, her stomach grumbled again, and she chuckled. "Too bad I can't control my wayward stomach."

The corner of his mouth turned up, and he placed the tray on her lap. "Eat up. It's plain but hardy."

She devoured everything on her plate and drank the entire glass of juice. She wiped her mouth and sighed. "Delicious. I feel better."

"Now we can talk."

Her chin trembled, but she nodded.

"You still don't remember your name or how you got to the creek?"

"I tried to recall, but hunger controlled my thoughts."

"Let's sort this out."

"Right. I remember I woke up to Rusty licking me and I begged him not to leave, but he didn't listen." Her shoulders slumped.

"He acted strange when he returned, so I followed him. The storm was coming, but something was wrong. Rusty fetches me when an animal in my care needs attention. A veritable panic button." He gave her a half smile and patted Rusty's back.

"I think I must have hit my head because I had a tremendous headache. I tried to follow him and must have blacked out. That's all I remember."

"Since you can't remember your name, I'll call you Lass. Is that OK?"

"Sure, whatever." She lifted one shoulder and smoothed

the patched blanket.

"This cabin is in the middle of nowhere in the hills of West Virginia. The nearest place is a farm twenty miles away. I can't imagine why you were all the way out here. Were you on a hike? You had on work out gear and hiking boots."

The soft shirt she stroked was four sizes too big. She paled.

"You were soaked and shivering. I had to get you into dry clothes. I'm sorry, but I had to cut the sleeves of your jacket. Your wrist was too swollen to do anything else. I cleaned the cuts on your face and hands and set your wrist. I'm sorry I had nothing better to use."

Lass flinched. "You took off my clothes?"

He sensed color flooding his cheeks. Even his beard wouldn't hide it. "I covered you with a sheet while I changed you. You're my patient."

"Did I have any identification? Why didn't you call an ambulance?"

"No ID. No ambulance."

"Why?" Her body tensed.

"Because the phone lines are down, and no cell, television, or internet out this far. And with the storm, the truck would sink into the mud, making it even more difficult to leave later on. Best place for you was to stay here, where it's warm and dry."

"But…" Her face gave away her thoughts.

He had to protect her even if she was frightened by waking in an unknown place not knowing who she was. And with a strange man. A scarred man.

"I won't hurt you. I promise. Besides, you have Rusty to protect you." The dog jumped on the bed and snuggled to her side. She absently watched him as she stroked the dog's forehead.

17

"You must have been hiking and fell, but it doesn't explain the glass shards I found in your cuts." Sean watched her face to see if she had any recollection, but only a blankness and a hint of frustration marred her gorgeous eyes.

"I don't know." She tilted her head and gave him a blank look. "I can't imagine glass in the middle of nowhere."

"Neither can I and if Thunder wasn't so afraid—."

"Who is Thunder?" Lass said.

"He's my horse."

"You have a horse?"

"Why can't you drive over to the next farm? Why ride the horse?"

"Because more than likely the bridge is out, and it's faster to get there by horse, but Thunder can't swim across flooded and fast-moving creeks. He's older, so I only take him on gentle rides."

Lass grimaced as she moved in the bed.

"Are you in pain?"

"My wrist hurts."

"How are the cuts on your face? And your ankle?"

"The ankle throbs and cuts on my face sting. I'm sure I'd have the starring role in a horror movie."

His lips curved. "It's not so bad, the bruises and cuts will heal."

"How'd you get the scar on your face?"

The Lass went for the jugular. He resisted the urge to lift his hand to the jagged scar stretched from his eye socket to the corner of his mouth and instead clenched his fists. His shoulders tensed and his voice clipped. "I fell off a horse."

"Thunder?"

"No." He didn't want to talk about his accident and definitely didn't want to remember the pain of loss.

"I like your accent. Have you been here long?"

"Seven years." His curt answers seemed to make her squirm, but she continued to stare at his face. His accent became more pronounced when confronted with his past. Stranded in a remote cabin with a beautiful woman asking personal questions tested him.

"Get some sleep. It'll help you heal." He gnashed his teeth and clamped his jaw shut.

Lass nodded, blinked. and smothered a yawn. "I guess you're right."

He got up, fussed with her covers, grabbed his laptop, and left the room. He'd check on her in an hour.

He paced in the living room and scrubbed his hand through his beard. The accident in Ireland was ages ago. *Please help her to focus on who she is and not on who I am.*

Chapter 3

For hours, the rain pummeled the window. Pine trees blocked the daylight. Lass's heart sank and fear rose in her throat. What if she never remembered her name? Or if she had no one to care for her? Was she destitute? Why had she been out in the middle of nowhere?

Shannon had saved her from the awful storm, and wariness filled her, but not enough to make her leave the warm bed to escape the situation.

Maybe if she studied her shoes and clothes, she'd remember her name. With that encouraging thought, she closed her eyes and fell into a deep sleep.

She awoke with hunger pangs and the tantalizing aroma of fresh-baked bread.

Shannon stepped into the room and cocked his head. "You're awake. Dinner is almost ready."

"Do I smell fresh bread?"

"I use a bread machine when I'm here." Shannon shrugged and his face colored. "I don't want to drive an hour to get groceries so I filled the freezer and pantry to last the duration."

"When did you get here?"

"Five days ago."

"How long will you be here?"

The corners of his eyes crinkled. "Until I finish my manual."

"Manual? Aren't you a vet?"

He heaved a long sigh. "I am, but I'm writing a manual on old-fashioned animal husbandry."

"Like from olden times?"

"Exactly."

"Can you get me my clothes and shoes?"

His expression showed her the question confused him. "Why?"

"If I touch my clothes and boots, I might remember something."

"Good idea."

Shannon was an attractive guy despite the scar and beard. He probably kept the beard to cover the scar. Understandable. Tall and muscular, he'd have to be strong to care for animals. Kind, too. Her heart thumped faster when he spoke with his Irish accent.

She couldn't afford to ponder him, his good looks, or his delightful speech. It could be dangerous for her and for him. She stared at her hands. No wedding or engagement ring. But that meant nothing. Did she have a husband or boyfriend?

While Shannon took excellent care of her, she couldn't be sure he was as courteous as he portrayed. Something in her heart made her fearful of interaction with men. Unable to understand her emotional state, her stomach flipped. Discovering who she was had to be her focus.

She recognized an immense kindness in his eyes when he brought in the folded items and shoes. She winced as she lifted her hand to touch the boots. He placed the clothing on her lap and she rubbed the ripped jacket and pants.

He dropped into the plaid chair next to the bed. "I'm sorry I ruined your clothes. They're expensive. The boots, too."

Her clothing told her she wasn't destitute. "Apparently."

"Remember anything?"

"No." She let out a heartfelt sigh. "I hoped I'd see them and remember something."

"A good idea, but no matter. In time you'll remember." His soft words eased her heart.

"I worry I won't remember. Then what? I can't stay here forever."

"Your family is most likely on a search for you. I can't get to Grogan's farm because of the storm. In the years I've come here, I've never seen a storm this extreme." He shook his head and gazed out the window.

"What do you see?"

"Rain and wind. Not as much wind as when you slept, but it's still windy. Trees have fallen, and the ground saturated and that'll topple more trees if it doesn't stop raining."

"Where's your horse?"

"In the barn."

"You have a barn?"

"And a few chickens for fresh eggs."

"Who takes care of your chickens when you're not here?"

"I brought them with me."

She widened her eyes. "You brought chickens with you?"

He grinned. "How else will I have fresh eggs?"

"What other animals did you bring?"

"Only Rusty, Thunder, and the chickens. Are you hungry?"

She nodded with vigor. "Can I sit at the table? You don't have to serve me in bed."

Sean helped her and her limp was less noticeable. The rest she'd gotten helped.

They stopped when they entered the living room. The river rock fireplace blazed with a roaring fire and gave the small cabin a homey coziness. Definitely a masculine room. The compact kitchen and dinette flanked the living room.

"How long have you owned this place?"

"Five years. I bought it as a retreat."

He helped her to the table and sat her in a chair that faced the fire.

"Where do you live?"

"Ohio."

She caught her breath. "I live in Ohio, too."

He gasped and blinked. "You remembered something." A smile lit his face and warmed her. "A step in the right direction."

"I don't know how I knew. But I can't remember where I live in Ohio." She breathed in. "But I like homemade bread. It smells divine."

"Your memory will return. Even if it's one memory at a time. We can't leave, but when we can, I'll take you to the nearest hospital."

Her stomach churned and her voice rose. "No!" She lowered her voice and looked away. "I mean, I'm afraid. Please don't force me to go." She placed her good hand on his arm. "Please." Her hunger dissipated.

He sat next to her and held her good hand. "We can't go anywhere until the rain stops and we don't know if the flooding will keep us trapped here. We'll deal with it as it comes, OK?" He patted her hand and left the table to get their food.

Now more than ever, she couldn't let him see she had a sore throat since she woke and had a headache in between taking aspirin. She breathed a sigh of relief. To leave this haven frightened her more than anything in her life, even her fear of water.

Her hand flew to her chest, and she hid her astonishment. She feared water? Why? She shivered, thankful he had turned away as he prepared their food.

"I trust a light meal is OK. Chicken soup, salad, and bread.

She peered at him as he set food on the table and she rubbed an unbandaged eyebrow. Should she be fearful of him? He said he wouldn't hurt her but she couldn't be certain.

Her stomach rumbled.

"Hungry are ya?" Sean chuckled.

She gave him a quick grin. "Yeah."

While they ate, he told her about the cabin and how he'd spent a month every year and vacations to work on it and the barn.

"Have you remembered anything new?" Excitement tinged his voice and he reached out to touch her hand. "You have, haven't you?"

She dropped one shoulder.

"Your name?"

"I'm...afraid of water."

"It's not much, but it's a start." He spooned soup into his mouth.

"Why did I remember a fear of water and not my name or why you found me in the middle of nowhere?"

"I don't know. It might be because your fear is linked to a traumatic event."

Mia's gaze traveled to the fireplace. "Could be."

While he did the dishes, she hobbled to the sofa.

He came in with the first aid supplies. "Let me re-wrap your ankle and elevate it on the coffee table."

"You don't have a television."

Shannon's lips turned down as he checked her injuries. "Don't like the distraction and don't want a dish or antenna. I come here for peace and quiet."

"Do you have any books to read?"

"Sure. What's your preference?" His face twisted. "Sorry."

His concern melted her heart, and she gave him a soft smile. "Anything except animal husbandry will do."

Nodding, he went in search of books for her to read until bedtime.

He laid several on the table. "Pick one and leave the rest for later. The Veronica Cannon book is the first in a series. So far there are eight. I have more when you've read these or if you don't like them, you can choose others."

"Thanks."

The wind roared and the rain beat against the tin roof and she hoped it continued until she remembered who she was. She didn't want to leave the cozy place or the man who took care of her. Too big of a world out there she had no recollection of.

He worked on his laptop in the soft leather chair across from her while she settled into the sofa and read the Veronica Cannon book. Something about the book gave her pause. She couldn't put her finger on it.

Soft cushions behind her shoulders comforted her, and she leaned into them and stared at the fire. Did she have a family who missed her and did they search for her? Was she far from home? She didn't know and it make her head ache.

"Are you OK?" he said.

"I'm drained and the wrist hurts."

"You should rest. I'll get you more aspirin."

She nodded, rose from the sofa, and he held her waist as he escorted her to the bedroom. She still favored her injured ankle. "Tomorrow I'll see if I can fashion you a crutch somehow. There's a plastic container in the bathroom cabinet under the sink with whatever toiletries you might need. Help yourself."

She shut the bathroom door and rummaged in the container to find the things she needed. After she brushed her teeth, she slipped into bed. He placed cushions under her injured ankle.

"I think you did too much with your hand tonight. Try to rest."

Rusty jumped on the bed and snuggled close to her. She welcomed the dog who saved her and patted his head with her good hand.

"Do you need me to stay with you tonight or will you be OK?"

"I'll be fine."

"Rest your wrist, Lass and I'll re-wrap it in the morning. I'll leave your door open. If you need me, shout."

The gentleness of the giant Irishman affected her soul. He had a resolute air about him and yet he showed compassion in every little detail—a trait seldom found in men today. How dependable. A man a woman could be interested in. His facial scar didn't bother her. Hopefully, she wasn't a woman who'd reject a scarred man.

Stop it. He cared for her because his dog found her and he wasn't a man to turn away an injured woman. That's what it was. Nothing else.

In her heart of hearts, she wished for more but couldn't go there if she didn't know her name or what she had done. *What had she done?* Had she fled a crime? A husband? She didn't believe so. How *had* she broken her wrist? So many questions and no answers. She wanted to curl into a ball and cry.

Chapter 4

As they neared the three-week mark, Lass had settled into a routine with Shannon. He checked her most severe injuries. They made breakfast, and she helped him feed the horse and collect the eggs.

And she avoided glancing at the creek waters that still flooded the bottom of the hill from the cabin.

Shannon said Thunder didn't trust strangers, but her soft touch and words calmed him as much as his owner. Thunder and Rusty distracted her from thoughts of her memory loss, but she couldn't use them like the crutch Shannon fashioned for her on the second day.

What would become of her? What skills did she have to get a job? And who would hire her with no home? Where would she go?

Each question pulled at her soul and caused an increased heaviness in her heart. She struggled every day to maintain a light attitude so Shannon wouldn't worry, but she'd reached the end of herself.

She came to terms with her situation, faced it, and would do what she must. No sense worrying about the unknown, but it swirled around her and had put the fear of God in her. Would Shannon allow her to stay here after he went home?

But that was unrealistic and would never work.

The cozy cabin, the sweet man who always made her feel welcome and at ease, and the location made her lack of identity a non-issue. Warm and comfortable. *I don't think I'll ever find a place that calls to my heart like this cabin.* She gazed around the rustic room and breathed in its essence. Or maybe Shannon captured her heart, but she knew better than to entertain those thoughts since she didn't know her name or if she had a husband and children.

Despite her misgivings, she'd allow Shannon to take her to the hospital for an exam and then call the police to see if by a miracle, she had family. Surely, the police have been involved in these situations and could help her.

She'd long ago stopped reading the novel in her lap and heaved a deep sigh. Shannon's voice shook her from her reverie when he stepped into the cabin. "Looks like the flood waters have receded."

"How soon do you think we'll be able to leave?" She forced a smile. The surprise on his face made her laugh. "What? Did you think I'd want to stay here indefinitely?"

Shannon scrubbed a hand over his scar and drew his fingers through his beard. "Well, at one time you didn't want to leave. Do you have cabin fever?"

"Yes, but I can't hide here anymore. I have to know if I have family or if I've done something terrible and face the consequences."

He sat next to her and took her uninjured hand in his and gazed into her eyes. "After spending time with you over the last three weeks, I know you've done nothing wrong. You're kind and helpful and Thunder likes you and that's a testament on your behalf."

"Still, I might be in serious trouble."

"Maybe. But I doubt it. I think it'll be resolved once we get to civilization."

"I'll miss you, Shannon."

He frowned and rubbed her good hand. "Who says we can't still be friends?"

"We live in a bubble right now. We don't know what the future holds, but we can dream about it." She forced a huge smile and turned her hand over to squeeze his.

Rumbling came from the vicinity of her midsection and caused both of them to laugh, altering the solemn mood.

"Guess that's my cue to make dinner."

Like an old couple who'd been together for years and knew one another's nuances, they tidied the kitchen after a flavorful dinner and sat in the living room. Both read books that she guessed he'd read a hundred times because she'd already gone through every book he owned twice.

Lass longed for more sound than the odd crackle of the logs. "How far along are you with the manual?"

"Done. I'll let it rest and go over it one more time."

She rose and roamed around the living room, fingered the ceramic dog and the candlesticks on the mantle, and warmed her hands by the fire. She sensed his gaze, but refused to speak otherwise every pain and heartache she held within herself would cross her lips.

"You seem nervous." Shannon's voice calmed her. He lifted his Bible from the side table. "Take a peek at the verses I've marked. Thought in time you'd be open to read them."

Her eyes met his and with a slow hand, she reached for the well-worn book. "Do you mind if I take it to bed with me?"

"Not at all. Hope you find something of value within its pages." His voice took on a faraway quality. "Helped me on more occasions than I can recall."

Clasping the book to her chest, she nodded, went to her room, and shut the door with a quiet click.

She took her time getting ready for bed but kept glancing at the well-worn book that laid by her pillows. When she had settled herself in bed, she opened the book to the first marked passage, then another one and then another until she came to the last one, Psalm 34:4 *"I sought the Lord, and He heard me, and delivered me from all my fears."*

Comfort seized her heart as she remembered a time on her knees when she begged God to forgive her.

Forgive her for what, she didn't know.

A memory. She remembered. After three weeks of only two memories surfacing, she had hope. Hope her full memory would return. She wanted to jump out of bed and tell Shannon, but he had taken Rusty out and hadn't returned yet.

Exhaustion overwhelmed her and took its toll. Her eyes grew heavy. The Bible slid to her chest, and she fell asleep.

Sean kept his door ajar in case Lass needed him, but she had slept well for days. He worried about telling her he'd go check the flood waters to see if they could leave, but she was ready now—and so was he. Or was he? He didn't want her to leave, but it was the right thing to do. And maybe once her memory returned, they'd explore something more. Then there was the whole name situation. He had to tell her soon that he was Sean and not Shannon, the name she'd pulled off the wall that seemed to bring her relief in her moment of terror. Explaining the lie could end everything. Why had he let it go on this long? Was it because he feared how she'd take it or if it was his own insecurity?

He laid on his bed and with his arm under his head. While he stroked Rusty's soft fur, he couldn't imagine his life without her.

A thump pierced the darkness. He stilled and listened with intent. Did she fall out of bed? When his breath stilled, he settled on the bed and closed his eyes.

His brow furrowed and Rusty stood on the bed. "What is it, boy?" The dog gave a soft whine and jumped off the bed and headed toward Lass's room.

Sean followed the dog and listened at her door. Whimpers came from inside, but when she screamed, he rushed in.

Her arms flailed, and the covers entangled her long legs. She kicked and moaned, but her eyes remained shut. Garbled words came out of her mouth and the tear track remnants on her cheeks broke his heart. He took quiet steps to the bed. He worried he might scare her when her voice became a high-pitched wail.

He slid his hand along her arm, captured her good hand, and crooned a few nonsensical things in her ear. He couldn't understand her words, but a terror gripped her. Something or someone had frightened her. She hadn't been that scared when she had awoken without her memory.

He stroked her arm, delighted in her softness, and held her good hand. "Lass. Wake up. You've had a bad dream."

She shook her head and her eyes opened to mere slits, then widened. "Shannon." She breathed his name as if it were a prayer on her lips. She raised her trembling body and hugged him. Her arms tightened around his shoulders.

At that moment, he could spend the rest of his life with this woman whose name he didn't know. Crazy and outrageous. He needed to clear his head. He'd only known her for three weeks. Maybe it was the Florence Nightingale effect?

He had learned his lesson the hard way, and he wasn't about to unlearn the lesson now, years later.

Her breathing became slow and rhythmic, and he took her hands from his shoulders and placed them on her lap. "Do you remember your dream?"

Her gaze shifted around the room then sought his face. "Snatches here and there."

He sat on the edge of the bed. "You want to talk about it?"

A charming shade of pink tinged her cheeks and her hands fidgeted. "Only if you hold me."

He straightened and recognized it as a mistake, but he wanted to know what had terrified her. He sighed and went around to the other side of the bed and crawled next to her on top of the covers and drew her to him. She felt so right in his arms, but he wouldn't go there. Dangerous. Given the situation and his past. And hers.

With her cheek on his chest and her hand over his heart, her words were soft. "The icy water surrounded me. No light anywhere. I forced myself to look for it, but the blackness covered me." She shivered in his arms and he held her close. "The life preserver kept me from choking on salty water and drowning. I didn't know how I came to be there."

"Your memory is returning. Not the best memory, though, is it?"

She shook her head and inhaled as he stroked her silky hair.

"Rest. In the morning, I'll check on the water levels and see if we can leave. Our supplies have dwindled and if we can't leave, we'll be forced to eat eggs or kill a chicken for food."

"You can't kill one of the chickens." She drew away from him and her voice rose. "You've named them. They're family."

He chuckled and tapped her nose. "Until they no longer produce eggs, then they become food, despite their names."

She grabbed his t-shirt when he moved. "Please don't leave."

"This isn't wise, Lass."

"Please. Just until I fall asleep then you can leave."

Sean sighed. This would be more difficult for him than for her, but he couldn't deny her his comfort. He listened to her soft breathing, but every time he moved to leave, she pulled him to her. He had to rest. His lids heavy, he struggled to stay awake until he gave in to his tiredness.

He furrowed his brow and thought he dreamed of her. Lass in his arms? Impossible. Early morning light came through the window and forced his eyes open. Her arms wrapped around him and her flowing hair tickled his nostrils with its unique fragrance. He gulped. Not good. He'd slept the night with her in his arms and he braced himself.

When he scanned her face, her eyes were wide, and she scooted nearer until her nose hovered inches from his. She touched his cheek and gave him a soft kiss. "Thank you."

He wanted to say, *you're welcome*, but he couldn't get the words out.

He stared at her lips as if they were an oasis in a barren desert until he couldn't stop himself, and kissed her with a force he himself feared. He savored her lips. Sunshine and moonbeams rolled into one and he struggled to pull away, but moved to the side of the bed and placed his forearms on his knees.

He couldn't look at her. "I'm sorry. I shouldn't have done that."

She placed a timid hand on his shoulder. "It's OK. I'm not offended or anything."

He chanced a look at her and noticed something faint in her eyes, but it couldn't be. Not yet. Not until they identified her.

His voice cracked. "Let me get breakfast, then I need to see about the flood waters." He left the room without a glance in her direction. If he did, he'd have to kiss her again and that couldn't be.

Leaning against his bedroom door, he called himself a fool to fall into a trap he had escaped years ago.

His peaceful haven would never be the same. Time to leave.

Chapter 5

Focus, Sean. Don't think about the kiss.

In the past three weeks, he attempted to ride to Grogan's farm a half a dozen times. But the depth of the water and the swiftness of the current kept him and Thunder a scant mile or two from his cabin.

He escaped the cabin so he wouldn't have to face her, left a note, and slipped over to the barn. Rusty's soulful eyes accused him as if he recognized Sean acted like a coward.

Guilt crowded his mind. Every time her lips formed the name *Shannon*, he cringed. She'd been in his care for a while and when he kissed her, his heart leaped, but it was wrong to deceive her. He had to get her to the hospital. If only for his peace of mind. She had been fearful and yet she trusted him. And he evaded the truth of who he was.

He sat next to her on the sofa in the evenings. They fell asleep a time or two and had awoken in one another's arms. Her warmth and softness made him feel whole again. A memory surfaced last night, and she had a breakthrough. And he kissed her this morning. He couldn't help himself and he had to get her away from the cabin before the situation became intolerable and things went where they shouldn't go. She'd leave and their little self-contained bubble would burst. Too often he fled to the barn to pray and spent time with Thunder.

The fast-flowing waters had receded enough that Thunder might cross it and make it to Grogan's farm to call for help, or better yet, get the rig packed and take them both out. He saddled Thunder and made his way to the creek.

A motor's rumble cut through the silence, and he craned his neck at the water-covered road. The ranch's Ford 250 pickup made its way to him.

His distant cousin, Brett Cooper, sat at the wheel with a grim look on his face until he spotted Sean. His cousin slowed the truck, rolled the window down and grinned. "You seem OK. Shannon worried for nothing."

He wanted to pummel Brett's smiling face and jovial manner. He didn't want Lass to get a look at his cousin. Brett attracted too many women.

"I'm fine. Why are you here? Why didn't Shannon come?" Sean chanced a glance at the cabin and Lass leaned over the cabin's railing and strained to see who talked to him. What was he thinking? He couldn't have his twin show his face here and expose the lie he'd created.

"Your father called. He's sick and told your brother he needed you to come to Ireland."

"Sick? Didn't Shannon call him?"

"Sure, but your dad wouldn't talk to him. He groused that your dad is stubborn and wants his firstborn to come as soon as possible."

Sean nodded. "Have the waters receded enough to get my rig through?"

"Got through with this monster. Just have to go slow."

Thunder nickered and Sean rubbed the horse's neck. "Have to close the cabin and get everything settled at the ranch before I leave for Ireland."

"I'll help you get things packed."

Sean panicked and his voice rose. "No." Then he lowered his voice. "I prefer to do things my way and don't want to rush. Da is melodramatic. I conferred with the doctor when he checked Da not three months ago."

Brett lifted one shoulder, removed his sunglasses, and squinted. "What are you hiding?"

"Nothing. Turn the truck around and take it to the ranch. Tell Shannon I'm OK and I'll be there sometime tomorrow. And then I'll make travel arrangements."

Sean didn't want to travel to Ireland. But in the seven years he had been in the states, his father never once asked him to come home when he felt poorly, so there must be a reason. Sean didn't care to think about it. He'd call him first, though.

"Shannon should go with me if Da isn't well."

"Can't. He and Wendy left this morning for equestrian competitions. Three times Shannon made the trip here, but the water levels hadn't dropped enough to get through. He and Wendy had to leave on their tour, so he sent me and hoped I could get through. Wants you to call him when you get in cell range."

Thunder stood in two inches of water and pulled at the bit.

"I have to go. Be careful. Flood waters can be treacherous."

With a salute, Brett turned the truck around and left.

Sean shifted on Thunder and they climbed the hill.

After he brushed the horse, Sean made his way inside. Once again, the skies darkened, and rain threatened. He'd forgotten to ask Brett about his animals and glad he hadn't asked if he'd heard about a missing person, otherwise his cousin would want to know why. And that was a conversation he wouldn't have wanted.

Inside, he spied a note and pen on the counter. She'd gone for a walk. He sighed his relief. She'd been grumpy and moaned about cabin fever in the past few days, but last night and this morning's kiss, well…the fresh air would do her good. And allow her to sleep better.

Last night had been the most restful sleep he'd had in a long time and he laughed at himself. Certain she'd slept well, too.

He could still taste her lips on his. He shook his head to change the direction of his thoughts. With her out for a walk, he'd pack the truck before she returned.

After he made several trips to the truck, a slight scratching came from her room. He spoke through the closed door. "Lass?"

Rusty whimpered, and he opened the door. "She didn't take you with her, boy?" The dog yawned and laid his head on his paws. His forlorn face spoke to Sean's heart.

He checked the time. Over two hours had passed since he found the note, and he wasn't certain how long she'd been gone since his cousin came to deliver the news. He wasn't worried—yet.

Packing the chickens proved to be more of a challenge than he expected. The wily creatures aggravated him. When he penned them and went outside the barn, a gentle rain fell. He hoped they wouldn't be trapped in the cabin for much longer.

She must have returned while he captured the chickens. Why hadn't she come to the barn?

Silence greeted him and wielded a coldness in his heart. Why hadn't he searched for her when the skies darkened? His concern for his dad and preparing for their departure in the morning consumed his thoughts.

It frightened him to think of her in the rain. He retrieved his slicker and flashlight and left the cabin with Rusty whimpering at his side. "We have to find her, boy. She's only recently recovered from her twisted ankle and her wrist isn't yet healed. I should've told her to stay in the cabin." Rusty barked, and he bent to rub the dog's ears. He shook the rain from his fur and plodded alongside Sean.

At war with himself over his lack of care, he tramped the way he came. The cold mist made it difficult for him to see. The darkened skies made him thankful he grabbed the flashlight before he headed out. The woman was a menace. She should have stayed indoors.

Rusty ran ahead in the same direction from where he found her. They got as far as the gully where she had been found, but she wasn't there. He doubled back a different way and still didn't see her.

His worry increased tenfold because the frosty air chilled him and she'd be wet. If she lost her way, it'd be more difficult to find her. He'd fetch Thunder and hunt for her on horseback. He grumbled about contentious women. She shouldn't be out on a day like today.

He continued to pray as he moved near the barn when Rusty's ears perked. "What is it, boy? You hear something?"

At the dog's bark, he stared as Rusty stood stock still and listened. Then he took off behind the barn.

Sean followed the dog around the rear of the barn and through the pasture. Rusty ran ahead like a thoroughbred Greyhound. He couldn't run like that and he couldn't afford to stumble and fall. Halfway through the pasture he spotted Rusty who ran to him and barked.

His steps quickened, but he spotted the dense cluster of trees beyond the pasture. The flashlight's beam split the darkness, but still nothing came into view. Rusty ran ahead and stopped at the wide base of an ancient oak tree.

As Sean stepped around the tree, Lass sat hunched under wet branches. He crouched next to her. The earthy scent of decaying leaves filled his nostrils. He checked her pulse, her eyes fluttered open, and her teeth chattered. "I'm so sorry. Shouldn't have gone for a walk."

Soaking wet and her skin clammy, her breath came out in raspy puffs.

"Can you walk?"

She grimaced. "No. I tripped on an exposed tree root and hurt my ankle again. I crawled to this tree to get out of the rain and have something to lean on. And I think I broke my other wrist when I fell and tried to catch myself."

He took off his slicker and wrapped it around her chilled body. A great wheezing cough made her shiver.

Sean watched the skies as she slumped against him and passed out again.

When he got her to her room, he removed the raincoat. She awoke with a start, her body chilled. "Can you get in the shower if I put a chair in there for you? Are you able to undress yourself?"

She gave him a withering look. "Yes."

He understood her reluctance for him to help her undress after he'd held and kissed her. But he had his doubts she'd accomplish it on her own. He hoped so. After the heated kiss that morning, he didn't need to see her soft body. He had to get out of his own head.

"Sit while I get what you need." Thankful he always left robes behind when he stayed there, he brought a stool and placed it in the shower along with whatever she might need. "Put your clothes on the floor and holler if you need me."

She nodded once and waited for him to leave. He listened at the door until the shower started. His confidence lagged and he hoped she could fend for herself. In the kitchen, he fixed an omelet for a late afternoon meal.

"Shannon."

He stepped into her room and rushed to catch her as she opened the door. "I don't feel well."

Placing her on the bed, he took her temperature. No wonder. She had a fever. She sat in the frigid rain for a long time. "I'm sorry I didn't search for you sooner."

Her hacking cough and wheezing concerned him. He hoped for light traffic in the morning so he'd get her to the hospital. She needed medical care. Now.

"It's my fault. I left a note. Did you see it?"

"Yes, but I figured Rusty was with you. Instead, you closed him in the bedroom."

"He slept, and I hadn't the heart to wake him, so I shut the door."

Another bout of coughing and wheezing.

"I made an omelet. I'll bring you hot tea along with aspirin for your pain."

She nodded and her eyes drifted shut.

Lass kept her newly broken wrist stationery as she fed herself with her other hand, but barely touched her food. He told her the flood waters had receded, and he'd take her to the hospital in the morning. Her newly broken wrist needed to be set and the other one examined.

His breath caught. "I'm worried about your cough."

She waved her partially healed hand. "I need to get warm and sleep. I'll be fine." But she didn't argue with him about a trip to the hospital. He hoped her painful wrists, fever, and coughing made her understand she needed expert medical care.

When he wrapped her wrist, the pain was so great she passed out again. Her breathing worried him. He was thankful he had the wisdom to make her eat and give her aspirin before he wrapped her wrists. The same ankle was swollen again. Holding her in his arms captured his mind.

Her temperature rose during the night and he knew he had to get her help. Thank God the bridge had been fixed and the roads were clear. And he should tell her he had to go to Ireland, but he didn't want to upset her.

The rain subsided to a fine drizzle and darkness crept in. While she slept, he continued his preparations to leave in the morning. He planned to leave by dawn. With the horse trailer and her sick, he'd have to go slow.

He'd packed the truck and readied last-minute items for their departure.

Her breathing rasped and her face flushed when he stepped into the room. The fall's unseasonably cold weather had given her a fever. He kissed her forehead. He'd sit at her bedside until morning. His worry increased by the minute.

Chapter 6

Dawn hadn't yet peeked through when Sean dressed and led Thunder into the trailer. With the last of his possessions covered by a tarp in the bed of his fifth wheel, he placed the chicken crates in with Thunder. He made a pot of coffee and peanut butter toast for breakfast.

Stepping into Lass's room, she had dressed but hadn't laced her boots. He laced them with quick movements. Her eyes dulled as a bout of coughing seized her.

He touched her forehead. "You have a fever. We need to get you to a hospital right now."

She leaned into his hand. "I don't know if I can walk, but—" Another bout of hoarse coughing doubled her over.

"Let me start the truck and get it warmed up. I'll get a blanket or two for the trip. It's cold and foggy this morning."

On his way to the truck, he poured coffee in a thermos and placed the toast in a bag for them to eat on the way.

When he returned, she slumped to the side of the chair, Rusty's head in her lap. "Lass. It's time to leave."

She struggled to rise from the chair and took one last look around the room and stared at the plaque as he wrapped her in blankets. He picked her up, placed her in the pickup, then belted her in. Rusty jumped in the backseat and laid his head near her headrest. She gave Sean a weak smile. After he slammed it shut, she leaned on the door.

He made a final sweep of the cabin to make sure he got everything, locked the door and strode to the truck. His forehead creased with worry.

"You want coffee? Toast?"

"The smell of coffee and peanut butter toast makes me nauseous."

The wheezing worried him, but he'd get her to the hospital. Well, as quick as he could, given the storm last night. His heart troubled him knowing he'd leave her stranded at a hospital with no one she remembered.

How had he become so attached to this beautiful woman? Her loveliness stood out and constricted his throat. She'd never long for him once her memory returned. Sean shook his head to clear his thoughts. Ireland and his sick father beckoned him.

Her breathing worried him, but he recognized they'd need to get to a hospital soon. When he hit an area with cell phone towers, he'd locate the nearest hospital, but as he caught sight of the gas gauge, he figured he'd have to stop for fuel. Sean wanted to hurry, but he didn't dare with the horse trailer in tow.

He stopped at the first gas station he found. She never stirred as he unplugged the cell phone from the car charger. He touched her forehead and covered her again, her labored breaths forced and raspy.

As he waited for the pickup to fill, he searched the internet for a nearby hospital, angry with himself. Why hadn't he known where the nearest hospital was? He chastised himself because he'd never had a need for it.

"Nice rig you got there," a man in the next aisle said.

"Thanks. Can you tell me, is the nearest hospital in Pershing?"

"Yup."

"Quickest way there is Route Ten, correct?"

"Been a pileup from the fog, so take Route Five."

"Longer?"

"About 10 minutes."

The man gave Sean directions, and he punched them into his phone.

When he got to the small hospital, pure chaos reigned with the number of ambulances and personnel rushing to take people in. He parked his rig in a far corner of the parking lot and opened Lass's door. Unconscious. He had to get her to doctors who could help her.

The triage nurse directed him to a treatment room to his left. A nurse stepped to his side and helped him place her on the gurney.

Sean studied Lass. "She has a fever and might have pneumonia. She's been coughing and is unresponsive."

Rolling her eyes, the nurse examined Lass. "I can see she's passed out. What happened to her face and wrists? Those aren't from the pileup. They're healing."

The nurse peered at Sean. She gave him a thoughtful look as if she gauged his truthfulness, but the doctor stepped in and kept a response from his lips and ground his jaw.

"This patient needs more care than we can give her. This is a rural clinic. With the accidents, we've depleted our resources. Any other time, we'd send her by ambulance, but with the various bridges out and the pileup, we'll have a medical flight transfer her to Columbus General."

"Who set her wrists? This break is recent, and the other appears to have been broken a while ago and set."

"I did. My dog found her near my cabin and I sheltered her. When the storm hit and the creeks overflowed, we couldn't get out. She doesn't remember who she is and didn't have ID."

"What about the lacerations on her face? Know how she got those?"

"No. She only remembered she's from Ohio and she's afraid of water."

The nurse gave him the once-over. He didn't like what her face told him and resisted the urge to touch his cheek. Did she think he had broken Lass's wrists or cut her face?

The on-call physician narrowed his gaze. "Are you a doctor?"

"No. I'm a vet. It's what I had to set the wrists and treat her cuts. She may have sprained her right ankle again, too." His jaw set.

"We'll take care of her. We'll stabilize her before we send her."

"See the nurse out front and explain the situation. See if there's a police officer who can take your statement about how and where you found her. Then you can follow her to Columbus General in your car."

Sean didn't tell him he'd leave her there or that he wouldn't travel to the regional hospital, but would head to his brother's ranch instead. The doctor didn't need to know and would never know. A low thing to do, but he had no choice.

"May I have a moment with her before I leave?"

The doctor raised a brow, gave a single nod, and left the room.

Sean touched her still form. They had administered oxygen to help her breathe, but she barely opened her exquisite blue eyes. He stroked his finger from her forehead to her chin, but she remained still.

"Lass," he whispered in her ear. "I have to leave. They'll fly you to Columbus to get you the care you need."

He kissed her forehead and stepped to the door. One last look over his shoulder and he left.

Emergency medical personnel struggled to manage the number of people in the waiting room in wheelchairs and gurneys in the hallways. They worked with efficiency but with the number of injured people they didn't have time to stop to talk to him. He stepped to registration, but the clerks bustled about and Sean didn't see a police officer. He couldn't afford to wait around for one. He'd call the police station when he got to the ranch.

I'm sorry, Lord. And I'm torn. Give me peace about leaving her. Bitterness rose in his throat. It had been one of the hardest things he had ever done, but he accepted it was best for them both. Nothing would ever come of his need for her, and she didn't need him, his moods or his ugly scar.

He jumped in his truck and pointed it to the ranch.

Rusty jumped into the front seat and whimpered. Sean rubbed his ears. "She'll get the best care, boy. Don't worry." He fought the sense of remorse in his heart.

The quiet in the cab allowed him to go over every aspect of his time at the cabin. He finished the manual, but hadn't edited it. He'd do that on the plane to Ireland.

His thoughts turned to Lass. Every conversation. Every hug. Every kiss. Not that there were many hugs and kisses, but the few they had shared rocked him to his core. He'd never experienced that before. Or maybe it was because he hadn't kissed or hugged anyone for a long time.

Sean frowned. He had sensed nothing like that with

Bridget, the woman who broke his heart. His mouth turned down. How could he try to see if what they had could develop into a deeper relationship? He didn't know her name or if she had a husband or if trouble followed her.

And now, he had no idea how to reach her at the hospital. What could he say? "A woman with amnesia had been on a medical flight transport. Can you tell me who she is?" Like the hospital would ever tell him anything. His stomach churned and grew into a huge ball of indigestion as the miles sped by.

With him on his way to Ireland in a few short days, he couldn't go to the hospital to find out who she was. Or maybe he could?

Chapter 7

Steve Nardelli and his best friend, Frank, strode into Columbus General's hospital corridor behind Dean Landers, the grim-faced detective. Sweat beaded Steve's upper lip and his heart pounded. He hated hospitals and for good reason.

Frank squeezed Steve's shoulder. "You can do this. God is with you."

With a nod, Steve acknowledged Frank's words. The last time he set foot in a hospital was to identify his dead wife.

The HIPPA law prohibited the hospital from giving the detective specifics of Mia's case, and he refrained from speculation. Hope filled his heart that his twin sister, Mia, would be OK.

When they arrived at the nurse's station, a young nurse introduced him to Dr. Garrett, Mia's attending physician, and escorted them into his sister's private room. Steve's breath whooshed out when he saw his sister's face and he fought his tears. His heart constricted and threatened to choke him.

He rushed to her side while Frank stood at the foot of her bed. Steve shut his eyes and controlled his breathing. When Steve opened his eyes, Doctor Garrett stood stone-faced and waited, but when Steve reached for her hand, the doctor grabbed his wrist.

Steve pulled away from the doctor's grip with a fierce scowl. "What—"

"She has two broken wrists and the one you wanted to touch is seriously damaged. She needs surgery on both wrists, but we can't do it until we get her pneumonia under control."

Steve's voice wobbled. "Anything else?"

"She came in through ER about an hour ago and the clinic started her on antibiotics, but with this strain of pneumonia we had to change the type and dose. We've sedated her for comfort measures and protection from further injury until we can do surgery. What happened to her?"

"We can only guess by where and how the car was found that she had a single vehicle car accident," Dean said.

"But most of her facial wounds have all but healed. Someone took rudimentary care of those and the less-damaged wrist, but she has a hairline fracture in her ankle and the other wrist has an extreme fracture. I'd guess her healed injuries are a month old."

"Three weeks." Steve frowned and crossed his arms over his chest. "What are you not asking?"

"Why wasn't she brought in when it happened? I have to file a report." The doctor's eyes flickered with disdain.

Exasperated, Steve turned narrowed eyes on the doctor. The same look he gave underlings when they didn't do their job. "Fine. Talk to the detective."

Dean Landers stepped over to the doctor with a purposeful stride. "I'll give you the information you need."

With a warning gaze, the doctor observed Steve over his shoulder. "The antibiotics are so strong she might have hallucinations when she wakes up."

Steve swallowed and pulled a chair close to the bed. He bent over her still face and kissed her forehead where it wasn't scarred, making sure he didn't dislodge the oxygen nasal canula. He sat and stared at his sister's broken body. The putrid hospital odors didn't bother him like they once had.

Frank stepped into the room. "Dean and I took care of

the doctor. He won't bother you anymore."

Steve's heart ached. He gave a slight nod, reached over and touched Mia's hair. Not once did he think she'd be injured to this extent. "Why were there fresh injuries? Where did she fly in from?"

"I'll look into it," Frank said.

"Thank you."

"From what we heard, sounds like it'll be awhile before she's well enough to go home," Frank said.

Steve's face set in an unmovable mask. "I'm not leaving her side. I'll have my assistant drop my laptop off and I'll work from here. Can you ensure I can stay? I don't want to deal with doctors and nurses. And I want a specialist to examine her."

"I'll make it happen."

He turned to his friend. "I don't know what I'd have done without you these past weeks, Frank. Thank you."

"I'll call your housekeeper and have her bring your clothes tomorrow. Let's take a minute to pray for her before I leave."

They laid hands on Mia's blanket-covered foot and Frank prayed. "Father, give the doctors wisdom in treating her pneumonia and guide their hands as they fix her broken bones. We pray a special blessing upon her that she would recover quickly. Amen."

After Frank left, Steve paced and rubbed the back of his neck. He'd messed this up…and he couldn't question his sister.

Her groan catapulted him out of the chair and he almost tripped over it to get to her. "What is it, Mia?"

Another smothered groan.

Steve listened with his ear near her lips, but her incoherent ramblings frightened him. He remembered what the doctor said about hallucinations. He frowned. Maybe she hallucinated.

This is not good.

Then he heard it again. "Shen"

What's a shen?

Now he'd rack his brain trying to figure out what she said.

For two days, Steve sat, watched his sister, waited and worked on his laptop.

Thankfully, the hospital allowed him to shower and shave, and though exhaustion seeped into every bone, he soldiered on.

After three days, she responded well to the antibiotics and her lungs cleared enough so they could do surgery on her wrists. The ortho guy wanted to break the other wrist and reset it at the same time. While whoever set the bone, did a good job, but without surgery, it could cause problems later on.

Someone from the surgical staff took Mia to surgery and Steve wrung his hands. Frank stopped by and after they prayed for his sister. He recognized he had to put the whole situation in God's hands as he'd only renewed his faith since Mia went missing. He half smiled. Mia had prayed and had the church pray for him to get right with God.

Fiona, his housekeeper, was like family, and she stepped in the room. "Laddie, pacing won't make the doctors go faster. Come eat. I brought your favorites."

While the hospital food was palatable, he relished his favorites. "How are the girls?"

"They want to visit their aunt."

Steve gave her a hard glare. "No."

Fiona's stiffness told him he had little hope of winning in a battle of wills in the long run.

"Any news about where she's been all this time?"

"Someone dropped her off at a rural clinic the day of the big pileup, but the doctor who treated her is on vacation. The nurses vaguely remembered her. She was one of three who were on a medical flight."

Fiona touched her cheek. "Strange. Wouldn't the person who took care of her want to find out if she was OK?"

Steve lifted his chin. "You're right. Nothing we can do until Mia comes out of surgery and is cognizant enough to answer questions. It's a mystery."

He considered the situation from so many angles his brain hurt.

"You need to rest. You're a mite bit peaked."

"I'll rest when I know she's OK."

Sympathy filled Fiona's eyes. "The girls miss you. And they miss their friends."

Steve grunted and ignored the reference to his daughters' friends. "I'll be home soon and we'll plan a big welcome home party."

Again, with the shrug. Then the doctor came in and Steve jumped from his chair.

"The one wrist was worse than we thought. She now has a plate and pins, but with good physical therapy she may regain full use of it. The other wrist was better than we expected and we only had to do a minor fix. She'll have use of that wrist faster than the other one."

Words stalled in his throat, but Fiona saved him. "Thank you."

"You can wait in her room. They'll bring her back in about twenty minutes."

"I'll wait with you so I can see her. Plenty of time before I need to get the girls."

He nodded and paced until they brought Mia to her room.

Kissing his sister's forehead, Fiona's eyes glistened. "Need to do something about those scars, Laddie."

"I'll get her the best plastic surgeon around. Don't worry."

His housekeeper dabbed her eyes and left the room.

Working on his laptop was out of the question, so he continued to pace. When her eyes flickered open, he rushed to her side. "You're awake."

Confusion filled Mia's face and her voice scratched. "Where's Shannon?"

"Shannon who?"

Her brow scrunched, and she shook her head.

"We're so glad you're OK."

"Who are you?"

Stunned, he stepped back. "Who am I?"

He was thankful the nurse stepped in because his sister's agitation concerned him. Mia reached to grab the nurse, but her arms had been immobilized due to the surgery. She moaned, then took a deep breath. "Please. Shannon...where is he?"

Steve's voice choked. "We don't know who Shannon is. Is he the one who found you?"

She nodded as her eyes filled with wariness. "Drink?"

The nurse gave her a few sips of water. "There now. You need to rest. You've been through a lot these past days."

Mia's voice croaked. "Days? My wrists hurt. I want Shannon."

The nurse's gentle voice crooned. "I've got something for your pain right here." And she administered a shot in the IV portal and put Mia out within seconds.

Steve shook his head. "Can you get the doctor in here? This is something else we'll have to deal with."

Pacing once again, he drew both hands through his shaggy hair. When the doctor came in, Steve calmed his stance.

"Doc—"

"Nurse filled me in. This is a new wrinkle. She was conscious when she was brought in but didn't make much sense. This could be the strong antibiotics and the anesthesia."

"What if it isn't? It makes sense now."

The doctor's perplexed look made Steve want to laugh in this not-so-funny situation. "Think about it. If she lost her memory, then she wouldn't have been able to find her way home and she couldn't tell her rescuer who she was or where she belonged."

He scratched his chin. "Could be. But I caution you about telling her too much at one time."

"She'll be in serious pain for the next couple of days. I don't want her upset and causing herself more pain."

Steve sighed. "What can I tell her?"

"Maybe only her name until she's more coherent." The doctor checked her bandages and smoothed her covers. "But if she asks you for more information, then you can tell her, but divulge nothing that might upset her."

"Understood."

His shoulders slumped with weariness. And when the doctor left, he yawned and sat on the chair next to her bed. He wanted to be right there in case she awoke. He laid his head on the bed near her knee, placed his face next to her less injured hand, and fell asleep.

Tomorrow they'd talk.

Lass winced at the pain in her arms and gazed around the room. No Shannon, but that guy was still there working on his laptop.

Blinking away the grogginess, she cleared her throat, and the guy's eyes met hers.

He got to his feet and came close to the bed. "You're awake."

"How long have I been out?"

"In and out for a few days. Do you remember anything?"

"Who are you, again?"

"I'm Steve."

She squinted. "Do you know me?"

"Yes, I do."

A doctor with a long lab coat stepped in the room.

"Thank heavens. I have a big black hole where my brain used to be. And my mouth tastes like cotton. Can I have a drink?"

Steve held a glass with a straw so she could drink.

"So, you want to tell me my name?"

"Well, I guess that answers that question," the doctor said.

She shifted her gaze from Steve to the doctor. "What question is that?"

"We believed the strong antibiotics caused issues with your memory," the doctor said.

"I don't know what caused my memory loss, but are you going to tell me my name?"

"Mia Nardelli." Both men answered in unison.

She arched her brows. "Mia Nardelli? Doesn't ring a bell. It's disturbing." She liked Lass better.

"I'll say," the doctor said.

"I'll leave the two of you to chat. Remember what we talked about, Mr. Nardelli," the doctor said.

"Mr. Nardelli?" Mia swallowed and whispered. "You're not my husband, are you?"

Steve coughed. "Good grief, no. I'm your brother."

"Thank God."

"Gee, thanks." Steve chuckled.

"No offense."

"None taken."

Mia shifted in the bed. "Your aftershave smells familiar to me somehow."

"The sense of smell holds the strongest memories."

Her eyes, just like his, stared back at him. "You want to tell me what happened?"

"We only know you had a car accident. We found your car in a ravine. Tell me where you've been for the last three weeks."

"I had a car accident?" She pondered the words, then nodded. "Makes sense."

"Why?"

"Because Shannon found glass shards in my face."

"Who is Shannon?"

"He's the guy who rescued me."

"He didn't know you had a car accident?"

"No," she said.

"Then, where is he? I'd like to thank him. I don't understand why he didn't bring you to the hospital sooner."

"He couldn't. We were trapped at his cabin. The area was flooded and we couldn't get out. When the waters receded, he took me to the hospital, but I don't remember the ride."

"Makes sense based on what the hospital said."

"Tell me more about my life, then. Something. Anything to jog my memory."

"The doctor doesn't want me to upset you with too much information."

She blew out a long breath. "I'll be more upset not knowing what I ought to know about my life."

Steve glanced at the door and probably hoped someone

would bail him out of an explanation, but he sighed and told her about her life.

She peppered him with questions. "When will I meet your daughters and Fiona?"

"Soon."

"I have a lot to think about."

The nurse strolled in with a wide smile on her face. "How are you today?"

"My wrists hurt. Can I have pain meds? The noise in the hallway disturbs me. Please close the door when you leave."

"Of course." The nurse helped Mia take two tablets.

"Tell me more about Shannon," Steve said.

Chapter 8

When Sean pulled into his brother's ranch four days ago, he put Thunder into the horse trainer's care and the chickens in their elaborate coop behind the farmhouse.

Guilt plagued him. For the entire trip to the ranch, his thoughts drifted to Lass, and the sense of loss that captured his soul. He detected her unique scent of vanilla in the truck's cab and pictured her as he'd last seen her. He grimaced. Alone in an unfamiliar place. Then his father's face popped into his head. Both were sick. Well, one was sick and one was injured and sick and he was torn between the two. But he had responsibilities, and he had to fulfill them.

He called his father, but Mrs. Monahan, his dad's longtime housekeeper, answered. "Dearie, your father's asleep. You need to come home."

"I'll call the doctor."

She blew out a raspberry. "What good would that do? He hasn't gone for a visit in three months."

"Right."

"Please come quickly."

He'd never heard Mrs. Monahan so stressed and his heart ached. She'd been a surrogate mother since his mother died. "Are you OK?"

"Yes, dearie." Her breath whooshed out. "A little flustered. Let me know when you'll be arriving. I have to go."

Sean slid the phone into his back pocket and he fingered his scar. *Flustered?* Even after his accident, Mrs. Monahan supported his family with strength and grace. He cast unseeing eyes toward the wind-rippled lake behind the farmhouse. His father always grabbed the phone out of the housekeeper's hand whenever he or his brother called. Not so today and every day since he returned days ago. *What aren't you telling me, Mrs. Monahan?*

Brett stepped through the door and his eyes filled with empathy. "You look harried."

Sean grunted.

His cousin crossed his arms and gave him an intense look. "Did you book your flight?"

"Yes. And visited one too many animals before I handed the last two horses over to my colleagues."

"Careful you don't lose your patients to other practices."

"I have no choice."

Brett's mouth quirked, and he touched his cousin's forearm. "That's why I'm here. You should revamp your website."

Sean gazed heavenward and shook his head. "Not that again." A sense of weariness overcame him. "You're like a dog with a bone."

Crossing his arms, a stern look came over Brett's face. "I'm serious, Sean. Who knows how long you'll be in Ireland? When you return, you might not have a practice."

Sean rolled his eyes as he poured water into a glass. "I'll always have a practice, even if I only treat my brother's horses."

"Will you at least consider a new website? Yours is old and outdated."

"I'll think about it."

"Great. I'll email you some ideas and I think you'll like them."

He gulped the glass of water. "Fine, but I won't make any promises."

"Fair enough. Have a safe trip. And keep us posted about your dad." Brett slapped his cousin on the back and headed out the door before Sean could say goodbye.

Sean's thoughts turned to the two problems that caused a burning sensation in his stomach and, at the moment, a new website for his practice wasn't either of them.

His father worried him when he wouldn't come to the phone. His dad might truly be sick and Mrs. Monahan's demeanor enhanced his worry. Her reaction alarmed him.

Lord, whatever is happening in Ireland, keep a hand on my father and help Mrs. Monahan cope until I get there. And please help me find Lass. I'm desperate.

He made an effort to reach his father several more times while he prepared for the trip and arranged for colleagues to care for his patients. Sean called the clinic to speak to the on-call physician the day he dropped Lass off, only to be told the doctor was unavailable because he went on vacation, which left Sean with no information. The nurses weren't helpful either. His frustration rose to an all-time high. And the hospital couldn't tell him anything because he didn't have a name. A crazed idiot made more sense than he did.

He'd leave late this evening for Ireland and he'd make one last-ditch effort to find her before he left. He had to confess his lie, divulge his real name, check on her condition and learn her name.

For the entire day, thoughts of her filtered into his mind. Mostly he worried about her respiratory issues and her wrists and if she remembered anything more.

He packed his bags, shoved them in his truck and drove to Columbus General.

Coffee. He needed coffee, and he strode into the shop to the right of the hospital's lobby. In an isolated corner, he inhaled the richness of the brew. The hospital was huge. He snorted. He had very little hope of finding her without a name.

His shoulders slumped. Why had he come here? He needed to leave for the airport, buy a paperback and go wait at the gate for his flight. He could only pray for a miracle.

Two policemen gave him a single nod, grabbed their coffee and sat at the next table. Sean distracted himself and listened to their conversation.

"Where've you been?" The blond officer nearest him blew on his coffee.

"On vacation," the portly officer said.

"You missed it."

"What?"

Blondie sipped his coffee. "That woman we searched for showed up as a Jane Doe a few days ago."

Sean straightened in his chair. He trained his ear, but pulled out his phone. They spoke in quiet tones, as if they prayed in a chapel.

"From where?" The beefy one said.

"She was on a medical transport flight on that day of the pileup on Route Ten."

It took everything Sean had not to give himself away or smile. Instead, he scrolled through his email and acted as if he wasn't aware of anything around him.

"I saw that on the news. Deaths and lots of injuries. Were her injuries serious?"

"Injured but not from the pileup. Someone dropped her off. Craziest thing ever."

Please say her name. Please.

"Did they get a name?" The portly one said.

"You forgot her name? Mia Nardelli?" Blondie blew an exasperated breath. "The detective kept after us to find her long enough."

Thank you, Lord, for answered prayer.

"Not her, you idiot. The person who dropped her off."

"No. But the detective checked into it."

Sean rose from his seat and almost upended the chair. He nodded at the officers and strode to the reception desk. The clock on the wall said he had four hours until his flight to Dublin. He'd tell Lass, er...*Mia* everything and promise to call her when he arrived in Ireland.

His heart soared and the dark cloud of his father's illness faded. He'd deal with his father when he got to Ireland. He'd found Lass, and he needed to see her. Now. He'd been a wreck for four days trying to get information on her.

The information desk gave him her room number. Mia. It suited her. He'd have a hard time calling her Mia, but it didn't matter, he'd learn. His smile widened.

Pushing the elevator button several times, he willed the elevator to open. The woman next to him glared, but he didn't care because getting to Mia was more important than a stranger who cast disparaging glances at him.

A hint of antiseptic filled his nostrils as he quick stepped past the deserted nurse's station. His preference was to ask about her condition before he visited her but her room was two doors away and he couldn't wait. Taking a deep breath as he stepped into her room and he froze. There she was, but a man half-sat on a chair and half-laid on the bed with her hand nestled on his face. Sean blinked and his heart dropped. His hands fisted. Who was this guy who touched her? His greatest fear came true. She had someone in her life.

His gaze flicked to the cards and colorful fall flowers lining the window ledge showing him she was well loved and he thanked God for her family and friends who cared about her. Then he took in the man who held her hand. Tall and somewhat muscular, he was perfect for her.

Mia. The second woman in his life who'd break his heart. It wasn't intentional. What happened with Lass was his own fault. He shouldn't have involved himself, but he had. And look what it got him. Another shattered heart.

He backed away from her room, his brain on auto-pilot, and he moved in the wrong direction to the waiting area at the end of the hall where he dropped into a chair. He couldn't tell her anything now.

Should he fight for her? Could he fight for her? He shook his head. He was leaving for Ireland in three hours. He didn't have time to win her heart. The man in her room was whole whereas Sean's face was ravaged with an unsightly scar. He slouched, leaned his head on the chair's back and stared with vacant eyes, hoping the answers to his questions would somehow flash across the ceiling.

His head cocked to the voices chattering from the adjacent break room.

"She doesn't remember him, but Mr. Nardelli's been here since she came in. Never left her side. Not even to go home and change or sleep. That's devotion for you."

"For sure," another person answered.

Sean jumped out of the chair, not wanting to know about how the woman he loved had a devoted husband. It didn't matter whether he lied by omission because pursuing her was out of the question now. They'd have nothing together.

But he'd inquire about her condition and make sure

she was recovering. At the nurse's station, he found the head nurse. "Can you tell me Mia Nardelli's condition?" He choked out. "I stopped by her room, but she's sleeping and I didn't want to disturb her."

"She's doing as well as can be expected. She should recover and be out of here within the week." The nurse eyed him, but he kept his scarred side away from her line of vision. "Can I tell her who stopped by?"

"Shannon. Just tell her I wanted to make sure she was OK." His heart sank as he left the woman of his dreams behind a second and final time.

The nurse nodded.

Slivers of his heart dropped with every step he took away from Lass until not a piece of it remained.

Chapter 9

The next two weeks were a whirlwind for Mia. Seeing her nieces called to mind her life's memories before the accident. They tumbled upon one another until her brain ached, but she welcomed them. An improvement over the black hole.

"Are you ready to get out of here?" Mia's brother, Steve, lounged on the chair that had been his bed since she'd been admitted to the hospital two weeks ago.

Happiness and sadness warred within her soul. She had a family who loved and cared for her, but she missed Shannon, the man who came to mean so much to her in those lost three weeks. How could she have believed she'd been married or involved? Now she knew she'd been married, but her brief marriage came to a painful end years ago.

"I'm so ready to escape and go where I can get tasty home cooking." Mia's legs dangled from the side of the bed as she waited for the nurse to bring the release papers. "Why does it take so long for them to get the paperwork done?"

"Bureaucracy. Can't release you until every piece of paper has been reviewed and signed."

She groaned and fell onto the pillow. Her casted wrists slung over her stomach. "I want to go home."

"Quit whining." He laughed. "I've been here for the duration, and I'm not complaining."

"I still can't believe you thought I ran away. What would ever make you think such a thing?"

Steve leaned closer and his voice became serious. "You did it before."

She reached over and touched his hand. "I told you. When you married Laura, I lost my best friend. Then when Mom and Dad died, I couldn't handle those losses. I'm older now. Wiser."

"I'm not trying to guilt you." His voice took on a faraway quality. "When you came home and took over the household duties, I was so grateful, but never told you. I'm sorry."

"No apologies. Only happiness, OK? Especially now since you realize my friend Cassie wasn't involved. I know she took excellent care of your daughters while I was gone. You need to make amends with her, Steve."

"My priority right now is to get you home and settled. I'll deal with Cassie later."

"If you say so. She came to visit, you know. I think she's in love with you."

Steve jerked and raised his eyebrow. "Matchmaking again, hmmm?"

Mia frowned at her fingers and wiggled them. "I wonder why Shannon didn't return, and it bothers me."

Steve's voice sharpened. "Shannon was here? When? Why didn't you tell me?"

"I learned about it last night. The nurse said someone named Shannon came, but I was sleeping. He never returned." She worked to conceal her despair.

Bustling in with the swish of the wheelchair, the nurse curtailed Steve's answer. Her arms held the documents for Mia's release. "If you'll sign these forms, we can get you home to your adorable nieces."

Mia smiled, signed her name, and settled herself into the wheelchair.

The nurse set the foot rests for her. "Did you ever find your knight in shining armor who brought you to the hospital? The young nurses have been enthralled with your story since they heard it."

Groaning, Mia covered her face with her hands. She didn't want to think about it.

Steve stepped behind the wheelchair. "We've been searching for him but..." His voice went soft. "It's as if he disappeared off the face of the earth."

Mia adjusted herself in the SUV's bucket seat and Steve belted her in. The bouquets' aroma filled the vehicle's confined space and made Mia nauseous. She opened the window until they were on their way.

Her curiosity got the best of her. "What did you do to find Shannon?"

Steve gave her a sidelong glance. "Called the clinic that transported you, but with the massive pileup that day, no one remembered much of anything. We can do whatever it takes to find him, Mia. I want to thank him for caring for you."

Mia picked at her slacks and scrunched her shoulders. "Sad thing is I don't know his last name. Not sure why I never asked. I was so focused on remembering my past that knowing his last name seemed unimportant somehow."

Steve reached over and touched her hand. "Don't worry. We'll find him."

"No. I'm angry with him because he left me alone at the hospital and then came to visit and didn't awaken me. It makes no sense. He was so kind and gentle. I want to find him myself. Besides you need to take care of your business and deal with Cassie. You can't put it off any longer. Quit letting the past rule and get busy living life."

Steve pinched his lips, but nodded.

Mia remembered that look and wouldn't push it. "I can't wait to see the girls. Since my memory returned, I miss them."

"We placed a bed in my office so you don't have to climb the stairs to the garage apartment. When your ankle is healed, you can move back."

"You won't be able to work in there."

"No worries. You won't be in there except at night, anyway." His bright smile lightened her heart. "How's the physical therapist working out?"

"The left wrist is tough, but the right is coming along and Pam has become such a good friend. She's a hoot."

"How so?"

"Talks to the two parts of her derriere."

A laugh burst from Steve's lips. "What?"

"Calls them Betty & Bertha. Makes me laugh and forget I hurt when she works my wrists."

"If it works, why not?"

Mia grinned. "She keeps doing it even when physical therapy is over."

Steve quirked his lips as he shot a glance to her. "Do they answer her?"

"Of course not, silly."

"Don't tell the girls or they might say something inappropriate to her."

"I won't say anything, but I can't guarantee Pam won't talk about her pals when the girls are around. She'll be at the house later this afternoon."

He drew out a breath. "I wish she wouldn't."

"Then keep the girls occupied when Pam comes."

Mia's nieces, Stella and Tina, raced to the car to welcome

her home with hugs and kisses. They took Mia's flowers and cards into the house. For having gone to the hospital with nothing except the clothes she wore, she amassed enough clothing and toiletries to warrant a suitcase.

Steve lifted her from the car and carried her in. She couldn't believe how tired she was from her hospital release and the drive home. Mia's eyes drooped when she sat in the familiar breakfast-nook chair and drank in the brightness of the homey kitchen.

"Aunt Mia, will you color with us?" Tina's soulful blue eyes pleaded.

Steve squatted to be eye level with Tina. "Your aunt is worn out. Let's give her time to rest before she plays with you, alright?"

Tina frowned and hugged Mia. "Are you gonna be OK?"

Mia received the hug with a sigh. "I'll be fine."

Tina nodded, pulled away, and stared at her dad. "Can we watch a video instead?"

He laughed and waved his finger at both his daughters. "Just one."

Fiona bustled around her. "Let's get you into bed and I'll make you a hot cup of tea. It's gotten cold out since you've been gone."

Steve gathered Mia in his arms and carried her to her makeshift bedroom.

"I'm exhausted, Fiona." Mia's mouth drooped. "How about if we wait on the tea until Pam gets here for PT?"

Mia awoke from her nap when Fiona led Pam into the room and shut the door behind her.

"Well, sleepyhead, I bet you're happy you got sprung from the ward. You ready for PT?" Pam smiled as she put her bag on the floor and glanced around the room. "Your brother went all out, didn't he? Got you a hospital bed and put it on the first floor. The question is, is there a chair around here where Betty & Bertha won't fight amongst themselves?"

Mia laughed. "I think you can use Steve's office chair. It's on wheels so you can get close."

"Great. Have you heard from Shannon?"

Mia winced as Pam worked her wrist. "No. But he came to visit."

"Was he as handsome as you described him?"

A tear threatened to fall. Was it because of the pain in her wrist or the pain in her heart? "I didn't see him."

Pam stopped and narrowed her gaze. "You didn't?"

"No. He came when I was sleeping." Mia arched her neck and shook her head. "I guess it was last week."

Pam continued to work Mia's stiff wrists. "Last week? And he hadn't returned?"

"No. I don't understand it. It makes no sense. How did he know how to find me? And why didn't he visit again?" Mia breathed out a groan.

"What do you mean?"

"He didn't know my name—so how did he know what room I was in? It's a big hospital. And why didn't he return?"

"Both good questions. You going to find him?"

"As soon as I'm well enough to hunt for him."

Pam pushed a little harder than Mia thought necessary. "Take it easy, will ya?"

"You want to get better to find Shannon, don't you?"

"Yes, but I don't want to be in pain."

"You may not believe it but you've made progress. Two

71

weeks and you'll be turning cartwheels." Pam smiled and patted her hand.

"Yeah, right."

Pam frowned and glared at the squeaking chair. "Bertha, will you please quit pushing Betty against the side of the chair? She doesn't like it. You're giving her chair burn. So be nice."

Mia barked out a laugh. "Will you stop?"

"Not until we get this PT done. Bertha is a naughty girl these days. Always pushing Betty around. It's not right."

"You need to get those girls in line." Mia chuckled.

Pam sighed. "I sure do and I'm thinking about horseback riding again. And I'm hopeful the pounding will put them in their place."

Mia stared at her new friend. "I have a favor to ask."

"Sure."

"Will you help me find Shannon?"

Pam leaned into the chair. "I don't know how I can help, but I'll do whatever I can."

"Call the clinic where I came from and see if they have a name."

"Didn't your brother already contact them?"

"Yeah, but as a medical person, you might have more clout. Someone might talk to you rather than my brother."

"I don't know about that, but I'll give it a shot."

"Thank you. Are we done?"

"For today. You'll be sore. Take some extra-strength aspirin for the pain. How's the ankle?"

"Still sore. But I'll be able to walk without limping in a few days. My brother insisted on carrying me in."

"He's a good guy."

Fiona came in and carried a tea tray. "Ready for your tea, now?"

"Thank you, Fiona. My favorite! Blueberry scones and lemon curd."

"Well, Betty & Bertha sniffed the scones and they're clamoring."

Fiona looked perplexed, opened her mouth, but clamped it shut when Mia cocked her head.

"Did Steve get things right with Cassie?"

"Not yet." And Fiona left the room.

Pam eyes held a question.

Mia's mouth puckered at the tartness of the lemon curd. "Long story. I'll tell you about it sometime."

After they had their tea, Pam stood over her and touched her arm. "I'll be here on Monday and let you know what I find out."

Mia nodded and closed her eyes.

Chapter 10

Sean grabbed his bag at the luggage carousel in Dublin and headed to the rental car company. Ireland. Home. He pulled his cap low on his forehead as he made his way to the car. In an hour, he'd be at his childhood home and would deal with his father's illness.

Before he left the parking area, he called his father. Mrs. Monahan answered, her cheery voice a balm to his shattered heart.

He passed a hand over weary eyes and stared at the unusual sunny day. "I'm in Dublin and I've left the airport, but wanted to call before I get on the road. How's Da?"

"Doing well today."

"Can I speak to him?"

Mrs. Monahan's voice got quiet. "I think he's in the bathroom."

No point in pushing the issue with her. "All right, be there in an hour."

His childhood home looked the same as it had three years ago when he returned for his Da's surprise birthday party. Smoke curled from the chimney and the soft gray stones of his childhood home gave him a peace he only found at his cabin. He took a deep breath of his Irish homeland and reveled in the whiff of wood smoke. The trees had already turned to their bright fall colors and the crisp, cool air invigorated him despite the circumstances of his visit.

He grabbed his coat and bag and went to the front door. The door opened before he could knock. His Da stood there and seemed older than the last time Sean had seen him.

"Son." Angus McDermott embraced him with a tight hug. His eyes were clear, but troubled.

"Da. It's good to see you. How are you feeling?"

"I'm fine. Just fine."

He stopped mid-stride and studied his father's face. "Why haven't I been able to speak to you on the phone, then?"

His father led him into the study where Sean had spent many weeks recovering from his fall. Nothing had changed. The fire in the hearth crackled and his father's Bible sat on his footstool open to the Psalms.

Angus grabbed Sean's arm and pulled him into the room. "Are you hungry? Mrs. Monahan has been cooking since you called. She'll bring tea in a few minutes."

The strength with which his father grabbed his arm and the clearness of his eyes, told him his father was fine, but something was grave enough for his Da to go to such lengths to make him return to Ireland.

With a deep breath, Sean dropped into his mother's chair. "Well, Da. I can see you're well…now. You've been sick. What's going on."

"Aye, that." A deep sigh escaped Angus McDermott's lungs. "I'm sorry we had to lie to you. But I didn't know how else to get you here without telling you over the phone."

"Tell me what?"

"Let's wait for Mrs. Monahan to bring tea. Actually, I could use some strong Irish coffee right about now."

His head snapped. Da never drank which showed him this was serious enough for his father to want to drink alcohol. Not good.

Taking the bull by the tail, he stood over his father. "Spit it out, Da. Are you dying?"

Mrs. Monahan opened the door and brought in a tea tray with Sean's favorite cinnamon scones, cream and a teapot. "He's not on his way out, the old fool. He should have told you and not made you worry."

His father glared and grabbed the teapot. "That'll be all, Mrs. Monahan."

She gave him a scowl and shut the door with a distinct thud.

"We've established you're not dying nor are you sick. You didn't have to lie."

His father sighed, then poured tea for both of them and muttered, "My past has returned to haunt me."

Sean took his cup. The familiar taste of Irish tea soothed him, and he clenched his jaw. "What are you talking about?"

"I'll explain, but first let's pray."

Sean's uneasiness grew. While his Father always prayed before meals and afternoon tea, it usually wasn't to this extent.

The silence deafened him. "I'm waiting, Da."

His Da leaned into his chair and an intense look of pain crossed his face. "About a month ago a woman came here with a boy. She was from social services."

"I don't understand. Why would social services be at your door with a boy?"

"Mrs. Monahan took the boy to the kitchen while I spoke with the social worker. The boy…Andrew, Drew for short, is seven years old."

Sean's confusion made him sputter. "Why did a social

worker bring you a boy?"

"Drew is your son, Sean."

"What?" Sean's voice rose to a thunderous level.

"He resembles you and Shannon when you boys were that age. I couldn't deny he was yours."

Sean rose and placed his hands on his hips. "Well, you should have."

His father turned saddened eyes upon him. "There's a birth certificate with your name on it."

He paced and became more agitated. "So—?"

"Think about it, Sean. Where were you eight years ago?"

Sean slumped into his mother's chair. "Bridget."

"Yes, Bridget. She came here a few months after you left for America. Told her to leave. Didn't believe her then, but the evidence is plain. I'm so sorry I didn't believe her or ever told you. I thought she was trying to palm off someone else's child on you. But his birth certificate lists you as the father, and he favors you."

His voice broke. "But it can't be. I used—"

"It's not fullproof, son." Tears welled in his father's eyes.

"But why now? Where's Bridget?"

Angus reached across to grip his son's shoulder. "Dead. Died two years after Drew was born. His Nana took care of him, but she developed Alzheimer's and died about six months ago, then he became a ward of the state. You can't turn away from him, Sean. He's blood, even if you didn't know he existed."

"Where is he now?"

"At school. He should be home in an hour. Need to get your heart in order, son. He's a little boy who's suffered enormous loss. The one person he loved more than anyone."

"I've no intention of turning away from my son, but I

want a paternity test to be sure."

"Certainly. But when you see Drew, you'll know he's your son."

Sean rose, stepped to the window, and blinked. His heart skipped a beat. *I have a son.*

Da lifted himself from his chair, stood next to his son and put his arm around his shoulders. "Everything will be OK, son. You'll see. But Drew needs a lot of love and attention."

"I need to go for a walk."

Angus squeezed his son's shoulder. "Seek the Lord for guidance. It's a huge shock to you. I felt the same way…we'll talk more later this evening."

Sean pivoted. "There's more?"

"You have the bulk of it where Drew is concerned. He's coming around, but he was sullen and angry for the first two weeks. He misses his Nana. But the horses are therapeutic for him."

Sean nodded and pulled on his jacket. "I'll be back in an hour."

With purposeful steps, he made his way to his parents' favorite tree and the bench that sat beneath it. It had become a favorite place for him to think after his accident. *Father, this is beyond my ability and an enormous shock. Show me the way and give me wisdom in every aspect of fatherhood.*

His world crashed. It wasn't enough he lost the love of his life, but now he had a son. "The Lord gives, and the Lord takes away." Sean leaned back, plucked leaves from the willow tree and rubbed them between his fingers. He couldn't think about Lass…Mia anymore. He had a higher calling. Sean had to learn how to be a father. He didn't need a woman in his life to have a family. He had a son and he had his brother. His twin. *Does Shannon know?* He guessed Shannon hadn't been told either, but he'd find out soon enough.

Sean grinned. Little Drew would have more family than he thought possible when he brought the boy to America. Sean frowned. Would the boy want to go? Could he get his son a visa? Many questions that needed answers.

He'd be gone more than he expected. Sean sighed. One thought led to another. Brett's visit before he left was timely. He'd send Brett an email to tell him to start on his website. He had a son to support now, and he didn't know when he'd return.

Sean returned to the cottage with a spring in his step. Decisions had to be made. Maybe his father would come to America now. So why not?

He wiped his feet and stepped into his father's study. His Da snoozed in his chair with his glasses perched on his nose. His hand on his beloved Bible.

Sean tiptoed out of the room and into the kitchen where he stopped short. There he was. His son, Drew. Sean took a deep breath and made his way to the table where Drew's face lifted and he stilled.

Mrs. Monahan bustled around the table and motioned for Sean to sit across from his son. "Well, Drew, what do you think of your Da?"

God bless Mrs. Monahan, but Sean didn't know what to do, so he sat and stared at his son. His father was right. Drew did take after him and Shannon when they were boys.

Drew tilted his head, then pointed to his face. "How did you get that scar?"

Mrs. Monahan gasped and a bitter laugh escaped Sean's mouth. "I fell off a horse. Or rather, a horse threw me." Sean sensed Mrs. Monahan's relief.

His son's eyes got huge. "You allowed a horse to throw you?"

Sean spread his hands. "Sometimes a horse has other ideas."

"Grandad says you take care of animals. You're a veten... vetnari...vet–"

"Vet is fine. Yes, I do care for animals. Lots of different animals."

"Horses and Dogs?" Drew's voice rose with each word. "Cats and Sheep?"

"Those plus chickens and an occasional bird."

Sean laughed at Drew's scrunched-up nose. Animals would be the path to forming a tight bond with his son.

"You like animals, Drew?"

Drew gave a vigorous nod. "Especially horses."

Mrs. Monahan stood by the boy and regarded Sean with loving eyes. "Your Da wanted you to take a peek at the horses. Can you do that before dinner and take Drew with you?"

"If he wants to go."

Drew popped out of his chair and ran to grab his coat from the hook next to the door. "Can we go now? I want to see you check the horses. Grandad said you're a good vet."

Sean rose and leaned in to hug Mrs. Monahan. "Thank you for preparing the way," he whispered.

She patted his scarred cheek, her touch tender and loving. "Be back in an hour."

He nodded and followed his son out the door.

The boy stared at his feet as they strolled into the barn. "Can I ask you a question?"

"You can ask me anything."

"Why didn't you come to find me?"

Sean stopped, put his hand on his son's shoulder and squatted in front of him. Staring into eyes much like his. "I didn't know you'd been born. Neither your mother nor your Nana ever told me. But now, I do know and I'll take care of you."

The boy nodded. Sean measured his steps to his son's small stride. His son. His heart, while broken for the years he'd missed having this wonderful little boy and the pain of losing his true love, was now full because he could spend the rest of his life redeeming lost years. His son asked questions about his life in America as they examined the horses.

It might be too soon to ask him if he wanted to live in America, but Drew knew no boundaries.

"Are you taking me to America?"

"Would you like to live with me in America?"

Drew kicked stones on their way back to the cottage and then stopped. "Will it be just you and me, there?"

Sean smiled, held his hand out to the boy and told him of his other relatives who would be eager to meet him.

Sean held his breath.

His son's smile transformed his face. "Always wanted to see America."

After dinner, Sean helped Drew with his homework, helped him prepare for bed, told him a story, and waited until the boy fell asleep.

When Sean came downstairs, Mrs. Monahan had left for the evening and his Da sat before the fire staring into the flames.

Sean stepped into the room and his father turned damp eyes toward him. "Went well with Drew?"

"Yes. He does need a lot of love and care, but he'll find that in abundance in America."

They discussed how long it would take to get a visa for

Drew and what his life would look like there.

"Da, why don't you come to America, too? You've kept your American citizenship so visas are not an issue."

His father's voice quivered. "No."

"But now it makes sense. You've sold the horse business. Shannon is married and will have children soon and then there's me and Drew."

"My home is here."

"So? Keep it. Come to America for part of the year and spend part of the year here."

"There's a reason I won't go back to America."

"Why?"

Angus sighed, and he gazed into the fire. "My heart nearly broke when Drew showed up on my doorstep. It brought back so many memories I'd buried from long ago."

"What memories?"

"Like yourself, I was a young man who fell in love with the wrong woman. She left me and I went after her, but she didn't want me so I returned to Ireland to heal my heart."

"That was before you met Ma?"

He gave a single nod and sorrow etched his Da's voice. "Her sister wrote and said my girl and our child died when she gave birth. I tried to find the sister, but she moved and left no forwarding address. I hired an investigator, but they couldn't find anything, not even the baby's grave."

His father's revelation shocked Sean and ripped at his heart.

"So, I understood what you were feeling. I never got to know him...or her."

The deep sorrow his father had buried came to light because of his circumstances. How could history repeat itself and cause so much pain in one family?

Not wishing to hurt his father further, Sean wondered if

his mother knew, but he'd never ask.

"My Louise knew and had a special place in her heart for my pain."

Angus wiped his face and blew his nose. "Enough of that. It's old news."

That was his mother. The most loving woman he'd ever known. He wished she were alive so he could ask her advice.

"What are your plans, son?"

"First things first. A paternity test for my peace of mind and I'll get a visa for him. But I'm guessing it'll take time to get those documents. In the meantime, I have to contact Brett about my practice."

Angus nodded and sighed. "I think Drew will be fine. He's a good boy despite the pain he's suffered in his young life."

Sean nodded. So much to do and yet, throughout the days and weeks, Mia's face popped into his mind. He shook his head. She was married and unavailable, and he stiffened his spine to forget her.

Chapter 11

While Mia was over-the-moon excited that Steve finally got his game going and decided to win Cassie's heart, she'd been shocked to see how fast the relationship developed. When it was right it was right, she guessed. Her excitement for her brother's engagement and subsequent Valentine's Day wedding only increased her heart's loneliness.

Why can't I find Shannon? What did he do? Disappear off the face of the earth? It had been months since she'd seen him. Valentine's Day had come and gone and Shannon was nowhere to be found. She had scoured the internet for all the vets in the area, but none of them were named Shannon. It didn't make sense.

Steve had taken her to the crash site and she shivered remembering what he said about the car being under water, but with the winter snow and frigid creek water, they hadn't been able to hike to where she'd fallen.

Classes to learn new photography applications and getting a handle on the updates to the applications she already knew weren't enough to keep her mind from thoughts of him. Angry? Oh, she was plenty angry. When she found him, he'd get a piece of her mind.

Her phone chirped Betty & Bertha's ringtone as Mia

updated the website she planned being live soon. She'd been reluctant to pull the trigger on the website, but she had to get her business off the ground. She needed an income, and she needed it now.

Now that her brother had married, his new wife had taken over the care of his daughters and she couldn't mooch off him and his new family forever.

Pam's cheerful voice came across the line. "You've been in a funk lately. How about we go horseback riding?"

"Isn't it too cold for that?"

"If you layer your clothes, you'll be warm enough."

Mia perked. "That's not a bad idea. When?"

"How about now? It's a gorgeous day. The sun is shining and although we're at the tail end of winter, the air smells fresh, and I'm at your front door."

Mia laughed, shut the program, and raced to open the door. "You're incorrigible."

Pam leaned against the door frame and pointed to her derriere. "Betty & Bertha want to exercise. And you could shoot fantastic end-of-winter scenes."

Mia struggled not to laugh, but her friend's smiling face always seemed to give her hope. "Come on in."

"I marvel every time I visit. I'd have never guessed this over-the-garage apartment was so cozy and cute. And bonus, you have Fiona and Cassie's tasty meals so you don't have to cook."

"Yeah, it's convenient. But I may be moving. Not sure yet, though."

"Why?"

"To give Cassie and Steve privacy."

"You don't live with them."

"True. But I don't want to inflict myself on them."

"Have they said anything?"

"No."

"Then forget it. Get dressed and we'll go."

Mia pulled on her silk long underwear, jeans and sweater then grabbed her puffy jacket, hat, and mittens. Mia winced as she threw her camera case and purse over her shoulder. "Ready."

Pam caught the wince. "Your wrist bothering you?"

"Only when I turn it a certain way. I'm worried I won't be able to use my hands to take fantastic shots."

"You're a brilliant photographer. I can't see you not taking great shots."

When they settled in the car, Mia adjusted her seatbelt. "Where are we going?"

"To a ranch I found online. They breed horses and I want to buy one."

"That's terrific. I know how much you love them." Mia fumbled in her purse. "I want to text Cassie. We could have dinner out."

"Absolutely. Have you searched for Shannon again?"

"No. I'm so angry I'm about done with the search for him. If he doesn't want to see me, then forget it. I don't want to see him either."

Pam shot her a glance. "You don't really mean that, do you?"

"Yes. No." Mia sighed. "I don't know. I want an explanation why he abandoned me, came to the hospital, and then just disappeared."

"Something might have happened to him."

"Like what?"

Pam's breath whooshed. "Heck, I don't know. But something had to keep him away from you."

Did something happen to him? Mia lowered her head.

Maybe it did and maybe it didn't. Her brain hurt from thinking about it.

Mia strained to see everything as Pam pulled the car into the ranch's gravel parking lot. She itched to get her camera out of her bag.

The white-washed barns with the red trim were unusual and stuck out among the various other dreary red and brown structures. Horses pranced on wet mud clumps while the shaded areas held patches of slow-melting snow.

The cold and deserted farmhouse sat apart from the other buildings and Mia wondered if it was vibrant in the summer. She'd have to come later in the season. If the owners planted flowers, it'd be gorgeous.

Pam beamed at her. "It's beautiful, isn't it?"

"Yes, it is."

"Come on, let's get our horses."

"I haven't ridden in years, but I'm looking forward to it."

Pam led the way to the barn where field hands worked with the livestock. When their horses were saddled, Pam held the camera while Mia mounted, then gave her the camera pack. Pam mounted and led Mia to the trails around the ranch. "I wish we could go farther afield, but since the horses don't belong to us, we're confined to one of three riding trails."

"That's OK by me." She wagged her finger and adjusted the pack on the pommel that held her camera. "But we'll stop along the way to take photos."

Pam smiled. "I can handle that. The fresh air and taking pictures will give you joy." They rode a narrow trail that gradually rose behind the barns, became wider, and overlooked the ranch. "Let's stop here. I want to take some shots." Mia loved that she could check the digital photos to see how the shot turned out.

She looked through the viewfinder and told her heart to lead her to the shots she should take. She snapped off a dozen photos of the scene before her and sniffed the spring-like air.

"Pam, can you hold the horse still?"

"Why?"

Mia held the camera in the air and pointed to it.

"I don't want pics of Betty & Bertha on your website." Pam's voice caused her horse to sidestep.

Mia's breath whooshed out. "Relax. I'll only take pictures of the horse. Betty and Bertha can find another photographer to take their pics. Now hold him still."

Mia then leaned sideways and snapped shots of the horse's profile, Pam's boot in the stirrup, and the horse's hooves. The churned ground with clumps of snow and mud could make an unusual background, so she shot various photos of that, too.

They moved into the sunshine when a horse whinnied from beyond the trees in front of them.

Pam stared ahead and frowned. "Who do you suppose that is? The foreman said no one was out today."

Mia shook her head and got her horse moving. "Let's go see."

They came into a meadow that sprouted early daffodils amid tufts of brown grass. Mia's eyes widened, and she struggled to not bounce on the horse. "I need shots of this."

As she moved her viewfinder over the meadow, a pang came over her chest when she remembered Sean's meadow. "I bet it'll be glorious in about two weeks."

"More like three," a masculine voice said.

Mia turned and almost unseated herself while Pam scowled at the dark-haired man sitting astride a huge gray stallion.

He tipped his cowboy hat. "Hello, Pam. Haven't seen you for a while."

"Last-minute thing." Pam scrunched her lips.

Mia narrowed her gaze at her friend. She'd never seen Pam so off balance. "I'm Mia, and you are?"

"Brett Cooper. You a photographer?"

"Gee, what clued you in?" Pam said in a low voice.

Brett smiled. "Still snarky, I see."

She cocked her head and glared. Something was going on, but Mia was clueless. Pam never talked about her personal life. They'd concentrated on the search for Shannon since she got out of the hospital and Mia never considered Pam might be interested in someone. *How self-centered can I be?*

Mia cleared her throat. "Yes. I'm a nature photographer."

"Is that a fact? I'm a web designer and I'm always on the lookout for original photos for my clients."

Mia's heart pounded. Could this be her big break? "I'm new in the business, but I'm open to whatever possibilities are out there."

"Perhaps we could have coffee or something," Brett said.

Pam harrumphed.

Mia studied her friend. "Possibly. You want to keep riding, Pam?"

"No. Let's go. You promised we'd go to dinner."

"What are your plans for dinner?" Brett said.

Pam's hands tightened on the reins, and the horse moved sideways. "We're not sure and you're not invited."

"Whoa, there. Treat the old boy kindly, will ya? The ranch owner will have a conniption if one of his horses gets abused," Brett said.

Mia darted glances between Pam and Brett. "You know the owner?"

"Yeah. But he's out of a town. I'm surprised the hands allowed you to ride today."

Pam was through with the conversation and trotted to the trail with Mia following and Brett behind her.

When they reached the barns, Pam dismounted, gave the reins to the foreman, and stomped to the car. Mia turned to Brett who still sat on his horse. "I'm sorry. I don't know what got into her. This is unusual for her."

"Funny. She's been prickly around me from the day I met her." Brett pushed his hat away from his forehead and scratched his chin. "Why that is, I have no idea."

Mia raised her eyebrows. "You have a business card? I'll call you and we'll arrange something."

Brett reached into his flannel shirt pocket and gave her his card. "You have a card?"

"Sorry, no. I don't have my ducks in a row yet for cards."

"Ok. I'll wait for your call. Best to reach me on my cell."

She nodded, waved, and left him sitting on his horse.

Pam peeled out of the gravel parking lot as if the devil himself chased her.

Mia breathed a sigh of relief when they were once again on the highway. Her voice shattered the silence. "You want to share what that was about?"

"Not particularly. Dinner might not be a good idea. I'm not up to it."

"Look. You've been there for me for months with the Shannon search. The least I can do is listen to your troubles. How about we order a pizza, instead? I've been hungry for spicy sauce."

"I don't know."

"Come on. My cozy apartment?" Her eyes lit and her lips curved. "We'll have a sleepover. I haven't had one of those in years. It'll be fun."

Pam cast her a sideways glance. "I'm not twelve, you know. And Betty & Bertha will hog the covers, but it might be fun."

Mia grinned. "That's more like it."

When the pizza arrived, Mia prepared plates and handed one to her friend. "Want to tell me what's going on?"

Pam sat with her legs tucked under her in Mia's warm living room, gazed at the crackling fire, and heaved a long sigh. "Betty & Bertha got pinched with a bit of the green-eyed monster. That's all."

"Why?"

Pam gestured and her voice rose. "Look at you. You're slender, beautiful and talented. Who could compete with that?"

"Are you kidding me?" Her voice squeaked with disbelief. "You're beautiful."

"Ha! If you call hefty with Betty & Bertha hanging out all the time, beautiful—"

Mia grabbed Pam's arm and stared into her eyes. "Will you stop?"

"Mia, I'm sorry," Pam whispered. "My insecurities got the best of me."

Maybe if she could make Pam see that even if a woman was slender or what some called beautiful, it didn't matter when it came to insecurities. Everyone had them in one area or another. Maybe if she shared her own insecurities, Pam would see herself in a better light. Mia had never shared about her New York life with anyone in the five years she'd returned to Worthy because it was so painful to her, but she'd put her own pain aside, if it meant it would help her dear friend. She was no psychologist, but she had to try.

Mia stared at her friend. "Maybe I should tell you about my life in New York City."

Pam's head shot up. "New York City?"

"Yeah, I left here after my parents died. Steve had married his first wife, Laura, several months before. I couldn't stand it. He was married, and I had no one—not even my parents. It felt like he abandoned me, his twin sister."

Pam grinned. "I love that you two are twins."

Mia smiled back. "Yeah, me too. Anyway, I couldn't take either loss and left for New York. I started out in a small fashion house and made a name for myself. Soon the bigger houses hired me. Then I met Brad. The epitome of every young woman's dream man. He owned a modeling agency. He was so handsome and built. I fell head over heels."

Pam's eyes got as big as saucers. "What happened?"

"I was mad at God and left my faith like a snake shedding its skin. I didn't realize the fashion business was taking me further and further away from God. When he asked me to marry him, I figured he was the answer to my loneliness. But I didn't know I married a serial gambler who owed the mob money. A lot of money."

"Oh, no." Pam breathed, and she touched Mia's arm.

"I found out by accident, but I was prepared to sell everything and get him help for his addiction." Mia's gaze lingered on the dark skies through the window and she shivered. "We took his godfather's yacht on a late honeymoon trip along the coast, but a storm came out of nowhere. Somehow he'd forgotten or didn't bother with the maintenance work on the boat and it exploded, threw me in the water, and killed him."

Pam grasped Mia's hand. "I'm so sorry."

"It was a long time ago, and I never told my brother. It was too painful. Then when I came home and saw my nieces…" Her shoulders slumped. "The wounds their mother left behind…" Mia shook her head. "I buried my hurt and focused on my family's healing."

Pam embraced Mia. "I don't know what to say."

Mia pushed Pam away. "I didn't tell you because I wanted your pity. I told you because I've lost two men in my life. Brad wasn't the man I believed he was and it almost destroyed me. So it's not just you, all of us have insecurities. And then there's Shannon…" Mia sighed. "Might be another Brad. I'm not interested in Brett other than how he can help my fledgling career with nature and other photography." She inhaled the zesty pizza and bit into her slice.

"Why not fashion photography?"

"Too many memories and I'd have to live in New York and my home is here. And it could suck me away from my faith again and I won't do that. Besides the well-known models are pure divas. I want to do animals and scenery. They don't mouth off…well, at least the scenery doesn't." Mia laughed and then sobered as distressing memories surfaced. "I spent the night in cold water and thought I'd drown which led to a fear of water. And because of it, I had to sell almost everything to take care of my husband's debts." Telling her new friend about the accident that made her unable to have children was out of the question. No one knew and that's how it would stay.

"I'm flabbergasted, Mia. I would have never guessed. Then the car crash with your injuries…"

"These wrist injuries and the facial scars…" Mia gave her a wistful smile. "Doesn't matter."

Pam leaned into the sofa with a thoughtful look on her face. "Now, more than ever, it's important to find Shannon."

"And it's important you go after the man that you care about despite your reservations. Will you promise me you'll do it? Or at least think about it?"

Pam looked away. "I'll think about it."

Mia wasn't sure she'd ever find Shannon and even if she did, she wasn't sure he was the man for her. If any man was for her. Not now.

Chapter 12

The accident insurance money allowed Mia to buy a used SUV, but she was still adjusting to its size when she parked at the local café. She jumped out, pulled her fuzzy cap on and made her way inside. The scent of the rich espresso filled her nostrils. Brett wasn't there yet, so she ordered her favorite latte, found a table near the electric fireplace, and opened her laptop.

She watched for him, sipped the milky brew, and fretted over the outcome of this meeting while she listened to the muted conversation around her. If nothing came of it, she'd be no further ahead than before. This morning she had prayed for wisdom and favor.

Brett walked in, waved and pulled the electric blue scarf from his neck. She pondered if she could get him and her friend together. In the past two weeks, Pam refused to talk about him. At the counter, the clerk flirted with him and he responded.

Not a good idea to get involved in Pam's love life. Heck, she couldn't even handle her own love life. She wouldn't be a party to heartache for her friend. Pam would have to do it on her own.

He pulled a seat next to hers, set his coffee on the table, and dropped into the chair. "Been waiting long?"

"Five minutes."

"Great. Show me your portfolio."

For the next hour she showed him her recent nature shots, but Brett's attention span waned. "Now show me your fashion shoots."

"What?"

Brett raised an eyebrow. "I researched you, Mia. You were a hot-shot fashion photographer five or six years ago and well known in the industry."

Mia frowned. "I'm not into fashion photography anymore."

"But that's what will sell you in nature photography. You already have the clout. Show me anyway. Please." His forceful eyes told her he'd not take no for an answer.

When she showed him the various mood boards she'd done, he perked up. "Hey, those are amazing."

She narrowed her gaze. "Fashion photography is off the table."

Brett's face registered confusion. "But why?"

"My reasons are personal. Besides models can be draining."

"What if they weren't models?"

Her curiosity got the best of her. "What did you have in mind?"

Excitement lit Brett's eyes. "I can use the nature photos for the various ranches and ancillary businesses. No question. But remember, animals don't always cooperate."

Mia laughed. "No, but they don't mouth off either. I'll make adjustments for their natural habitat and shoot those accordingly."

He frowned. "The market is small for those. Equestrians and ranches who specialize in breeding horses have ongoing needs, especially the breeders. They foal horses then sell them. Professional photos, when creatively done, give buyers that wow factor."

"Equestrian jumpers." Mia gave his words consideration and raised an eyebrow. "Are they divas?"

Brett chuckled. "Most are down-to-earth girls and women who love to jump horses."

Mia nodded. "I think I can handle a handful of divas. And they wouldn't be photographed together, right?"

"No, it'd be one-on-one."

"Groups of models can be catty."

"I bet. How about photos for big ticket houses and ranches for sale? There's always an abundance of those. With seasonal changes, they need new photos."

Mia leaned in. "Now you're talking. I'd love to do that."

"How about kids and babies? Parents always want their kids' pictures taken."

"No thank you. Parents can be worse than models."

Brett chuckled. "What? You don't enjoy children?"

It wasn't that she didn't love children, but it was her own inability to have them that haunted her, so having to face that realization every time she took a photo of a plump toothless baby would cause her untold grief.

Mia tightened her grip on the mouse. "I love children. I'd rather not be a children's photographer."

He leaned in. "Can I ask you a personal question?"

Her lips set in a straight line as she eyed the handsome man. "Depends. And only if I can ask one of you."

"Deal." He pointed to her face. "How'd you get those scars?"

Mia touched one of the three scars that plastic surgery couldn't erase. "Car accident. My turn. Why don't you like Pam?"

Brett's shocked look surprised Mia, and he blustered. "I never said that about Pam. What gave you that idea?"

"When we were at the ranch, you seemed..."

He stiffened and gaped. "Let me set you straight. Pam is

a beautiful woman, and I wanted to get to know her better, but she turned prickly and I have no idea why."

She gave him a twisted-lip grin. "Is that a fact?"

"Do you know something I don't?"

Mia raised her brows. "No. But I saw you flirt with the clerk who's been giving you goo-goo eyes since you sat down."

The dumbfounded expression on Brett's face made Mia laugh outright.

"What?"

She smirked, shook her head, and crossed her arms. "Do *not* tell me you're oblivious to women giving you the eye." She followed the heat rising from his collar to his cheeks and laughed.

Grumbling under his breath, Mia barely caught his words. "You women are all alike. Chat with a lady and right away, other gals think I'm hitting on her."

Mia stared at him and frowned.

Brett gazed at her and raised his chin. "I'll make you a deal. You get me a date with Pam and I'll get you appointments at the ranches and realty companies."

She slammed her laptop shut. "You think I'd trade a business deal for my friend's happiness? No way." She slid her laptop into her bag and grabbed her coat.

He grinned and touched her arm. "Checking to see how good of a friend you are."

"That was underhanded."

Brett sighed. "Yes, it was. But could you put in a good word for me?"

She gave him a side-long glance. "I'll think about it."

"Good. Send me your price sheets and we'll schedule appointments with my clients. We'll start with the ranches in the area."

She nodded and knew she had her work cut out for her.

There'd be no time to search for Shannon. No matter, though. Hopefully, her business could take off soon and she'd have no time to think about him.

Mia relaxed her wrists and did the exercises Pam insisted helped with the stiffness. Overuse and the cold caused her to lose her grip. She couldn't wait for warmer weather. She sighed when her phone rang.

Pam's excited voice flowed through the phone line. "I think I have a lead on Shannon."

Mia straightened and blinked. "You do?"

"I think I found the cabin."

Finding Shannon had become a priority over the various opportunities Brett offered her yesterday. "How do you know?"

"Because I went out there on my day off and it's exactly as you described it. The gentle sounds of the flowing creek soothed me, but that brown cabin faded into the hillside. I swear buttery biscuits cooked in the oven and my mouth watered for them. Must have been hungry."

Mia laughed and grabbed a granola bar from her stash. "You're making me hungry. How did you find it?"

"My brother's friend overheard me talking about finding Shannon. He does a lot of hunting in West Virginia and I described the cabin. He said he thought he knew exactly where it was. Now, what's important is if it's the right place. You available for a road trip to find out?"

Her breath caught in her throat. When her brother took her to the crash site months ago, she remembered the creek. When the snow melted, she trekked to where she fell, but she didn't know which direction to go or how far. The search had been futile after that. "When?"

"I'm off today. How about an hour?"

Mia groaned. Research would have to wait. She'd get the rest of the preliminary pricing done and she'd do a final review before she met with Brett the next day. "Make it two and you have a deal."

"Two hours then."

The overcast day couldn't quell Mia's excitement. Her price sheets were done, and she texted her sister-in-law she'd be gone for the rest of the day.

Mia grabbed her camera case and headed for Pam's car.

Pam turned her head as Mia shoved the camera case on the floor. "What's with the camera?"

She smiled and rolled her shoulders. "I want shots of the area."

Her friend chuckled. "Course you do."

As they made their way to the highway, Mia turned in her seat. "I met with Brett last week."

Pam's head swiveled and she frowned. "Why?"

"To explore a business opportunity with him and his clients."

Her friend snorted. "I'll bet."

"Will you stop? It wasn't like that."

"So, tell me how it was?"

"We talked about my services for his various clients. I have to give him price sheets and he'll schedule appointments for me."

Her friend raised her brow. "And that's it?"

Mia sighed. "Not exactly."

Pam leaned forward as they entered the highway. "That's what I thought."

"You know I've searched for Shannon for months. I need to find out if what we had in the cabin was real or my imagination gone wild. Sure, Brett is attractive, but I've had one like him, remember?"

"Sorry, Mia. He's way too handsome for his own good. And charming. I've seen him in action and I don't trust him."

"He's oblivious, you know?"

Pam gave her a side-long glance, her fingers tightened on the wheel. "No, I don't. Explain."

"We met at a coffee shop. The barista flirted with him, but he didn't have a clue his flirting affected her."

She snorted again and pulled the car into a rest area.

"Why are we stopping?"

"Because this conversation could cause an accident."

"Fine. But what I've said is true." Mia pulled her seatbelt free and turned to face Pam. "And I'll tell you something else. He thinks you're beautiful, but prickly. He wanted me to get him a date with you."

The stunned look on Pam's face caused her to choke. "I hope you didn't trade a date with me to get your business going."

"Of course not. In fact, I made it clear he could take a hike. He gave me this big smile and said, 'Good. I'm glad you're a good friend'."

Pam released a long breath. "I've never had a friend like you, Mia."

She patted her friend's hand and her lips twitched. "But—"

"Oh no.—" Pam groaned and closed her eyes.

"He wanted me to put in a good word for him. I think you should date him."

Pam sighed. "Betty and Bertha won't let him have a word

in edgewise."

"Stop." Mia laughed then crossed her arms. "He said you were beautiful. That means *all* of you is beautiful, even your pals. Can I give him your number and tell him to call you?"

"I don't know." Pam picked at her fingernails.

"Take a chance. What's the worst that can happen?"

"He won't like me?"

"Nope. Already told me you're beautiful. And you are. Period."

"Give him my number and we'll see if he calls." Pam sighed, shook her head and gave her a half-smile.

She clipped her seatbelt on. "He will. Can we go now?"

Pam laughed and started the car.

They made their way to the narrow black-topped side roads. Mia didn't recognize the area. She grabbed her camera, opened the window and shot the stark trees and decayed wet leaves. The branches whistled with short bursts of wind. "Are we close? I don't remember any of these roads."

Pam glanced at Mia. "Almost. It's up that hill."

Mia held her breath as Pam pulled the car into a graveled lane. Mia's breath caught as she saw the cabin for the first time since her memory returned. She jumped out of the car then stopped every five steps to click the shutter on her camera. The crunch of gravel told her Pam waited right behind her.

They climbed the three steps onto the covered porch, knocked on the door, and waited. No answer. Mia's shoulders slumped, but she cupped her hands and peered through the front door at the quaint dinette table and remembered the many tasty meals he prepared.

Then she caught sight of Shannon's Bible and remembered the scripture verses he'd highlighted for her. She'd forgotten he was a man of God and yet, he left her at the hospital and then didn't bother with her after that initial visit. Didn't make sense nor did it sit well.

She knew he didn't visit the cabin often, but she prayed he'd be there. If for no other reason than to get an explanation.

Mia leaned on the rustic railing. "I was hoping he'd be here and he'd answer questions. Then I'd have closure."

"At least you know where to find him even if he's not here now. You can always come back another time. Let's take a peek around back." Pam moved to the side steps and disappeared to the rear of the cabin.

Mia followed her friend and grumbled. "We're peeping toms."

The hillside trees surrounded the cabin, but didn't hide it from the main road. The place looked desolate, but peaceful. The pain in her heart caused a lump in her throat. What if she met Shannon here now that she knew who she was? Would he feel any different about her?

"I'm afraid he's not here. I'm sorry, Mia."

Her heart ached, but Mia smiled. "Don't be sorry. At least now we have an address. I'm sure one of Brett's clients could help us."

Pam frowned. "I don't see how."

"They can get a last name for the owner of the cabin." Mia hugged her friend. "Thank you."

Realization dawned on Pam. "Let's go, then."

"Wait. I want to leave a note. Just in case he comes and I miss him again." She wrote him a note and included her telephone number and placed it under a large rock in front of the door. Hopefully, if it rained the paper would remain intact.

Her excitement welled. She'd finally gotten a good lead on Shannon's name and could find him.

Chapter 13

Sean smiled as his small son's eyes grew to the size of giant marbles as he watched bags drop onto the luggage carousel. Leaving his Da had been difficult. Drew's sniffles as he hugged his grandfather and Mrs. Monahan, broke Sean's heart, but his life was in America and he wanted his son to take advantage of everything America offered.

A woman strolled through the crowd and reminded him of Mia. Funny, in the time he'd been in Ireland arranging for their return, he hadn't thought of her much. He counted on Drew to keep his mind occupied.

"There's our cases, Da." Drew shouted and darted between scowling adults. Sean caught his son as he fell onto the conveyor belt. He pulled him from the slow-moving carousel, lifted both cases, and gave the smaller one to his son.

As he and his son exited the airport arrival center into the blustery March air, Shannon tooted the horn, and they made their way to the SUV.

Drew stopped and stared at the two men. "Da, he looks just like you. Except you have a beard and a scar."

Shannon laughed and slapped Sean on the shoulder. "Spitting image, eh? Welcome home."

Sean introduced his twin to his son. Shannon swooped

in and gave the boy a hearty hug while lifting him in his arms. He whispered something in the boy's ear, then let him slide to the ground.

His twin grinned and lifted the luggage into the trunk. "Wendy and Mrs. O'Neill cleaned, cooked, and baked since you texted your itinerary. And drove me nuts."

Sean chuckled at Drew's expression when he buckled him in his car seat. "There are videos you can watch."

"Super." Drew fiddled with the video and put his earbuds in.

Shannon gave Sean much of the ranch news since he'd left over six months ago. Sean had been glad to spend Christmas with his father and son, but he missed his twin. He wished his father would divide his time between Ireland and America so they could be together. Ohio wasn't anything like the New York his father recalled and he hoped, between Shannon, Drew and himself, they'd convince his father to visit.

"Brett wanted me to tell you he found a top-notch photographer for our websites. He's working out the pricing."

"He emailed me. I hope to drum up business with a fresh website."

"When your clients find out you're back, you'll be inundated."

"Yeah, I'm concerned over balancing work and home life." Sean stole a glance at his son who stared at the video screen. "I need to make time for my son. He's still so little."

Shannon frowned and maneuvered the vehicle into traffic. "That was a shock, I'm sure."

"More than I can say." Sean let out a long breath. "We'll talk about that later, but there is something I need to talk to you about."

"I know that tone. It's not good." Shannon flicked a

glance at his twin.

Sean sighed. "It's about Da. I pressured him to come to America…if only for six months out of the year."

"Great. When can we expect him?"

"He won't come and told me something that staggered me."

A worried frown covered Shannon's face. "What?"

"Da, are we there yet?" Drew called from the back.

"Almost, son." With a warning look to Shannon, Sean silenced further conversation.

Sean eased out of the SUV and grinned as Wendy flew out of the house and hugged him. "You must have watched for us."

"Da, I can't get this belt undone," Drew said.

Wendy moved to unbuckle the boy's belt and gathered him in her arms for a tight hug. "You look like your dad and uncle."

Drew shuffled toward his dad after she released him. "That's what my grandad says."

"Let's get you guys in the house for some food," Wendy said.

His son tugged on his pants. "Da, can I go riding?"

"Not today, son. We've had a long trip and we both need to eat, settle in, and rest. We'll have the entire day tomorrow to check out the horses and explore the ranch."

Drew dragged his feet and directed longing glances at the barn before they entered the farmhouse. Sean elbowed his brother when he was about to open his mouth. Shannon pinched his lips and answered Brett's ringtone, then hung up. "He arranged for the photographer to be here next week."

Later, after a hardy meal, Wendy poked Sean. "Need

some help?"

Sean shook his head. Drew's eyes drooped, and he stumbled and made Sean smile. He lifted the boy and carried him in his arms. "Come on, buddy. Let's get you to bed."

Mumbling, the boy wrapped his arms around Sean's neck. "Don' wanna go to bed." Sean's heart melted once again for his son.

Drew was asleep before Sean could get him into his pajamas. *Thank you, Lord, for this extraordinary gift you've given me. I'll take special care of him. Bless him and help him to fit into his new life here.*

Sean found Shannon in his study working on accounts. The scowl on his twin's face told him Shannon hadn't gotten the ranch out of the red yet. "What's the verdict?"

"No good."

"I can take a loan out on my practice."

"Why should you? You had nothing to do with my bad judgment."

A furrow appeared on Sean's forehead. "A few tough years doesn't make it bad judgment. Every ranch in the area has suffered."

Shannon slammed the laptop shut. "I can't take money from you now that you have a son." He drummed his fingers on the orderly desk and stared at his twin. "You need a wife."

Crossing his arms, Sean's jaw stiffened. "I don't need or want a wife. It's Drew and me. That's it and that's how it'll always be. You need money. I've put money away and the proceeds from the manual will help. That'll be enough, right?" It was a stand-off between him and his brother, and like other times in their lives, he'd win it.

The chair creaked as Shannon swiveled it and eyed his brother. "No. You've been saving for years to build a building for your practice and I won't take that away from you."

"You're not taking, I'm offering."

"Doesn't matter. After what you've been through, you continue to put yourself out to help others." Shannon shook his head and gripped the edge of the desk. "When will you live for yourself?"

Sean spread his arms and cocked his head. "I *am* living for myself. Drew came into my life at the exact moment I needed him. And we'll have a grand time discovering one another and caring for animals."

His twin lit a fire in the fireplace and sat in the armchair near the door. "Tell me the whole story. You didn't want to talk about it over the phone and we couldn't talk about it in the car."

Sean took in the gleaming bookcases on either side of the fireplace. He sipped the last of his hazelnut coffee and breathed in the burning oak logs. "I never realized how much this room looks like Da's study."

Shannon nodded. "A bit of Ireland right here in America."

The crackling fire reminded Sean of the day he arrived at his childhood home and found out he was a father. Sean took the other seat and told Shannon about Bridget, Drew, and his Nana. Weariness settled in his bones and he wanted to sleep for a month.

"And what's this about Da?" Shannon said.

"History repeated itself." Confusion marred his twin's face and Sean settled into the comfortable chair. "When Da lived in America, long before he found his faith and married Ma, he fell in love with a young woman and got her pregnant." Sean wanted to laugh at the shock on Shannon's face, but it wasn't funny.

"Da? Our Da? Can't be."

The flickering fire drew Sean's eyes, and he muttered, "All these years and we never knew a thing."

"We have a sibling?"

"No. Apparently, the child died at birth along with the mother but that's the extent of his knowledge of the situation. If you could have seen Da's face when he told me I was a father and couldn't abandon my son." Sean heaved a sigh. "I had never seen a more tortured expression in my life. Like a knife had carved his heart out."

"I don't understand."

"He tried to find her, but her sister had sent her away. When the young woman died along with the child, the sister wanted no more contact with Da. Moved away. He tried to find her and the graves through a detective agency. but nothing ever came of it."

Shannon stared into the fire. "That must have killed Ma."

"He said Ma understood, and she supported him for whatever he had to do. For that, he loved her more than life itself. I pondered some things he said to me when I recuperated from my accident. His cryptic remarks make sense now. At the time I was in no condition to question him, and then we left."

Curious eyes exactly like his own stared at him. "What did he say?"

"He said he understood my affair with Bridget. Made sense why he'd pounded it in our heads to stay pure." Sean's breath whooshed. "Drew needs a father figure to guide him and other strong males to emulate. His Nana worked hard to give him a loving home, but he misses her. Counseling will help him and his adjustment into the American lifestyle."

Shannon's face hardened. "Another reason I can't take your money. Counselors cost."

He stood and leaned over his brother. "Will you stop? A check will be on your desk Monday, and I'm not taking no for an answer."

"I won't talk you out of this, will I?" His twin heaved a sigh and flattened his lips.

"No. Plan to pay off the ranch bills."

Shannon scowled. Sean could almost see the gears grinding in his twin's head, then his face lit. "How about I give you part ownership for the money?"

Sean considered the option and smiled. "That I'll do."

"I'll call my attorney on Monday and have him draw up the papers."

"Don't you have to talk to Wendy first?"

Shannon's face closed. "I will, but I know she'll tell me I have to do what's best for the ranch. Besides, I want her to concentrate on her equestrian thing and not worry about the ranch. She knows I'll make it profitable."

Sean dropped into the chair again. "I'm exhausted."

"You thought about school for Drew?"

"Not yet. I want him to get accustomed to his new environment for a week or so before I plunge him into a new school."

Shannon stood and stretched. "For years we've not been able to get Da to come to America. If we'd have known this before, we wouldn't have pestered him."

Sean fingered his scar. "It must have wounded him every time we bugged him about it."

"But now that he knows he has a grandchild and maybe more—"

"Is Wendy—"

"No. We want to wait." Shannon grinned.

Sean moved to the door. "I'm headed to bed. Have you met the photographer? I hope he does great work."

"No. We'll meet him next week."

His thoughts turned to Drew and his time spent in Ireland with his Da. Mia's face popped into his head and wished with all his heart it could have been different. But he knew he couldn't think about what could have been. Especially now.

Chapter 14

Excitement coursed through Mia's veins. The cloudy March day didn't dampen her spirits. She'd meet two of Brett's ranch clients today.

She dressed in her best jeans and boots, taking special care with her makeup and hair. She fussed over her camera equipment and triple-checked she had everything she might need along with any documents. *Lord, help me make a good impression.*

She arrived at the Shady Dale Ranch and saw Brett's jeep, but didn't see him. The ranch appeared to be moderately successful with the number of people who roamed the place. The horses in the corral next to the barn seemed healthy, but she couldn't tell much from this distance.

As she maneuvered the SUV to a stop, she readied her camera to take a few shots of the farm. Instinctively, she knew the place would look much better if the sun came out and there were pops of color near the barn. But that's something Brett would have to deal with.

She focused her camera on the frolicking horses in the corral and wrinkled her nose at the fresh earth churned by them. When a little boy came out of the barn, she adjusted the camera and took a few shots of him. When he spotted her, he ran to her.

Out of breath, he stopped next to her. "You the photographer?"

She beamed at the cute little guy. "I am."

He watched her take a few shots, then tugged on her jacket. "Can I take a picture?"

The little boy had an accent similar to Shannon's and it warmed her heart. She never let anyone touch her camera equipment, but there was something about the little boy that stirred her heart. "Let me show you what to do."

She held her breath while he gently, and with reverence, took a few shots. Then she showed him his photos, but he caught sight of hers and his face crumpled. "Mine are no good."

Mia crouched to his level. "What's your name?"

"Drew."

"That's a great name. When you take a picture, you have to look with the eyes of your heart and not just your eyes."

He smiled, but confusion crossed his face. She'd have to explain it better. "When you look through the viewfinder, take a picture of something that touches your heart. Something that makes your heart happy."

His little face grew serious and he nodded and took the camera again. Drew enthralled her. His darling accent reminded her of Shannon and she wondered if there was a connection. Her heart ached. *Concentrate on the work.*

Soon his face became animated. He pointed and dropped the camera and Mia's stomach with it. She snagged it before it hit the ground. "Sorry. I want to take a picture of my Uncle Shannon and Aunt Wendy." When Mia followed his finger, her heart dropped, and vomit rose in her throat. Not fifty feet from her stood a clean-shaven Shannon with his arms wrapped around a beautiful woman.

He was married? No wonder he didn't return.

The little guy pulled at her jacket. "Can I take a picture now?"

Without thinking, Mia adjusted the viewfinder for him and regarded the couple's embrace. They were oblivious to anyone around them. She allowed Drew to take a few pictures, but she couldn't stand it any longer and had to leave.

She gently took the camera from the boy's hands while straining to keep her tears at bay. She swallowed. "Drew, it was nice meeting you, but I have to go," she whispered.

He stared at his uncle, then at her and ran after her. "Wait. I want to see the pictures I took."

Over her shoulder, she said. "I'm sorry, Drew, I have to leave. Stay there. I don't want you to get hurt."

Mia jumped in the car and left as if the devil's minions threw fireballs at her. Sobs erupted from the pit of her stomach. She spent months searching for a man who had moved on.

Had he been engaged when he found her? Married? He never told her and she never asked. But maybe that's why he'd been reluctant to kiss her and spent so much time with Thunder. It had nothing to do with her having a husband, children or being in trouble. It had to do with him having a wife. What a fool she'd been! *Lord, heal my heart.*

Sean and Brett stepped out of the farmhouse and Sean checked his phone. "Your photographer is late."

Brett frowned. "It's not like her."

Sean raced to his son as Shannon crouched and rubbed his son's back. He sobbed in his uncle's arms. "I wanted to see the pictures."

"What happened?"

Shannon stood and steered Drew to his father. "The photographer arrived, and she allowed him to take pictures, but she took off like a bat out of—" Wendy poked him in the ribs and he glared. "An underground cave."

Brett narrowed his eyes and put his hands on his hips. "What did you say to her, Shannon?"

He rose to his full height and growled. "I didn't say anything. I didn't even meet her. Before I could reach her, she bolted."

"Something set her off. Let's figure this out." Wendy squatted, turned Drew to her, and wiped his face. "Can you tell us what happened, honey?"

Drew's sobs stopped and nodded. "I saw her car and wanted to meet her. Uncle Shannon told us we should welcome everyone that comes to the ranch." He glanced at Shannon for confirmation.

"That's right."

"I asked her if I could take a picture. She showed me how, but I couldn't do it. She told me I had to—" He scrunched his face as he remembered her words. "See with the eyes of my heart and not my eyes. Then I saw uncle Shannon and you in the paddock. I wanted to take a picture. She let me, then she ran away."

Brett scratched his head. "That's not like Mia."

Sean's knees buckled, and he squeezed his son's shoulder. "Mia?"

Drew grabbed his father's hands. "Da, that hurts."

He drew a deep breath. "Sorry, son."

Shannon turned, waved the foreman over, and pushed Drew toward him. "Why don't you see if Gingerbell is ready for a ride, Drew?"

Wendy placed her hand on Sean's wrist. "Are you OK?" Worry colored her voice.

Sean stared at her hand, watched his son trot to the foreman, his pictures forgotten. He shook his head. His voice failed him.

Brett eyed him. "What is it with you, man?"

Sean cleared his throat of the bitterness and his voice rasped. "What is the photographer's full name?"

"Mia Nardelli. I looked forward to meeting her and discussing my ideas for a photo shoot for my next competition," Wendy said.

Sean's voice took on a harsh note. "Cancel my appointment with her, Brett. Find another photographer for my website. Better yet, I'll find someone."

Shannon moved in front of his brother. "You want to tell us what this is about?"

He pushed Shannon aside. "No." He sensed they followed him into the house and he wished he were a drinking man because right now he could use a belt.

If he and Brett hadn't been delayed, he couldn't imagine the confrontation with Mia. He shook his head. For months he kept her out of his thoughts and she arrives at the ranch. And was his photographer. No way.

He slumped into a chair in Shannon's study and waited for them to swoop in. He gripped the chair arms until he had no feeling in his hands.

Troubled looks covered their faces. Shannon plopped into the chair next to him, a scowling Brett leaned on the fireplace with crossed arms, and Wendy sat on the ottoman next to her husband.

"You want to tell us why you're upset?" The softness of Wendy's voice did him in. He couldn't take the overwhelming compassion in her eyes. They wouldn't let him be. He'd have to confess what happened and suffer his brother's wrath and rightfully so.

Sean took a deep breath. "I rescued Mia last fall when I was at the cabin."

Brett straightened and anger flashed in his blue eyes. "And you never told us?"

"I didn't know she was a photographer. She'd been injured and didn't remember her name. I dropped her off at the clinic the day after you came to the cabin. Because of the pileup that day, the clinic put her on a medical flight transport to Columbus General. I called the clinic and the hospital to find her, but I didn't know her name."

Brett paced behind him and made him nervous. Sean expected his cousin to pop him on the head every time he went by. "Will you stop with the pacing?"

Brett stopped next to him. "I can't believe it. All this time and you knew her."

"I knew her as Lass."

"Lass?" Brett said.

"Aye, I didn't discover her name until the day I left for Ireland."

Shannon reached across and touched his arm. "If you didn't know her name, how did you find her?"

"Only by God's grace. Two cops in the hospital's coffee shop had searched for a missing woman."

"Mia." The three spoke in unison.

"We spent three weeks at my cabin and waited for the floods to subside. I took care of her and—"

"Fell in love with her." His brother finished for him.

Sean swallowed and rested his forearms on his knees. "I raced to her hospital room only to see a man who slept with his head on her bed and her hand on his face. She had cards and tons of flowers.

"Then what happened?" Wendy's voice seemed so far away.

"I backed out of the room and went to the waiting room at the end of the hall. The nurses said he'd been there day and night since she arrived. I overheard the nurses talking about Mia and her husband—then I left."

Brett's eyes went wide. "Husband? Mia isn't married."

"Heard it with my own ears. The nurse specifically said Mr. Nardelli. That means husband."

"Could be a brother," Wendy said.

Sean leaned into the chair and stared at the ceiling. "A brother wouldn't hold his sister's hand to his cheek. He was her husband."

Wendy glanced at Shannon who tilted his head.

Brett pulled out his phone. "Well, I don't believe it. I'll call and find out."

Sean jumped out of his chair and grabbed Brett's arm. "Do. Not. Call. Her."

He pulled away from the fierce grip. "Ease up. I wasn't planning to call her. I'll call her best friend, Pam." He left the room.

Sean dropped into the chair. The silence in the room closed in on him. Everything seemed to go so smoothly, now this. He wanted to flee to his beloved Ireland, but his history of running away from his troubles had to stop and he had to face the consequences of his decisions.

Everyone's eyes focused on Brett as he strolled into the room. "You're an idiot, Sean. She's not married. The man you saw was her brother."

Shannon grinned. "Great. Now you can go after her."

Sean's heart shattered again. "Shut it. I have to think

about Drew. He needs stability. He's been torn from his Nana and his country. I won't subject him to a woman who may or may not be married."

"She's not." Brett's frustration came off him in waves.

"It doesn't matter, and I'm not convinced on the whole married thing. And even if Drew weren't an issue. I lied to her."

Shannon straightened and leaned in. "Don't tell me…"

Sean nodded and misery permeated every fiber of his body. But if Drew weren't an issue, the lie would haunt him.

Shannon's breath whooshed. "Why, Sean? Why would you do that?"

Wendy drew her gaze from Sean to her husband. "Care to clue us in?"

"I didn't know if she *was* trouble or *in* trouble and when she saw the plaque on the wall, I didn't correct her. I knew it was wrong, but I wasn't sure if trouble would visit me."

Shannon cocked an eyebrow. "No, but you'd let trouble visit me."

"What plaque? You're talking in riddles and it's frustrating," Wendy said.

Shannon rubbed his wife's back. "It was a joke. Sean had a plaque made that said 'Shannon's Place' and hung it in the spare room so I'd have a place to call my own when I visited. She saw the plaque and assumed he was Shannon. We often played those tricks when we were lads."

"So now what?" Wendy said.

"He tells her the truth." Shannon's voice trailed, and he stiffened. "That's why she left. She thought I was you. I hugged my wife, and she probably thought you were a real jerk. Having a wife and playing around with her."

Sean growled. "It wasn't like that." The heat rose on his neck.

"Well, it was something because she left like a tornado chased her. And by the color on your face, I'd say it was more than a rescue. Hope it's not a repeat of Bridget."

Sean got in his brother's face. "Shut it. Don't talk about her like that."

Shannon leaned forward and his mouth curved. "Glad to see you're such a gentleman. But you have to tell her the truth, Sean. It's not right for her to think I'm you."

Sean slumped into the chair. "I know it. But after today, do you really think she'd meet with me?"

Brett frowned. "No, she wouldn't. She's a stand-up gal. I'll call her and make it happen. Pam will help us."

Wendy touched his arm. "You've had a great shock, Sean. Why don't you rest until dinner? Shannon and Brett can handle Drew."

"I need to check on the horses but let me sit here for a few minutes."

Wendy leaned in to kiss his cheek, Shannon squeezed his shoulder and Brett punched him in the arm as they left the room.

He leaned against the chair, closed his eyes, and when he awoke, his son sat in the other chair watching him. "You ok, Da?"

"Tired and had to do some thinking."

Drew climbed into Sean's lap and turned worried eyes on him. His warm body full of the pungent horse aroma. "You're not sick, are you? Nana got tired before—"

"No." Sean smiled and hugged his son. "I'm fine, son." At least in body. The heart, not so much.

Chapter 15

The rest of the day Mia gorged herself on the decadent taste of triple-fudge ice cream and watching old action movies. She periodically checked emails and voicemails, but decided she would return calls later after she pulled herself together. She couldn't even pray, though she knew that was the best thing for her.

When Pam arrived the next night with a pizza and soda, Mia didn't want to let her in but Pam was insistent. "Betty & Bertha are here to give you a good talking to, girl."

"Go away. Your gals can't help."

"Mia, please. You haven't returned any of my voicemails and your texts were confusing. It's not like you to not call back."

She banged her forehead against the door. "He's married. For months I've been an utter fool."

"Please open the door. Betty & Bertha want to sit down and I'd like to eat this pizza while it's still hot."

Mia relented and let her in.

"Goodness, girl. You look awful!"

"Gee, thanks."

"Come on. Eat. It'll make you feel better. I got your favorite." Pam lifted the box, made an exaggerated sniffing sound, set it on the table, and plopped the soda next to it.

After their stomachs were full, Pam settled her ample self on the sofa. "You want to tell me why we haven't been able to connect?"

"I found him, Pam."

Pam frowned and crossed her arms. "I gather from the wrinkled pajamas, the bed-head and the sticky ice cream spoons over there, the meeting didn't go well.

She shook her head. "Betty & Bertha sure know how to kick a girl when she's down."

Pam cocked her head. "Well?"

"He's married. He took care of me, kissed me, and made me fall in love with him."

"How do you know he's married?"

She choked out the whole sordid story. Pam gathered Mia into her arms and hugged her. "Are you going to spend the rest of your life hiding in this apartment? Your family is worried. Cassie called and then Steve called. I promised I'd come and see you. I gave you twenty-four hours, but now your time is up."

She blew her nose and wiped her eyes. "I'll be fine. I just needed a little time. I'm hurt, but I have to come to terms with it. He's out of my reach."

"What about your business?"

Shaking her head, she sighed. "I can't work with Brett now. He probably thinks I'm a flake. Besides, I want nothing to do with that ranch."

"I don't blame you but you still have to make a living. What about the other ranches?"

"Brett left me several messages, but I haven't responded. I need time to rationally explain what happened. And I'm embarrassed and afraid."

"You? Mia Nardelli? The woman who fearlessly worked

through her pain and the prognosis you'd have limited use of your wrists even with physical therapy? You proved them wrong, my girl."

Mia gave a half-hearted chuckle. "That's more of a testament of your bullying. And Betty & Bertha's quips."

"Here goes nothing." She grabbed her phone and looked at the number of messages on her phone.

"You have so much to give, Mia. You are talented and beautiful. Please don't let this stop you from your dreams."

"Twenty voicemails."

"Some are mine."

Pam sipped her root beer while Mia listened to her voicemails.

Mia sighed and leaned into the tufting on the sofa. "I can't believe it. He doesn't know what happened at the ranch, but he still wants to work with me and begged me to meet him."

"When?"

"Tomorrow morning for coffee. Will you go with me?"

"Of course. I want to make sure he doesn't give you grief over it. Where and when?"

"Chuck's Cafe at ten. I've never been there. You?"

Pam arose and put the pizza and soda in the fridge. "No, but I know where it is. Put some ice packs on those eyes and get some sleep."

After Pam left, Mia checked her email, and a dozen emails popped into her mailbox from Brett begging her to meet him. She couldn't think about Shannon. He was a dead issue and she wouldn't work with him. But her heart mocked her. Her goal of reinventing herself as a nature photographer had morphed into something much different from what she had imagined, but she couldn't walk away from it.

The next morning Mia descended the steps as her twin, his wife, Cassie and the girls were leaving. "Taking the girls to gymnastics?"

"Yes. We'll be back late. Mia, are you OK? We missed you at dinner."

Mia lifted her briefcase. "Been working on some proposals. Say a prayer for me."

Steve hugged her. "You know you don't have to do this, Mia. I'll take care of you."

"Don't, big brother. I need my wits about me. Besides, I have to do this for me."

He gave a single nod, got in the car and pulled out of the driveway as Pam pulled in.

Mia hopped into the car and adjusted the seatbelt. "You know, we talked about my problems last night and I didn't even ask you about Brett."

Pam narrowed her gaze. "What about him?"

"Now don't get all prickly. Tell Betty & Bertha to stand down." Mia laughed at her own joke.

"My, but you're much more chipper this morning."

"The wonders of a hot bath, cool mask, and a good night's sleep."

"I guess."

Mia poked her. "So, what gives?"

"He called."

"And?"

"We're going horseback riding."

"When?"

Pam sighed. "After your meeting and I take you home."

"I could have driven."

"True, but I wanted to support you."

Mia leaned in and hugged Pam's arm. "You always do. You're the best."

Spring was upon them and the day was sunny, but had a chill in the air. Tucked among quaint shops, the small café had an old-fashioned air about it despite it being in a trendy part of town. Benches and retro lights dotted the street. Brett met them at the door and ushered them to a quiet booth in the back.

"I'll get us coffee. Your usual, Mia?" Pam said.

Mia nodded, took off her jacket, and slid into the booth. Brett sat next to her. "What are you doing?" And she scooted closer to the wall.

"Thought it'd be easier to see the proposals if we sat next to one another."

"Oh, right."

Pam brought Mia's coffee and told them she'd do some window shopping while they did their business. Mia removed papers from the briefcase and laid them on the table.

When she looked up, Shannon slid into the booth opposite her. "Hello, Mia."

She felt the color drain from her face and her heart pounded. She struggled with her voice. His aftershave filled her nostrils, her mind remembered the rich taste of his lips, and she cringed. "What are you doing here?" She turned accusing eyes on Brett. "What's going on?"

Brett nodded toward Shannon. "He's our client and a distant cousin."

Shannon reached across the table and touched her hand. "Lass—"

Mia jerked her hand away. "Don't touch me. And my

name is Mia."

Shannon's face paled. He lowered his gaze, and he muttered. "I told you this wouldn't work."

She grabbed her papers and stuffed them into her bag. "No wonder you seemed nervous, Brett. You were in on this. Let me out of this booth."

"Wait," another voice, so much like Shannon's said.

Her jaw dropped when the man slid in next to Shannon. Except for the scar and beard, they were identical. Her gaze bounced from one man to the other, she leaned back, and crossed her arms.

"Mia, there's been a misunderstanding." Shannon's doppelganger said. "When you saw the plaque at the cabin, you assumed…" he thumbed his hand toward Shannon. "…he was Shannon, and he didn't correct you." He glanced at Shannon. "But I'm the real Shannon McDermott and your rescuer is my twin brother, Sean McDermott."

She stared at one brother, then the other, and chuckled. It dissolved into deep belly laughter. She held her stomach until she saw the fear on their faces.

"Lass, stop." Sean reached across the table again.

Wiping her eyes, she lifted her chin and directed her gaze to the real Shannon. "So, it was you I saw the other day at the ranch." When he nodded, she sat back. "I wondered about the clean shave." Both men touched their faces in the same way.

Sean hung his head. "I'm really sorry, Mia." He seemed genuine and contrite but Mia couldn't forget he left her at the hospital or that he'd left without a word.

"Tell me one thing, Shan—Sean. Why did you leave me at the hospital when you knew how afraid I was? You were the only person I knew."

"I was called away to Ireland on a...family matter. I wanted to tell you that morning, but you were unconscious. Then they flew you to a bigger hospital. I called the clinic and Columbus General, but neither were helpful because I didn't know your name.

She raised her cup to her lips and narrowed her gaze. "But you came to see me, didn't you? How did you know how to find me?"

"I went to the hospital right before my flight. Two cops were in the coffee shop and discussed a missing woman who'd shown up with amnesia. I knew it was you and I waited until they mentioned your name. I raced to your side only to see a man holding your hand on his face." He took a deep breath. "How's your husband, Mia?"

The sweet taste of hazelnut invaded her mouth and drowned the memories of his lips. "He's dead," she whispered. When the silence became unbearable, Mia stared at the twins' shocked faces.

"I'm very sorry, Mia," the real Shannon said.

Mia wrinkled her brow and snapped. "Why should you be? He died over five years ago."

Sean's head shot up. "Then who was the guy in your hospital room?"

She took in the twins' identical gazes, saw their shock, and she smirked. "My twin brother."

"You're a twin?"

Mia nodded and gripped her cup so they wouldn't notice how much she shook inside.

Sean's eyes bored into hers. "Will you forgive me?"

Her memory flooded with every minute detail of their time together. She stiffened and trained her gaze on the table. "I'm angry. You left me at that hospital by myself,

127

Shan—Sean." She bit her cheek. "Whoever you are. I don't know that I can."

Brett squirmed next to her and turned to plead with her. "Can we shelve this discussion and try to salvage our business relationship?"

When Mia nodded, he breathed a sigh of relief.

Then the real Shannon looked at his brother who had gone white. "Please find it in your heart to forgive us."

"You did nothing wrong, Shannon. There's nothing to forgive."

Sean grimaced, opened his mouth, and clamped it shut again.

"I admit my brother lied—by omission. But it wasn't malicious. He doesn't have a mean bone—"

"Shut it, Shannon." Sean gripped the table. "Mia, thank you for listening."

"No everyone shut it!" She grasped the table with her damaged wrist and nudged Brett so hard he tumbled out of the booth. "You boys and your games…You need to move on because I have a business to run, and I'm meeting with my partner." The very idea they'd show up at her meeting incensed her.

Mia scrambled to gather her laptop and remaining pages from the table and moved toward an empty seat two booths away. "You comin, Brett?"

"Yes, ma'am."

She sat facing away from them and didn't look back.

Pam slid into the booth across from her and touched her hand. "I'm right here."

"Didn't you go window shopping?"

"I couldn't leave when I saw them sit with you. I didn't know they would be here, Mia." She flashed an angry look at Brett and elbowed him. "If I had known I wouldn't have put you through it. I crept in behind you in the next booth and heard the whole thing. Are you OK?"

Mia saw Brett stiffen. She couldn't speak what was in her heart while Brett looked on. "I'm fine…now."

Pam looked past her and snorted. "You gave them what-for. Good for you. You should see their faces. They're still sitting there, still as statues, staring at your back. I think they're leaving now.

Brett followed Pam's gaze and gave the briefest of nods. He cleared his throat and sneaked a glance at Pam's mulish stare before he turned his eyes on her. "I'm sorry I deceived you both, but I thought if I told you the truth, you wouldn't meet with me, much less do business with any of us. Both Shannon and Sean still want you to do their photos and Wendy is chomping at the bit to have you do hers. Can we proceed?"

Mia sighed. "I don't know. I need time to think about it."

"I can't wait forever on this. They need to have this portion of the design finished soon. Let's talk pricing."

Pam scooted to the edge of the booth and gave Brett another angry glare. "Now I *will* go window shopping while you two finish your business."

Mia nodded and Brett's worried gaze followed Pam out the door.

"You're smitten, aren't you?" Mia lips lifted in a half-grin. When his cheeks turned red, she knew she'd hit the mark. "Don't answer that. I can see it on your face."

"Doesn't matter. She's furious. I don't think she'll even

talk to me now. I'm surprised you're even talking to me," he muttered.

She patted his hand, then pulled out her paperwork. Anything she could do for the two of them, she'd do. As for her and Sean, she'd put that in a corner of her heart and mull it over later. Right now, her business was more important.

They went over the numbers and Brett gave her his client list with next week's appointments.

"You've been busier than a colony of ants facing a hard winter, haven't you?"

Brett burst out with a nervous laugh. "Good one. These appointments were tentative until we discussed actual pricing. My clients gave me the go ahead." He gave a dismissive wave of his hand. "And you're reasonable, so I'll confirm the appointments and send you service requests."

She closed her folder. "I think that wraps it up."

"Just about." Brett took her hand. "Mia, Sean is a good guy. The best, actually. Please forgive him—for everything."

Mia frowned as she walked away with enough work to last her well into the summer months. Her heart pulled her in different directions and she couldn't make sense of how she felt. She needed prayer. Her sister-in-law Cassie understood this situation more than anyone because she had suffered in almost the same way.

Her heart ached. Could she forgive him? Should she? *Lord, help me with my indecision.*

Sean stumbled to his feet and trudged to the rear door of the café with Shannon in hot pursuit. He jumped into Shannon's SUV and leaned his head back and stared at the dark clouds approaching. It reminded him of the day he found Mia. What made Brett and Shannon think this meeting would end any other way than it had? He felt like his entire body had been ground into the dirt by hooves of every horse he'd ever treated. How was he going to get through this pain? It was a hundred, no, a thousand times worse than when Bridget left.

Shannon buckled his seat belt and smirked. "That went well, don't you think?"

"Shut it, Shannon."

His twin turned in his seat. "You're going to have to talk about this, Sean. You can't retreat into yourself or run away. I saw your face and I felt your pain."

"I expected I'd have to grovel for my stupidity, but I didn't think she'd go off like that." He pinched the bridge of his nose between his thumb and forefinger and breathed a deep sigh.

"I guess the lie and facing both of us after so many months did her in. I was worried about her. And I called the hospital to see how she was until she was discharged."

"You called from Ireland?"

He gave a single nod. "And I didn't even get a chance to tell her I was worried about her. She thinks I'm a heel for having left her." He turned in his seat. "I did the right thing for my father and my son…but she doesn't know about Drew either. Another lie of omission that'll seal my fate forever where she's concerned."

"Just take it a step at a time. Maybe Brett will convince her to do the photography for your website and you'll have another opportunity for forgiveness."

"Maybe. But I'm not counting on it."

"Pray about it, brother."

His chin dropped. "I wanted to ask her about her wrists.

Did you see how scarred they were? I hadn't realized how much damage was done to them." He leaned forward and rubbed his wrists.

"No. I missed the wrists. I was looking at her face. She has some scars. Did you sew her up?"

He gripped the arm rest. "No. I'd left my bag at home so I could only butterfly the cuts. Even if I had my bag, I'm not skilled enough to suture a person's face so there aren't any scars. She'd need a good plastic surgeon and it looks like she's had some of them fixed, but even he couldn't erase them all."

Shannon turned the key. "Nothing a little makeup won't cover."

He drew a deep breath. "She had makeup on."

His twin studied him. "What are you going to do?"

"I don't know." His chest tightened.

Shannon pulled into traffic to go back to the ranch outside of town and his voice was determined. "We need to ask God for wisdom in this situation."

Sean didn't answer. He couldn't. For all his brother's bravado in trying to fix the situation, insisting they both meet with Mia, he was no closer to forgiveness than he was before. He was further away. Seeing Mia and her injuries left a hollow pit where his heart used to be. He needed to pull it together before he got home and he needed time to think and pray, but his son's needs came first. He'd deal with his failures alone.

Chapter 16

Mia rolled her shoulders. A week of back-to-back meetings and photo shoots at various companies and locations left her with more work than she could handle. She barely saw her family while running from shoot to shoot. Despite her happiness doing what she loved, getting into deadline mode proved more difficult than she imagined and left no time for introspective thoughts where Sean was concerned.

She groaned when a barrage of knocks came at her door and Steve's voice called out. "Mia, open up. I have your dinner."

She could do without her twin's chastisement. "Coming." Opening the door, she grabbed the food and was about to shut the door in his face when he stuck his foot in and shook his head. She knew she wouldn't get out of it, now.

Her brother's stubbornness was how he found her car all those months ago. He never gave up on her. She sniffed the plate. "Smells fantastic."

Steve sat at her miniscule table and dwarfed everything around him. "You eat and I'll talk." He looked around the small, but tidy kitchenette and the pictures that cluttered the living room. The workstation in the corner of the living room was just as neat. "I haven't been up here in years. You've made it cozy and warm."

"Thanks. What'd you want to talk about?" Mia sat opposite him and dug into her food.

"I'll get right to the point."

She groaned but kept eating.

"You're burning the midnight oil and I'm concerned."

She wiped the remnants of Fiona's delicious casserole from the corners of her mouth and she narrowed her gaze. "How do you know that? Have you been spying on me?"

Steve shook his head. "I had cameras installed around the property when there were break-ins down the street, remember? I monitor them on my phone and saw your lights on at all hours."

She leaned into her chair and crossed her arms. "So? You used to work all hours, too."

"Because I didn't want to face the truth."

"What truth would that be?" Mia pointed her fork at her older sibling. "That you needed a life—and a wife?"

"I got the wife and the life. But before that, I needed to forgive Laura."

Mia's mouth dropped open just as the fork clattered on the dish. "How do you forgive a dead wife?"

"That's not important. What's important here is that I forgave her. And when I did, the hundred-pound cross I carried around for years became lighter and lighter until it disappeared into nothingness. You need to forgive Sean, Mia."

"It's not that simple." She counted off on her fingers. "He left me with strangers. He came to visit and left. And worst of all, he lied about who he was."

"C'mon, Mia. Do you hear yourself right now? After all we've been through, he's hardly the bad guy you make him out to be. He saved your life. Do you know what he did to take care of you before you even woke up? While I was searching for you and thought you might be dead?"

She picked at crumbs on her placemat. He had a point.

"He had good reasons," Steve continued. "And it's not like you to not forgive. I don't want you to carry that burden of unforgiveness. It eats away at you." He got up. "I've said what I came to say. Pray about it. I promise once you forgive him, you'll feel much better." He bent to kiss her on the forehead. "And get some sleep. All work and no play—"

"Yeah, I know." Mia got up and hugged him. "What you've said makes sense. I know I have to forgive him and I promise I'll pray about it."

When Steve left, Mia eyed all the work she needed to do. God would help her get things done if she put time aside for him. She pulled out her well-worn Bible, sat in her reading chair, and read Psalms. A peace came over her. She closed her eyes and prayed.

After her prayer, she felt energized in a way she hadn't felt in weeks. She knew she had strayed, and she offered a prayer to her heavenly father for moving away from him instead of rushing to him.

Before she tackled the work at hand, she shot an email to Brett about meeting with Shannon and his wife about the proofs they wanted. She didn't mention Sean because she could only take baby steps right now.

The work seemed to go quicker than usual and she was done before midnight. With a sigh, she organized her computer files and checked her email. Brett had emailed the meeting time at the Shady Dale Ranch. Two days to get her heart in order because chances were, she might see Sean. She had to start to think of him as Sean. Then she remembered, he must have thought of her as Lass. He'd have to remember her as Mia.

Nerves assailed her as she pulled into the gravel parking lot at the ranch. She wondered about little Drew and if he'd be there. She'd forgotten about the delightful little boy who wanted to take pictures and realized she must have hurt his feelings. Was he Wendy's nephew? Or maybe Sean and Shannon have another sibling? No matter, that little guy deserved an apology from her. She'd been in apology mode for days now.

Brett pulled in beside her and helped her carry her photography equipment into the farmhouse that had been spruced up. Tulips and daffodils sprouted along the walkway and the house must have been pressure washed. They went all out.

Wendy met them at the door and gushed her enthusiasm. "It's so good to meet you, Mia. I've been looking forward to it."

Shannon stepped into the hallway.

Mia extended her hand. "I'm so sorry I bugged out on you two weeks ago."

Wendy took her hand, her eyes soft. "Don't apologize. Understandable. I felt the same way when I realized Shannon had a twin."

Shannon grinned, then sobered and squared his shoulders. "If it wasn't for Sean's beard and scar, we'd be able to still play childish tricks."

Brett accessed both websites so they could determine the shots they wanted. Mia nodded and grabbed her clipboard. "I think the shots for the ranch's website are a given. Unless Shannon had some other ideas."

"Great pictures of the horses are my only concern. Maybe the barn and out-buildings?" Shannon said.

Mia made a note. "I suggest we wait a bit for the buildings when more flowers are in bloom."

"Those flowers should be in bloom in about two weeks. Then we can add them to the site," Brett said.

"We can put some potted flowers on the porch." Wendy's voice rose with excitement. "And whatever else will make the barns look good."

Mia brought up a few other web sites. "Strategically placed hay bales will work for the barns. Maybe some antique ranch items, too." They gathered around her and gave comments about the things they liked and didn't like. Mia took more notes for her client profile. "Now that I know what you like, we can go from there. Now, Wendy, what did you have in mind for yourself?"

Wendy's enthusiasm bubbled. "I want you to make me glamourous like your fashion shoots."

Mia shot a killer glance at Brett.

"He didn't tell me, Mia. I had a friend in New York who raved about your original photo shoots. And I've seen them. They are bold, daring and fabulous."

"Fashion photography is off the table, Wendy. I'm sorry." Her voice pinched, and she crossed her arms.

Wendy shook her head. "I'm not asking for a fashion shoot. I want what you do best. Crazy awesome." She gave Mia a wide smile. "I want my photos to stand out. To give me more of an edge. So people will pay more attention to my riding because they've seen top-notch photos."

Mia gave her a brief smile. "In that case, I'll do my best."

At that moment, Sean walked in and Mia caught her breath. The tension in the room choked her. Sean stood still and held her gaze while the others scurried from the room.

When he broke eye contact and plunked into the chair next to her, her breath caught.

"Lass." His quiet voice unnerved her.

Her voice barely above a whisper. "Don't."

The pain in Sean's eyes disappeared before she could say it was there. The ticking of the grandfather clock in the corner of the well-appointed room, the only sound.

Mia rose from the chair, turned away from him, and stared through the window at the frolicking horses. "I've had some time to digest the situation and think about the entire chain of events."

She heard movement behind her, sensed him standing to her left, and inhaled the scent of him.

"I never meant to hurt you."

"I know that, Sean, and I've prayed about it." Out of the corner of her eye, she saw him raise his brows. "I don't want to carry unforgiveness in my heart. It's a burden I don't need or want."

"Now what?" he whispered.

"I don't know." She tucked her hair behind her ear and lowered her eyes. "I just need time, I guess."

"Can you shoot pictures for my website? I won't ask for anything more of you."

She turned to face him. Sean's eyes seemed to bore through to her damaged heart. Her slight nod caused him to breathe a small sigh of relief, his face still held remnants of remorse.

"But I can't do anything today. I'm booked with Shannon and Wendy's photos."

"Understood. Do you mind if I watch the process so I have an idea what to expect?"

"I suppose."

He nodded and left the room. Mia realized she'd held her breath. *Forgiveness is so difficult, Lord. How did you do it?*

Brett stepped in. "Are we good? Ready to shoot?"

Mia gave him a tentative smile and nod. "Just one thing. Where's the little boy, Drew? And where's Rusty?"

Brett stilled. "I believe Drew's in school. And Rusty is in the barn."

"Oh. I wanted to apologize for leaving without letting him see the pictures he took. I have them on a thumb drive in my desk, but wanted to give them to him. And I was hoping to see Rusty, but under the circumstances, I'll wait for another time."

"No worries, Mia. They explained what happened. I'm sure he'd love to have them. Give them to me the next time I see you, I'll see to it he gets them. And I'm sure you'll see Rusty at some point, but right now you have your work cut out for you."

"Right." Mia wanted to question him, but Shannon and Wendy stepped in the room and they jumped into the photo shoot.

She took pictures of them in the kitchen, in the study, and on the porch. Then they moved to the barn, and she shot picture after picture of the horses, always aware of Sean on the outer fringes watching her, which made her nervous and exhilarated her at the same time. How that was possible, she didn't know.

Shannon stepped over to her. "New horses will arrive from other parts of the country next week. Could you take some shots of them for the website?"

Mia gave him a single nod. "I'll text or email what days and times I have available."

Brett helped her pack her gear and then left. Sean stood

by and waited until Brett left and then stepped close to her. "I really need your help with the photos on my website, Mia. My business took a hit while I was gone."

Mia narrowed her eyes, then opened her car door. "I'll do what I can."

Sean nodded and walked away.

She watched him enter the barn without a backward glance and sighed. He seemed even more distant than the day she saw him in the coffee shop. Sadder. She shook her head. She couldn't think about him. There was too much work to do to get her business off to a great start. And yet her heart drew her to him. She remembered the fresh baked bread he made and her mouth watered. She knew she loved him but fought against it because of her past, her personal issues, and her business.

Their family's websites were a good part of her business, at least for now. She had to forgive him, but she couldn't get involved. Maybe spending time with him would push her to do just that. With a nod, she left the ranch.

Chapter 17

Sean's practice grew with his client needs and Shannon's crop of new horses. Spring flowers bloomed to full color, but the air still had a slight chill. Soon the rich scents of summer would fill his nostrils.

After checking the horses, Sean made his way to the barn office. When the foreman Shannon conferred with left, Sean shut the door and dropped into the cracked leather arm-chair opposite Shannon's paper-strewn desk. The strong odor of liniment filled the air.

He leaned into the chair and flicked a glance at his twin. "New crop is in fine shape except for the gray mare, Phoebe. She has some respiratory issues."

A look of worry crossed Shannon's face. Sean knew that look. If one horse was sick, chances were others could get sick. Shannon needed them healthy so he could breed or sell those he bred. This particular horse was one Shannon wanted to breed.

Sean crossed his legs and smiled. "Nothing a round or two of antibiotics won't cure. Keep her isolated for a few days and monitor her. Don't think it's contagious, but it never hurts to be cautious."

Shannon heaved a sigh of relief. "We've gotten a lot of

hits and new buyers with the website. Brett and Mia make a great team."

He twisted his lips and scowled. "I bet."

"Jealous, brother?"

"Shut it."

Shannon sighed and jotted notes in one of his journals. "Have an appointment for your photo shoot?"

His unwarranted surliness caused him to relax a little, and he rubbed his beard. "Haven't heard."

"Brett has been working some long hours. But he's effective. Hadn't realized he had such extraordinary creative talents. I'm happy for him."

Shannon leaned forward. "Me too. He likes to ride, but his heart wasn't in ranching. Hope he can convince Mia to work wonders on my website, too."

"I'm sure she will, but remember, it's a combined effort between them. And don't bristle. It's only business. He has the hots for her friend, Pam."

He smirked. "Good for him."

"I'd heard Wendy teasing him. When he turned red, I knew something serious was going on."

"About time he's off the market. Been a challenge for years with his constant flirting."

"Let's talk about you and Mia."

Sean clasped his hands. "There is *no* Mia and me." He warned Shannon with a dark look. "Drew and I are still getting to know one another. Can't think about anything else." Sean rubbed his scar and beard.

Shannon rose from his seat behind the desk and slapped his hands on the desk. "Don't even go there. I don't think she cares about that darn scar any more than anyone who cares about you does. I'm tired of you hiding behind it when you could have a full life with a lovely woman."

Sean's nostrils flared.

"She has scars of her own, doesn't she?" Shannon cocked his eyebrow.

His voice rose and registered disdain. "Those tiny scars? She can cover them with makeup."

"So? She still has them, so she understands."

He moved to the door just as it opened and Brett stepped in, whinnying horses filtered through the doorway. "Sean. Glad you're here. Mia has an opening. Can you fit her in your schedule on Friday?"

"Why didn't she call me?"

Brett lifted his eyes from fiddling with his phone and lifted one shoulder. "Doesn't have your number, hot shot."

"Why didn't you give it to her?"

"Didn't think of it. Been busy lately, you know? I can't keep track of your love life."

Sean frowned and pulled out his phone. "Ten?"

"I'll enter the appointment."

"You're privy to her calendar?" Sean's voice had risen. He glanced at his twin who frowned and crossed his arms.

Brett's lips tightened. "Only her work calendar. It makes both of our jobs easier."

"Ten at my office, then." Sean felt their eyes on his back as he left the room.

His website was the most important thing, even though his heart called him a liar. He closed his eyes for a minute before he started his truck. Paperwork and patients at the office called him. Friday would be upon him quick.

He couldn't think of Mia as a love interest. Drew's happiness was the most important thing to him right now. Besides, she couldn't forgive him. If she couldn't forgive him for all the misunderstandings and lies, then how in the world would she forgive another lie? His stomach churned. No. He only could hope for a great website and nothing more.

Sean stared out the window as he waited his turn to drop Drew off at school. *Spring rains.* It reminded him of his time with Mia. He'd see her this morning, but nothing could ever come of it. His scar and his lies, her unforgiveness, but more importantly, his son. Everything changed.

Drew turned questioning eyes on him. "Da? Why are you so sad?"

He forced a smile he knew never made it to his eyes. "It's just the rain. I long for summer weather."

"Will it be different here than in Ireland?"

A genuine smile crossed his lips. "Very different. Much warmer. Not as much rain. And it stays light late into the evening."

Drew's eyes grew wide. "Really? Does that mean we could ride late?

Sean chuckled and ruffled his son's hair. "For sure."

"I can't wait."

"You have a little over a month. How do you like school?"

His son rounded his shoulders. "It's OK."

Sean frowned and touched his son's arm. "Just OK?"

"The boys want to know about my life in Ireland and the girls…" Drew sighed.

Sean turned a sharp eye toward his son. "What about the girls?"

Drew grimaced. "They want to hear me talk all the time."

"That's OK, son. They'll get used to your accent."

His little face scrunched. "It's not me that has the accent, it's them!"

Sean pulled his lips in because the last thing he wanted to do was laugh at his son's predicament. He remembered well when he came to America how the women swarmed around Shannon and, to a degree him, too. But they were more interested in Shannon because his looks weren't marred by an ugly scar.

"Just be kind, OK?" Sean pulled forward and the teacher's assistant accompanied his son into the building.

He had met with Drew's counselor last week and the sessions seemed to help him with the loss of his Nana and his homeland, but still, Sean worried. He groaned and turned his attention to his meeting with Mia. His brittle nerves stretched beyond their strength when he arrived at his office.

His assistant was off today, but at least Brett would be there to serve as a buffer. He sipped his favorite brew, checked on the animals in his care, and prepared for her arrival. Rusty followed him around and sensed something big was about to happen.

Sean patted Rusty's head and updated the charts when the door jangled. Hoping it was Brett, he stepped out of his office to see Mia grappling with her camera equipment.

His heart sank. He expected Brett, but he moved to help her. His lab coat fluttered behind him as he grabbed the weighty bag slung from her narrow shoulders.

She smiled. "Thanks."

That was the most genuine smile she'd given him since they had been at the cabin. He smiled too, but then frowned. "Do you have more stuff to bring in?"

Rusty barked and ran to Mia. She dropped her stuff on the counter and crouched to give Rusty a hug and he licked her face. "You remember me! How have you been, boy?" Her exuberance was clear. Rusty barked and his tail wagged in sincere affection.

Once again, Rusty saved the day and made their meeting less awkward.

When she got up, Rusty nuzzled her legs. He gave Rusty a pat of his own.

Mia's laughing eyes turned to Sean. "I can't believe he remembered me."

His lips curved. "You made an impression." Their eyes locked and time stood still as Sean remembered their kiss until the door jangled again.

Brett shook his umbrella. "It's pouring out there."

Still at Mia's feet, Rusty cast adoring eyes at her.

"I think he's in love." Brett stepped closer.

Sean jerked his head. Mia's face turned that gorgeous rose color. Her clenched jaw told another story, though. Brett stared at Mia and then at him.

Brett bent and gave Rusty a pat, but the dog ignored him. "See? He can't take his eyes off you, Mia."

Mia gave a nervous laugh. "We had a little reunion before you came in." She turned to Sean. "Are you ready?"

He could only nod as he led them to his office. Uncomfortable, he put his hands in his lab pockets. "What do we do first?"

Mia sat in one of the two consultation chairs in the room and set her laptop on the tiny table between them. She pulled up a browser to the bookmarked pages to show him various websites. "See anything you like?"

Sean pulled the other chair closer and sat next to her.

Brett's phone blasted a funny ringtone. "Guys, I have to take this call, I'll be in the other room."

Sean rubbed his beard. "They're all good, but I wanted something, I don't know, with a wow factor. Like Wendy's pictures. Those were amazing."

"Thank you, but this is a different business, therefore a different application. Let's try something. Which do you like the least?"

He pointed out four of the seven mood boards.

"Good. That's a start. For your business, it's best to have images of you while you work with the animals."

Sean resisted the urge to touch his scar, but frowned. "I'm not photogenic."

She studied his face. "Sure you are. If the scar bothers you, I can shoot them so people can't see it."

Sean cringed and crossed his arms. "Why should I do that?"

She looked away. "I just thought you might not want to…"

When her voice trailed, he tightened his hands into fists and his voice roughened. "Look. The scar is part of who I am. It'll never change or go away, so I'm not hiding it." He hoped his words came out with conviction without any hint of self-pity.

"I totally agree." She held out her wrist, then swept strands of hair away from her cheek. "We all have scars and they aren't going anywhere. I only brought it up because of what you said. I'm a photographer, remember? I want you to be comfortable."

He was nowhere near being comfortable, and everything about the way she moved, smelled, and touched her hair made him want to hold her and never let her go. How had he gotten himself into this mess?

"Right." He nearly choked. "You're the professional. Photograph me however you want. I don't care about the scar."

147

"No one who cares about you does."

She stared and their eyes locked. This time Brett wouldn't be there to interrupt them. After a long moment, he looked away. "Where do we start?"

"Do you have any patients here?" Rusty had his head at her thigh the entire time and she stroked his fur as she spoke.

He cleared his throat and moved to the door. "Aye. Three dogs, a cat, and an owl."

"Very cool. I'd also like to use Rusty. I remember you told me he keeps you apprised if there are any problems. We'll work that into the spread. And I'd like to get some shots of your operating room, too."

Brett's soft voice drifted in from the other.

"Who do you suppose he's talking to?" Sean said.

Mia stopped short, turned her head toward Brett's voice and smirked. "Probably Pam."

"Your friend?"

She raised one brow. "You know about Pam and Brett."

"Just that he's interested."

Mia nodded. "Let's see those patients."

When he took her around, he could see she was moved by their condition and his heart pricked.

"Will you hurt them if you hold or check them?"

"No. What do you want me to do?"

She fiddled with her camera. "I want you to act naturally." Mia gazed at him and recognized his confusion. "What do you normally do?"

"I take them out of their cages, examine them, change bandages or feed them, and put them back."

"Then do that and don't pay attention to me. I'll walk around and take shots from different angles, OK?"

He nodded, lifted the Maine Coon cat in his arms, and

petted him. He tried to place the cat on the table, but the cat wouldn't cooperate and wanted to stay in Sean's arms. He leaned against the table, spoke in a hushed tone and examined the cat's paws. He adjusted the bandages, then placed him back in his cage much to the cat's mewling displeasure.

"You're amazing at what you do. I almost forgot to take pictures. You mesmerized that cat."

Sean laughed. "That cat is spoiled beyond reason." Then he pinched his lips. "His owner treats him like a baby thus, I must, too."

He repeated the process with the Australian Shepherd and the Pekingese and was conscious of Mia when she maneuvered around his examination table and snapped shots of him. The dogs were a little less tolerant of his extra ministrations. After Sean finished with them, he turned to see that Brett stood in the doorway.

"What about the owl?" Brett said.

"I think Sean's bread and butter is with domestic animals. Still, the owl is exotic and it might be a fun addition. And we can't leave out Rusty."

"Your new best friend? Course not," Brett said.

Mia frowned and gave Brett a warning look, Sean put the falconry glove over his white surgical gloves. "Brett come in or get out. And shut the door. If the owl bolts, I want him confined to this room." Brett stepped out and Sean took the owl out of his cage.

Since the owl had been in his care for some time, he was used to Sean fussing with him, but Sean didn't know if Mia taking photos with a clicking shutter would scare the bird. When Sean put the animal back in his cage and locked it, he breathed a sigh of relief and turned to Mia who looked at her camera.

"Is that it?"

"Just a few with Rusty in the operating room. But these are great, Sean. The ones with the owl are so cool. You want to see?"

Sean moved beside her and stared at the images as Mia scrolled through them. He didn't even look like himself. Is that what people saw when they looked at him? He shook his head.

He noticed her special scent and his heart pounded. Again. "They're great." Then he backed away from her.

Mia frowned, but she followed him to the operating room. "Rusty, can you get up on the table?" Like the obedient dog he was, Rusty jumped on the table, even though he knew he wasn't allowed up there. It appeared he'd do anything for Mia.

Sean scowled at him, but Rusty just laid down and put his head on his paws. He leaned in and whispered in his dog's ear. "This is the last time you'll be on this table." Sean didn't realize she took shots of him whispering to the dog. The dog looked at him with mournful eyes and turned to Mia to rescue him. "No way," Sean muttered as he moved his hand over the dog's back. He cocked his head, frowned, and felt around on Rusty's hip.

Mia stepped over to the table. "What is it?"

"Don't know. I'll need an x-ray."

The concern in Mia's eyes gave him a sensation of warmth. "It's probably nothing, but I want to be sure."

"Are you going to do that now?"

"Aye. You can take pictures if you like, but you'll have to wear a protective vest."

Mia put on the vest and raised her camera, snapping photos as Sean adjusted Rusty on the table. He took a series of x-rays. "Down, Rusty." The dog headed straight for Mia for consolation.

Sean developed and placed the film on the viewer. All the while Mia snapped shots of him and Rusty. He sighed. It was a growth, and he'd have to remove it.

Mia's small hand on his arm caught him by surprise. "Is Rusty OK?" He'd forgotten what her touch could do to him and made the mistake of staring into her glittering eyes.

Sean could barely get the words out. "He has a growth which needs to be removed."

"When?"

"Sunday afternoon when I'm off."

"Can it wait that long? Will he be OK?"

"Aye. I hope so."

She nodded. "I think that's it for the photos. I'll need your number so we can coordinate which of the proofs you like best. And I'd like to schedule time with the big animals, too."

He needed to find out what happened to her, tell her about Ireland, and his son. It wouldn't go anywhere but he wanted her to know the truth of why he left her. "Will you have dinner with me tomorrow night?"

She let out a breath. "Only if we can meet somewhere."

Sean stifled a grimace. She wanted a way to leave quickly, and he didn't blame her.

"How about Grafton's at six-thirty?"

Her voice wobbled. "Sounds good."

Brett's voice came through from the next room. "Are you guys done? It stopped raining and I want to get out of here before it starts again."

Mia laughed and walked in front of him. "Yeah. We're done, but we still have to get some big animal shots."

Rusty plodded by her side.

Sean frowned. *Whose dog are you, anyway?*

Brett looked at him and then Mia. "You two work out your own schedule. I have too much to do. Got three more clients, Mia. They want your expertise, too."

Mia groaned, but smiled. Sean was glad her business thrived, but he worried about his continued relationship with her. Maybe he should cancel dinner until she got the rest of the photos of him and the horses.

No, Mia wouldn't be unprofessional, would she?

Time would tell.

Chapter 18

Smoothing the little black dress, Mia observed herself from different angles, checked her hair and makeup. Maybe they could resolve any misunderstandings tonight and resume their friendship. Friendship? Who was she kidding? She remembered the way their eyes locked and how she desperately wanted to discuss their relationship. Maybe that's what this dinner was about? Mia shook her head, grabbed her pashmina and clutch, and headed out the door.

Grafton's wasn't a swanky restaurant, but it wasn't a dive either. Elegant with white tablecloths and subdued lighting. Soft music shielded the clinking of plates and glasses. Terrific ambiance for an intimate dinner.

Mia wrapped her shawl tighter around her shoulders, picked at her nails, and chastised herself. Waiting for Sean caused her nerves to spiral. Maybe he'd bail on her like he did at the hospital. That thought and another ten rolled around in her brain. Being abandoned again by the same man made her stomach churn. When she thought to leave, he stood next to the table.

"I'm sorry I'm late." He unbuttoned his jacket and sat opposite her in the quiet corner of the restaurant. "Shannon wanted to talk and there was a bit of traffic."

Mia's lips turned down, and she picked up the menu.

When the server took their drink order, Sean cleared his throat. "You're probably wondering why I asked you to dinner."

She stared at the dinner offerings without glancing at him. "The thought had crossed my mind."

"I wanted to clear the air about…everything." Sean's breath whooshed out and Mia's gaze hit his eyes.

"Like what?"

"Why I left you at the hospital, why I didn't come back, and what happened to you before and after you stayed at the cabin."

Mia placed the menu on the table and took a deep breath. "I know you went to Ireland, but why?"

After Sean had explained how Brett had arrived the day before they left with news that his father was sick and his father summoned him to Ireland, the server dropped off their drinks and said he'd be back in a few minutes to take their order.

"Why didn't you tell me before we left?" Mia said.

Sean seemed nervous, too. "I feared you'd revert to not wanting to leave the cabin, and I had to call my father."

"Did you call him?"

"Yes, but his housekeeper kept him from the phone or at least they both conspired to keep him off the phone."

"Why?"

Sean sighed and looked away. "Da wanted me to come home because he had something he wanted to tell me and he didn't want to do it over the phone."

Mia reached out and covered his hand. "Is he OK?"

"He's fine. Older than the last time I'd seen him, but his health was good." Sean pulled his hand away. That was telling. He couldn't even stand her touch. Mia placed her hands in her lap.

"How did Rusty's surgery go?" Mia said.

"It was a tumor, but it was benign. If you hadn't been there doing the photo shoot, I wouldn't have caught it as soon as I did."

She gave him a warm smile. "I'm glad. He's a wonderful dog."

Their order placed, there'd be a wait for their dinner since the restaurant grew crowded by the time Sean showed up. Not surprising for a Saturday evening.

"Tell me about what happened to you, Mia. How'd you come to be at my cabin? How'd you regain your memory?"

Mia smiled a half smile. "I had a car accident in the hills. Not sure how far your cabin is from the place where I crashed and then wandered along the creek before I fell since I remembered nothing after I blacked out." Mia sipped her iced tea, and it cooled her throat.

She told him how she had been on that hill, gave him a blow-by-blow account of the accident, and pointed to her face. "That explains the shards of glass you found in my cuts."

Sean scanned her face for the scar locations. "Looks like the plastic surgeon did an outstanding job."

"I can cover them with makeup, but without a lot of makeup, a few of them are still visible.

She leaned in. "Tell me about your scar."

He appeared to attempt a lighthearted jab at himself. "Well, I don't wear much makeup, so…" He frowned and looked away. "When I had my accident, the surgeon said the cut was so deep and ragged that to repair the damage to be flawless would be tricky. He could do it, but warned I could suffer irreparable nerve damage that could cause another set of problems. So, I opted against it."

Mia's heart hurt with an ache of understanding. She

didn't pity him but felt sadness that with the advances in medicine, and his own love and care for animals, he couldn't get his face fixed.

Sean jarred her out of her thoughts. "So how did you remember who you were?"

Mia sighed. "I didn't. I awoke in the hospital room with an oxygen mask, a nurse and a strange man standing by my bed. I asked for you, but they didn't know who you were. The man made me nervous, and I was upset you'd left me."

"I'm really sorry, Mia. I planned to tell you when we got to the hospital, but because of the massive pileup and injured people, there was complete chaos. The best they could do was stabilize you and send you to a bigger hospital as soon as possible. I was in the way, had to leave for Ireland, and you were passed out."

Mia's voice lowered. "I didn't know there had been an accident."

"I was thankful they could get you to a larger hospital to get proper treatment. I worried about your respiratory issues, wrists, and wounds on your face. Your memory loss, too."

The aromas of their served meals made Mia's stomach growl and Sean chuckled. "Eat up. You were saying?"

"When my brother told me my name, I still didn't remember. It wasn't until he brought my two wonderful nieces to visit that everything before the car accident rushed into my brain as if I fast-forwarded an action movie."

Sean flashed her a half grin. "That must have been wild."

"It was. Sorting out my impressions took a few days. I had surgery to fix the wrists. Both of them. The second break needed a plate and screws. But the one you set, they re-broke it and set it again." She gave him a warm smile. "The specialist did what they thought was best."

Sean frowned, put his fork down, and reached across the table. "I did the best I could under the circumstances and without an X-ray or proper tools, I made do with what I had available."

"No! I didn't mean…" Mia turned her hand palm up and shook her head. The scrumptious salmon clogged her throat. "I'm not blaming you for anything, Sean. You saved my life. Can you imagine what would have happened if you hadn't found me? With the amount of rain, I could have drowned in that creek." Mia shivered, looked away, then turned her gaze to him, and smiled. "Besides, the ortho guy told us you did a great job, and they didn't have to do much to the wrist you set. The other one, not so much."

Sean took her hand, turned it over, and his finger followed the scars making her stomach grow warm. "Does it hurt?"

"On occasion. I have to rest it sometimes when I've pushed it too hard. Usually after a long day of shooting."

Sean's lifted her wrist and his lips moved as if he wanted to kiss the scar. Mia pulled her hand back. "Steve, my twin, searched for you because he wanted to thank you for taking good care of me."

His face turned red. "No thanks necessary."

At that moment, Mia could tell he was thinking of their time together and that last kiss. A kiss she'd thought about for months.

"Then I searched, and found you. Or rather, I found your twin. I'm sorry I acted like a nut case. I must have hurt that poor little boy's feelings." Her chin trembled.

Sean's face paled, and he dropped his fork.

Her heart dropped. "What?"

"I'd forgotten you met Drew."

She searched his face. "I meant to ask you if you have

another sibling."

Sean looked confused. "Just Shannon."

Mia leaned back and she couldn't keep the look of shock from her face. "Drew is your son?" She didn't know where to look, so she stared at her plate.

The sound of laughter from other tables wafted across to their table.

Sean sighed and whispered. "He's the reason my Da wouldn't talk to me on the phone. I didn't know I had a son until I arrived at my Da's house and he told me."

Mia swallowed and turned confused eyes in his direction. "I don't understand."

"I had a relationship with a woman when I was attending university. I was in love with her and thought we'd be married and return to our hometown after graduation. She had other plans. After my accident, she broke the engagement and told me she wanted nothing to do with our hometown. That was the last time I ever saw her, then our son showed up on my Da's doorstep."

"Where's his mother?"

"Dead. Died a few years after he was born. He doesn't remember her."

"Who cared for him?"

"His Nana. By the time children's services realized there was a child involved she was in the final stages of Alzheimer's."

"I see." Mia fiddled with her napkin. "You became an instant father."

"Aye. He needs a lot of love and care. In the last year, he lost his Nana to a dreadful disease, and he didn't understand why she treated him so poorly."

"Poor little guy. And I went and traumatized that sweet kid when I ran away with his pictures."

"Aww, I don't think he was traumatized. Confused, maybe."

"Still, I'd like to apologize and make it up to him. He took some good pictures and I can let him take some more."

"I'd rather you didn't."

"Oh." Mia swallowed. There it was. *He doesn't want me near him or his son.* She couldn't blame him. After all, she hadn't told him she forgave him. What was the point now? She reflected about if they were to mend the chasm between them, he had a son who needed attention and love from his father and she wouldn't come between father and son.

She pursed her lips and inwardly ranted at her own personal issues. Then she caught the hurt in Sean's eyes. "I have forgiven you, Sean. Tonight has been—"

"Enlightening?"

"Yes." Mia kept herself aloof. This dinner had been to tell her about his son and make her understand he only needed her photography skills. So be it. She pulled her wrap around her and her professional demeanor kicked in. "Shall we arrange the session with the horses?"

Sean pulled his phone from his pocket and gave her a date and time. For a split-second, sadness appeared in his eyes, then it disappeared.

She added the appointment to her calendar, and he paid the bill.

So that was that. She could never tell Sean about her feelings for him. Between the needs of a little boy, her fledgling business, and her personal issues, they all spelled a dead end for their relationship.

How her heart ached. She wanted more but knew she couldn't have it.

This was worse than not knowing the truth.

Chapter 19

Sean arranged his son's covers and kissed his forehead. He couldn't imagine his life without Drew. He thought of the dinner he'd had almost a week ago with Mia as he brushed his teeth and prepared for bed.

He laid in bed with his hands behind his head and his mind drifted. His son was the most important thing in his life. Before his business and before Mia. Her expression told him everything. She'd never accept his son in her life and he'd never put himself or his son in that position.

The next morning Drew bounced into the kitchen in his green sweatshirt and jeans. "Da, can I ride Gingerbell this morning?"

Sean leaned in. "It's Friday. Why aren't you dressed in your school clothes? You can ride this afternoon when you return."

Drew's shoulders slumped. "You forgot."

Shannon ruffled his nephew's hair. "Forgot what?"

"No school today. It's a teacher's day."

"Teacher's day?" Shannon said.

"Aye. Teacher's in-service day. I'm sorry, son. I forgot." Until Drew felt secure in Sean's love, his preoccupation with Mia had to stop. He couldn't let her infiltrate his mind and he didn't know how long that would take. He'd do what it took to make his son happy.

"Can I ride Gingerbell, then?"

Drew's anxious face melted Sean's heart. "Only if Uncle Shannon says it's OK and someone goes with you."

Shannon gave his twin a half-grin. "I think I can spare one ranch hand."

Sean eyed his son. "Are you done with breakfast?"

Drew gave him a wide smile and nodded.

"Take your dishes to the sink and go brush Gingerbell. I'll be out shortly to saddle her for you."

Drew hugged Sean's neck. "Thanks, Da."

Sean patted his son's back and squeezed him tight.

When the door banged shut, Shannon laughed. "He slams doors just like we used to do. Now I know why Da got aggravated." He poured himself another cup of tea. "It's not like you to forget anything associated with school. What's going on?"

"Been thinking about my practice and the website." Sean lowered his head as he bit into a buttery biscuit.

Shannon smirked as he raised his mug to his lips. "Maybe a certain photographer has wormed her way into your heart and brain."

Sean swallowed the biscuit that had turned to cardboard in his mouth and gave his twin a hard stare.

"We're talking about this." Shannon leaned forward, a disgusted look crossed his face. "Ever since you went to dinner with Mia, you've moped around here like a lovesick puppy."

"Shut it."

Shannon slammed his mug on the table. "I won't shut it. You're in love with her. I saw it on your face when she was here that day. And I saw her face when we met in the coffee shop. You're the only one who can't see it."

Sean's chair scraped across the floor as he rose. "Well, you're wrong. She doesn't love me. How can she when she can't tolerate me having a son?"

His twin's eyes narrowed. "Why would you think that?"

Sean smashed his thumb on his chest. "I saw the look on her face when I told her about Drew. She's not interested in some other woman's son."

"You're wrong."

Wendy came in and hugged her husband. "What's Sean wrong about now?"

He gave Shannon a warning look.

Shannon gave his wife a soft smile and kissed her cheek. "Not important."

Wendy pulled back from her husband and turned to Sean. "Is that right?"

Sean nodded. "Let me get out to the barn before Drew pesters every ranch hand."

"I'll check on him and ride with him, Sean," Wendy said.

"Don't you have to practice?"

"I can practice later today. I'd love to take him."

Sean threw his napkin on the table. "Suit yourself."

Wendy snatched her jacket from the coat rack and slammed the door and Shannon frowned. "We're not done with this conversation."

Sean grabbed his jacket and shoved his arms in the sleeves. "Aye. We are." He closed the door with a quiet click and pulled out his phone to check his messages. The bright sun and earthy smell of the day should have made him happy, but it didn't. Mia would be here this morning to take the large animal pictures. Shannon would give him all kinds of grief and Drew would be here, too.

He groaned.

Mia dreaded her appointment with Sean. She'd heard nothing from him since last week's dinner disaster. But she hadn't expected to hear from him.

She analyzed every detail of their conversation. Every look and every word. He pulled away from her so many times during dinner, anything beyond a professional relationship was out of the question, even if her fertility issues weren't a problem.

The day was clear and bright. Blue skies abounded. The light perfect for outdoor shots. She'd take the photos and be on her way. Her demeanor would be cool and professional.

But her stomach kept somersaulting. Mia stretched to release her taut nerves as she got out of the SUV and grabbed the equipment. The smell of horses assailed her nostrils.

"Mia." Wendy's horse pranced as she took full control of the towering stallion.

Waving, Mia strode to the corral, and laughed. "I thought he'd throw you."

Wendy patted the horse's neck. "Nah. Smokey is a teddy bear."

Mia laughed. "That's one *huge* teddy bear."

"You here to take photos of Sean?"

Mia nodded.

Drew ran to the fence and Wendy smiled. "You ready to ride?"

"Sorry, Aunt Wendy. Gingerbell has a problem with her shoe and the foreman wants to fix it before I ride her. Told me she wouldn't be ready until later."

"I'm disappointed, but we can go together another time," Wendy said.

The boy noticed Mia fiddling with her camera equipment and his voice turned belligerent. "Why are you here?"

"Drew!" Wendy dismounted, tethered the beast and frowned. "That wasn't very nice."

He stared at the ground and pushed the dirt around with his boot. "She didn't let me see the pictures I took."

If there had been a hole somewhere near her, Mia would have crawled in and hid. She stiffened her spine and crouched to his level. "I'm very sorry I left without giving you a chance to see the pictures. I was a little distressed."

"You thought Uncle Shannon was Da." Drew shook his head. "I don't know how. Da has a beard and a scar."

Surprise made Mia force a laugh as she looked to Wendy for help, but Wendy's mouth hung open and she clamped it shut. The boy understood more than either of them knew. Maybe even more than his father knew.

Drew pointed at her camera. "Do you have my pictures?"

"Not with me, No. But I saved them to a thumb drive and I'll give them to your dad the next time I see him. OK?"

Drew gave her a wide smile and eyed her equipment. "You taking pictures of Da?"

"Yes, I am." Sean might get angry, but she'd do it, anyway. "Would you like to watch?"

A big smile flashed on his face and he nodded.

Wendy mouthed 'thank you' from behind him. "Why don't we do lunch if you can spare the time?"

"I wish I could but today is packed. Why don't we schedule something?"

"Works for me. See you later."

At that moment, Rusty raced out of the barn straight to them almost pushing her to the ground, licking her face and being all-around joyful. "Well, it looks like you recovered, boy."

Drew's gaze pivoted between her and the dog. "You know Rusty?"

"Yeah, I do." She smiled at the little boy. "He was at the office when I took photos of your dad. Such a sweet little guy. Are you and Rusty friends?" After the conversation with Sean, Drew didn't need to know Rusty had saved her life. If his father wanted him to know, he'd tell him.

"I love Rusty. He's the best. Can I help carry something?" Drew said.

Rusty would make Drew's life more joyful.

"You could take this bag."

Drew shouldered the bag and walked next to her. "Do you like my Da?"

Mia stopped. Her invitation might not have been wise. If Sean worried his son might glom onto a woman, he'd have to do damage control. She'd have to be careful how she answered the question.

"Your dad is a nice man."

The boy rolled his eyes and sighed. "But do you like him?"

Mia pulled her lips in to avoid laughing at his expression and schooled her features. "Sure, I do."

Drew puffed out his chest and gave her a single nod. "Da is in the office."

She followed the boy. Ranch hands tipped their hats as they strolled past neighing horses and Drew opened the office door.

"I'm telling you, you're wrong, Sean," Shannon said.

"Da, Mia is here."

A look of guilt passed over Sean's face. "I thought you and Aunt Wendy went riding." His voice took on a harsh tone.

Drew's face fell. He dropped Mia's case and backed out of the room. She reached back and brought him closer to her.

"I asked him if he wanted to watch when Gingerbell needed a shoe replaced."

Shannon moved to Drew. "How about we go check on Gingerbell, buddy?"

"But—" Drew's gaze bounced from his father to Mia and back again.

Sean nodded and gave his son a small smile. His voice softened. "Go on, son."

When Shannon shut the door, Sean moved in front of her and his harsh tone returned. "I don't appreciate your interference."

"It was my fault he was here with me. I invited him to watch, so I felt it my duty to defend him." Mia's breath whooshed, and she gave him a hard stare. She wouldn't back away from this conversation. "If you have a problem with that, it's your problem."

Sean heaved a deep sigh, shook his head, and sat on the edge of the desk. "I do have a problem with it, but the horse is out of the barn now."

Mia crossed her arms. "Excuse me?"

"Drew gravitates toward females in my life."

"So?"

He closed the distance between them and gave her a hard stare. "My son is the most important person in my life. I can't have any woman who can't or won't be a part of his life now and in the distant future have any impact on his life. I don't want him hurt."

"You think I'd hurt a little boy?" Her heart ached because she knew she couldn't be a part of his life the way she longed to be. But Sean had no right to prevent his son from having a friendship. But even in her mind, she knew she wanted more. More of Drew. More of Sean. But she wouldn't let him know that. That part of her life, would be something she'd never tell him.

His body stiffened. "Not intentionally. But he's already felt the abandonment of his grandmother. I don't want him to feel that ever again. And I mean it."

"I want to be Drew's friend. Why is that an issue? And I have nieces. I know where to draw the line from making it much more."

"I said I don't want him hurt, and I meant it. You're their aunt. It's a given you'll always be there for them."

"That's right, I will be. But I've had over four years of dealing with two little girls who lost their mother at a very young age. I always knew their father would someday find a woman to be their forever mother, and he has. So I had to make sure they understood I was just their aunt. Never their mother. Drew is no different. I'll be just a friend."

"That's where you're wrong. Drew is a little boy who desperately wants a mother. He's already attached himself to the two women in our household. They aren't going anywhere, but you…" He waved his arm toward the door. His protectiveness of his son endeared her to him even more.

"Well, it's too late. I've already invited Drew to watch the shoot. You're going to tell him he can't watch because I will not."

Sean rubbed his beard. "Fine, I will."

"Look. I can see why you wanted to distance me from him and I respect that. But he's interested in photography and if he wants to watch, let him. Either he'll be bored and take off or he'll still be interested."

Sean gazed at the ceiling and whispered. "I'm floundering here. Being a father isn't as easy as it looks."

"No doubt." Mia placed her hand on his forearm. "You

didn't have the luxury of growing into parenthood, it was thrust upon you a short while ago."

He stared at her hand, gave a single nod, and peeled her fingers off his arm. "How long will the shoot last?"

She stepped back and grabbed her bag. "If the horses and you cooperate, not more than an hour." He breathed a long sigh, more than likely from relief.

"Let's go then. Shannon wanted me to use two of his new horses. Inside or out?"

Mia followed him. "Outside. The day is gorgeous and the lighting will be fantastic."

Shannon and Drew met them in the corral, Drew's little face fearful. "Are you mad, Da?"

Sean squatted, shook his head and touched his son's cheek. "I'm not mad. I hadn't expected you to be here for the shoot."

Drew looked from Sean to Mia and back again. "I can watch?"

Sean gave him a single nod and stood. "Can you get the horses, Shannon? Mia said outdoors is better."

"Sure thing. You don't want them saddled, right Mia?

"Correct."

Mia took shots of Sean while he examined the horses and took a few of father and son. Then Drew piped up. "Can I take a picture of you with the horses, Mia?"

Sean frowned. "I don't think—"

"Of course, you can." Mia gave him a warning look. "Let me just move some of these photos to a drive and set the camera for you." She crouched to his eye level and touched his chest. "You remember what I told you?"

"To see with the eyes of my heart?"

"That's right." She smiled at the boy.

Mia used her knowledge of fashion photography and posed with the horse and Drew took the first photo and then moved around and told Mia to smile. She laughed when she saw how he imitated her.

"Da, I want one with you and Mia."

He stiffened. "I don't think…"

Sean's sense of duty was compelling, but it was mistaken. She wouldn't let him spoil the boy's joy.

"Come on, Sean." Mia chuckled and waved her hand. "I won't bite. I promise."

Drew laughed. "Smile, Da. You too, Mia."

When the boy was satisfied, he gave the camera back to Mia. "Can I see them?"

Mia flashed him a wide grin. "Of course."

The three of them crowded around the camera. "Drew, these are quite good," Mia said.

Drew's look of delight thrilled Mia, but Sean's lips flattened and he shook his head. When his son turned to him, he erased his unhappy expression.

"I'll make sure these are added to the other ones." Mia turned to Sean. "I promised Drew I'd give him a thumb drive with the photos he'd taken of Shannon and Wendy. I'll send them over when I have a minute."

The boy crooked his finger at her. "Mia."

"Yes?" When she crouched to his level, he threw his arms around her neck. "Thank you."

She removed his arms and stood. "You're welcome." She pulled out her phone. "Gosh, I have to go. I have another appointment shortly."

Sean placed his hand on his son's shoulder. "Why don't you check on Gingerbell? If she's ready, we'll go for a ride." The boy ran into the barn.

When he was out of earshot Sean stepped over to her. "Let me help you load your equipment."

"Not necessary."

Sean lifted his chin and reached for the case. "Now you know why I'm reluctant with him. I want to protect his heart."

She stared at his solemn face and gave him a single nod. Swallowing, she struggled to maintain an outward calm. "I'll send you the thumb drive. You don't have to worry about my interference. I doubt we'll see one another again since we concluded the photo shoot."

The realization she'd fallen in love not only with Sean, but with his son, too, hit her. Mia watched in her rearview mirror and wanted to cry. He didn't want his son around any woman. She hadn't expected this would happen. Never meant for any of it to happen. But it did. She'd have to focus on her work and only her work.

Chapter 20

The sun warmed Sean's back and beads of sweat pooled on his brow. "Let's ride the trail around the lake, Drew." His son grinned, followed him out of the corral, and hopped off Gingerbell to close the gate.

They ambled through the trail dotted with budding trees and the birds chirped overhead. Soon they'd be covered with leaves, and the barren landscape would once again be lush and green like the grass.

Sean stopped at a willow tree and allowed Thunder to feed on the new grass. He inhaled the scent of spring.

Drew dismounted and did the same, his face thoughtful. "Da, this tree is like grandad's tree in Ireland. Too bad there's no bench to sit on."

"We can sit on the grass for now, but that's a terrific idea, son. We'll buy one."

His boy nodded and dropped onto the grass. "Da, don't you like Mia?"

Sean cocked his head to stare at his son. "Why would you think I don't like Mia?"

Drew lowered his head and looked away. "Your face looked mean. Kinda like Nana's did before she went to heaven."

Sean pulled his son to his chest and wrapped his arm

around him. "I like Mia. She upsets me sometimes. Did you like the photo shoot this morning?"

He grinned and shook his head. "Aye. It was fun. Can we do it again sometime?"

Sean ruffled his son's hair. "Mia took all the pictures she needs for now so I don't think we'll do it again soon."

When his son's face fell, Sean wanted to kick himself. The last thing he wanted was to hurt his little boy. Parenting and navigating a child's disappointment and hurt was harder than his work with injured animals.

"I really like her, Da. She taught me to see with my heart eyes."

Sean smiled at how his son had changed Mia's words. "I'm sure she'll be at the ranch taking pictures for Uncle Shannon during the summer."

"I'm hungry, Da. Can we go back?"

"Sure thing."

Drew talked to Gingerbell and patted her neck while Sean rode behind him on the narrow portion of the trail on the far side of the lake. It gave Sean a few minutes to think about Drew's words 'she taught me to see with my heart eyes'.

Mia taught him that, and it appeared Sean worried about his son's involvement with Mia and he shouldn't have. Maybe he needed to reconsider his relationship with her. What relationship? He snorted and his son turned to look at him. "Something wrong, Da?"

Sean crinkled his lips. "No, just thinking."

"About what?"

"How much I'm enjoying this ride with you."

Drew's wide grin filled Sean's heart with joy. Maybe he could have it all. His son and Mia.

The house was quiet that evening when Sean went in search of something to read in the study where Shannon had covered three of the four walls with floor to ceiling shelves. There had to be something there he hadn't read. Shannon peeked in the room. "You want some tea to go with your book."

Sean didn't look up from reading a book's jacket. "Sure."

Shannon popped in with two mugs and handed one to Sean. "Find anything you like?"

"Is this a new Veronica Cannon?"

"Aye. Came out right before you came home."

"Enjoy it?"

"It's the first in a new series and the bookstore made a big deal about it. It has a lot less heat than her other series, but I like it. A lot."

Sean sat in the wing-back chair near the fireplace and flipped through the book. Even though the weather had warmed, he and his brother still liked a fire in the evenings. When summer came, it would be too hot to have one, but for tonight it was just right.

Shannon sat in the other chair. "What happened this morning with Mia?"

"I told her to stay away from Drew." The shock on Shannon's face made Sean chuckle.

"Why?"

Sean sighed. "Because I didn't want Drew to get too attached to a female. He's already attached to Wendy and Mrs. O'Neill. I don't want him hurt if…"

Shannon reached out and touched his brother's bicep. "It's a good thing he's attached to them. He needs female influences in his life. Thank God, we had Mrs. Monahan in our life."

"He's been through so much change. He doesn't need more turmoil."

"You can't protect him from hurt, Sean. So what if he gets attached to her?"

Sean's breath whooshed. "Doesn't matter, he's already attached. I didn't realize she had bonded with him from the first time he'd met her." Sean sipped his tea, the warmth coating his throat. He related the conversation with Drew earlier in the day.

Shannon smiled wide. "I'd say that opens the door for you to pursue a relationship with her."

"What if I do and it doesn't work out? Then what? My son's heart is broken and—"

"Mia cares for your son. Evidenced by how she defended him this morning. She had a mama bear look in her eye and you weren't going to harm her cub."

Sean chuckled. "She did have a 'don't touch my baby' look, didn't she? I thought she'd give me a matched set of scars after you left."

"Good for her. You need a kick in the pants sometimes. And besides, she's in love with you."

His smile left his face and his voice came out as a hoarse whisper. "How do you know that?"

Shannon rose, punched his twin in the arm, and grabbed his empty cup. "I have eyes in my head. I could see it when I first met her in the coffee shop. She only had eyes for you. She was hurt and confused, but there was love there. I'd stake this ranch on it."

Sean's jaw dropped as Shannon left the room. Could she be in love with him? What if his twin was wrong? Then what?

Too many questions for him to ponder. He'd sleep on it. Maybe everything would make more sense in the light of day.

Mia hugged Pam when she arrived at the Art café where they had commiserated on the search for Shannon. The café had a small courtyard tucked away on the side of the building. Wrought-iron railing wrapped around the patio with trees and shrubs that hid them from passersby.

Meeting Pam for lunch was enough to lift Mia's spirits along with the sunny days even though she'd spent her time working from her garage apartment. She rearranged a corner of her living room as an office for her photography which took an entire weekend, but the space comforted her and she had a terrific view of her brother's backyard. Not as much light as she'd like, but her brother and sister-in-law wanted her close by and insisted she not leave, even though she wanted to get a bigger place. She understood her brother's need for her to be near after her disappearance all those months ago. Besides, she loved being able to visit her nieces when she could.

Even the thought of Sean not in her life didn't distress her on this glorious day. The birds chirped from their perches in the blossoming trees and the fresh breeze filled her lungs.

Pam sat at a table in the patio's corner. "How's the wrist?"

"Still have bad days and good days. Good days are winning right now."

"That's great. How's business?"

Mia cracked a smile. "Like you don't know. Come on."

Pam blushed and trained her gaze on the menu she already knew by heart. "I don't know what you're talking about."

"Like I don't know you're dating Brett. For goodness sakes, he can't stop talking about you." Mia put her hand over her friend's hand. "For the record, I'm ecstatic for you."

Pam turned curious eyes in her direction. "And what about you?"

Mia sighed. "Sean and I had a confrontation three weeks ago when I did the last of his shots. Drew was there and wanted to watch, so I agreed. Sean was none too happy, but he allowed it."

"What happened?"

"We did the shoot then he walked me to my car and politely told me to stay away from his son."

Anger filled Pam's face and Mia wanted to laugh, but her heart broke for the man she loved and the boy who could never be hers. "I guess Sean saw his son become too attached to the women in his life and he didn't want him too attached to me." Mia sighed. "He wants to protect his son. I get it. I do. But—"

"You love him."

Her breath whooshed out. "Yeah, I do." It was the first time she'd admitted it out loud.

"Then why don't you do something about it."

Mia shook her head. "He doesn't want me. I don't go places where I'm not wanted. Besides, there are other factors...personal issues." Tears welled in Mia's eyes, but she fought them as she stared into her glass.

Pam leaned forward and whispered, "What personal issues?"

"It's not important. Those factors will never change."

Pam placed her hand on Mia's. "I'm your friend and I'd never betray your trust. You should know that by now. I've never spoken to Brett about your relationship with Sean and so far, he hasn't confided in me either and I like it that way."

Could she trust Pam with her most guarded secret? The one thing that had kept her from becoming involved with any man since her husband died? Mia sighed and bit into her pastry which tasted like sawdust, but another perspective on her dilemma could help her decide what to do.

Mia nodded and said. "Be prepared. It's an ugly story."

Pam sat back and grinned. "You know Betty & Bertha are great listeners even if I'm not."

That one quip broke the ice and Mia chuckled. "Remember when I told you about my husband and how we were on a yacht when it blew up?"

Pam nodded.

"I didn't tell you debris hit me in the side." Mia rushed on. "The doctor wouldn't give me a definitive answer if it was the cause, but he told me I'd never have children. How can I get involved with any man knowing that if the relationship progressed to marriage that I could never give him a child? I couldn't put him or myself through that."

The silence stretched until Mia thought she would scream. "Aren't you going to say anything?

"I'm stunned. Have you gotten a second opinion?"

"No. Why would I?"

"In today's world, you need a second opinion. And even if the results show the first doctor was correct, what difference does it make? Sean already has a son. I don't think it would matter to him unless it matters to *you* that he loves a son not born by you."

"Drew is a sweetheart with a darling Irish accent I hope he never loses." Mia smiled to herself. "I'd be proud to be his mom. But—"

"You've always wanted a child of your own."

Mia couldn't hold back the tears and they dripped to her chin. Pam handed her a napkin and waited like the best friend she was while Mia mopped her face and composed herself. "I do. But since that's not possible, I have enough love in me to love another woman's child like my own."

"So, what's the problem?"

"I told you." Her voice took on a hint of exasperation. "Sean isn't interested. He made it clear to me on a number of occasions including the last day at his cabin."

"I don't believe it for a second. I saw the way he looked at you at the café when he and Shannon showed up."

Mia shrugged. "It doesn't matter."

"Go get a second opinion to make sure the first doctor's prognosis was correct. And then, tell Sean how you feel. Sometimes you have to go first."

"Did you?"

"My situation is very different from yours."

Just then Mia spotted Brett coming through the door. "Here comes your beau. Let's ask him." A look of fear passed over Pam's face and Mia knew she'd never say anything to hurt her friend.

"I hoped to catch the two of you here." Brett dropped into a chair opposite Pam. Her face colored and amused Mia.

"Tell me you have more work for me," she said.

Brett pulled an envelope from his pocket. "I do, but that's not why I wanted to see you."

"Wendy wanted me to give you this." While Pam and Brett stared at one another, Mia opened the envelope that held an engraved invitation to the ranch's first annual *Spring Thing*. Mia rubbed her finger over the embossed words.

Pam craned her neck. "What is it, Mia?"

"It's an invitation to the ranch's first annual *Spring Thing*, whatever that is."

Brett grinned. "It's a time of celebration and new birth. They're having a barbecue and riding displays—courtesy of Wendy—and a way for clients and prospective clients to see Shannon's operation. I thought it was a brilliant idea. Drew thought of it, actually."

Mia turned to Brett. "Drew?"

"What can I say? He's a smart kid. Then I took it a few steps further, embellished the idea and came up with the name."

"It's snappy," Pam said.

Brett gave Pam one of his heartwarming smiles. Smiles he seemed to have only for her these days. "Thanks. They'd been working on it for weeks. I know it's short notice but not only are you invited as a guest, but I hope you'll be able to take pictures for the website, too."

Pam snorted. "That's crass, Brett. First you invite her as a guest, then you want her to work?" She shook her head.

"It's ok, Pam. I'd rather be there in a work capacity, anyway."

"Great. I'll tell Wendy you'll be there an hour earlier so you can take prep shots, too." Brett beamed.

Pam groaned.

His face had a look of incredulity. "What?"

Pam shook her head. "You're unbelievable."

Mia checked her phone's calendar. "It's in two weeks. Interesting. I have nothing planned for that day. I wonder why." She chuckled. "I have to go. I promised a catalog to the boutique." She wagged her finger at Brett. "And I'm still not happy about that client."

He lifted one shoulder and gave her a slight smile. "But the pay is great."

Mia punched his arm as she left the table.

Pam grabbed her arm and whispered in her ear. "Remember what I said you need to do."

Mia nodded and thought about making an appointment with her doctor. Maybe Pam was right, and it was time to revisit the issue. She'd always been sure of it.

Maybe she was wrong.

Chapter 21

Mia finished up the last of the shoots for the small boutique and remembered why she didn't want to deal in fashion and vowed to reject any other fashion client. In fact, she wouldn't take another fashion job even if it was a boutique type shoot. It only stirred memories for her that she'd rather forget.

Angry with Brett for scheduling this appointment, when she'd explicitly told him she wasn't interested in fashion photography, she slammed her car in gear, and wanted to be as far away as possible. Her breathing became more regular the farther away she drove.

Her phone chimed with a client call, but she let it go to voicemail. She never answered when she drove. Time enough to answer it when she got home. Home. Her tiny photography world calmed her. She longed for her laptop, a cup of tea, and losing herself in the proofs.

Once in her apartment, she stored her equipment and took the SD card for the shoot and placed it in the client folder. Her tidy corner office a haven.

She dialed Wendy's number since she had been first on the list of people who called. Soon she'd have to hire an assistant for the day-to-day operation, but she balked at a stranger inside her apartment while she was out.

"I'm so glad you returned my call." Wendy's voice seemed strained. "I'm in a bind. I promised my sponsor photos, but there are patches of snow in the shots I have."

"Not a problem. I can Photoshop the snow out."

"I don't think you can put leaves on the trees or colorful flowers in the ground."

The ranch's sights, sounds and smells flew into her mind and she laughed. "True. I can't do that."

"Can you squeeze me in tomorrow and have them ready the first of next week?"

"Let me check my calendar." She'd hoped to do paperwork and get mood boards done, but Shannon and Wendy had turned into her best customers and she wouldn't let them down. Plus, working with Wendy was more fun than work.

"I have a few tasks I need to do in the morning, but I can do it at one."

"Great! Come a half hour early and we can have that lunch we promised to have."

"You don't have to do that."

"Nonsense. I don't want you to fall over from hunger while we're doing the shoot."

Mia chuckled. "Not likely. Besides, I carry granola bars and water with me on every shoot."

"That's not lunch! Mrs. O'Neill would have my hide if she knew you were coming, and I didn't invite you for lunch."

"You twisted my arm. I'll see you at 12:30."

They hung up and Mia worried whether Sean would be there for lunch. She hadn't seen him in two weeks after the disastrous confrontation about his son. Most likely Shannon would be since he was always there when she visited. Hopefully, Sean would be off site tending to his client's animals and he wouldn't be around.

Sean's stomach had told him it was lunch time a half hour ago. He heard voices from the kitchen. Laughing, feminine voices, and then he stopped. Lass! She was here? Why was she here? Hopefully, not for lunch.

When he stepped through the door, his heart stopped. She was even more beautiful than his dreams of her. He stared until she squirmed and he sensed the color rise to his cheeks.

Wendy placed platters of food on the table. "Did you see Shannon on your way in?"

He shook his head and moved farther into the room. Mia was still, but watched him and Wendy as if she were an observer at a tennis match.

"Let me call him. I wouldn't want him to miss a meal." Wendy left the room.

"That won't happen. My brother can smell food before it hits the table." Sean sat across from her so he could gauge her reaction to him. "Hello, Mia."

Wendy popped in again. "Shannon wants me to take his lunch to the barn office. I'll return in a few minutes, Mia. Help yourself."

Great. Wendy left him alone with Mia. Maybe he could see for himself what Shannon saw. He was not about to put his heart on the line, but he sure enjoyed looking at her lovely face.

"Did you get the thumb drive I sent with Drew's photos?" Mia said.

"They thrilled Drew and he has a few framed in his room."

Mia smiled her killer smile. A softness in her eyes. For a flickering moment, he thought he caught a hint of sadness, but then it was gone.

She reached for a sandwich. "How's he doing?"

"He's fine." The last thing Sean wanted to talk about was his son. And not with Mia. He wanted to know more about her. Was she as interested in him as he was in her? He'd dreamed of her for weeks, and he still couldn't believe she'd be interested in someone like him. She could have anyone. And he wanted to know more about her dead husband.

Instead, he talked about something less personal. "How's business?"

"Brett keeps me busy." Mia forked some pasta salad in her mouth, chewed, then swallowed. "This is delicious. I must get Mrs. O'Neill to give me the recipe."

"I believe this is my recipe." Sean laughed.

"Right. I forgot you're a great cook."

Sean's face turned red. "Do you like to cook?"

"Not particularly. I can and I do, but there's not much need for it. Fiona and Cassie strong arm me to have meals with them. But I do cook on occasion."

His brows furrowed. "Who are Fiona and Cassie?"

"You haven't met them. Fiona is my brother's housekeeper. Was my parents' housekeeper before they died. Cassie is my brother Steve's new wife."

Sean wondered at Mia's choice of words. Did she imply he'd meet these people who were so close to her? "Do you live close to your brother?"

Mia chuckled. "In his backyard."

Sean bit into his sandwich. Enough talking. His stomach wanted food, and he had a full schedule this afternoon. Silence filled the room, and he wished Wendy would come back.

"Read any good books lately?" Mia said.

It seemed she didn't like the silence either.

Sean grinned. "As a matter of fact, I have. The new Veronica Cannon thriller series. Remember reading her books at the cabin? You seemed quite fond of them, if I recall." Waves of joy trickled through his system as he remembered their time together. How she sat on his sofa and became so immersed in the books that she forgot he was there and it allowed him to drink in her beauty. How comfortable they were with one another. They didn't need conversation to be content in their own little world. And when her ankle had healed sufficiently, how she tucked her legs under and covered herself with the soft throw he kept for chilly nights.

"I was and still am a huge fan of those books." Then she burst into laughter—

"What?"

"I know the author."

Sean's eyes widened. "You do."

"Yep. You like them?" Mia sipped her drink.

Her laugh made his day. With all his heart, he wished he could move their relationship forward, but if all she wanted was friendship, he'd couldn't allow her to destroy him...or his son when he wanted more. He wanted it all.

"Aye." He leaned in his chair and his mouth formed a straight line. "What are you doing here, Mia?"

She stopped, her eyes widened at the abrupt change of subject, and anger etched her face. "Wendy wanted some shots and invited me to lunch." Mia wiped her mouth and pushed away from the table. "I'm sorry I intruded."

"Lass, wait." His heart pounded. He clutched her arm and stared deep into her eyes. "I didn't mean you weren't welcome." His eyes bored into hers. He'd hurt her feelings and never meant to. Then he whispered, "You're always welcome here."

She stopped and stared at him, then narrowed her eyes. "Am I? What about being near Drew."

Sean sighed. "Just because Drew lives here with us doesn't mean you can't visit. After all, you have business here."

Mia nodded. "I do and I'd best get to it." She left him lurching for answers to the questions in his heart.

What did he say that offended her?

Mia didn't see Sean the rest of the afternoon, but Rusty showered her with so much affection she didn't miss seeing Sean. At least his dog loved her.

Wendy grinned and shook her head. "That dog is smitten."

"He saved my life." She rubbed Rusty's ears and patted his head.

Wendy's shocked eyes made her laugh. "He did?"

Mia shivered and wrapped her arms around herself. "If he hadn't found me, I would have either died from exposure or drowned."

A thoughtful look passed over Wendy's face. "I thought Sean rescued you?"

"Sean carried me to his cabin, but Rusty found me." Mia fiddled with her camera. "At least I think he carried me. I don't know. I was unconscious for hours."

"Really? Sean only gave the briefest of explanations of how he knew you. You know how men are. They skip the details."

Mia smirked. "My brother is the same way."

"You're a twin, too, aren't you?"

She didn't want to talk about her twin or her stay at Sean's cabin. Her mind traveled back in time to their time together there when she didn't want to think about her life or work. It was private. "How'd you meet Shannon?"

Wendy laughed. "It's a long story, but fireworks flew the first time we met and thereafter. I fell in love with him when he took me to church."

Mia's eyebrow rose. "He took you to church?"

"Our first date, actually. That was it for me. I fought it, but it didn't matter."

Wendy's dreamy expression gave Mia insight to her relationship with her husband.

"What didn't matter?" Shannon's voice came over her shoulder. "Hello, Mia. Sean told me you were here to take Wendy's pictures."

Mia smiled. "Almost done, too."

"Great. Since you're here, I have a new crop of horses I want you to see so we can schedule a photo shoot for them."

"I'll put the camera equipment away and find you in the barn."

"Let me help," Shannon said.

Wendy mounted her horse. "I'll see you before you leave, Mia. I promised myself a ride this afternoon."

Mia smiled, waved, and watched Wendy trot away. "Thanks for the invitation to the *Spring Thing*. Sounds like it'll be a fun time even if I'm working."

"Brett dreamed up the idea along with my nephew."

Her laughter rang out. "His enthusiasm sometimes needs to be curbed."

Shannon sobered. "Actually, it's a blessing you're working with him."

Mia stopped. "Why?"

"Because for a long time he floundered at what he wanted to do. It seems you've helped him find his groove."

"He's helped me, too. My fledgling business thrives because Brett pulled me along with him."

"You make a good team. What's next for you, Mia?"

"Doing what I love, photography." She spread her hands. "Meeting great people like you and Wendy."

Shannon stopped and peered into her face. "What about Sean?"

Mia studied the barn and her muscles tensed. Sean was a subject she chose not to discuss. "How about we stick to the horses?"

"They're in the paddock behind the barn. Most of them are feasting on the new grass. I see Rusty found you again."

Mia reached to pat the dog's head. "Rusty seems to be doing well. Sean said it was a benign tumor."

"He is. Sean fretted over it until the lab results came back."

Mia smiled. "I'm glad he's OK."

They were in the paddock and Shannon showed her the horses. Sleek and gorgeous. She especially liked the light tan mare who seemed to beg, but Mia had no treats for any of them. Shannon frowned on excess treats. The amazing animals were for sale.

"Precious seems to have taken a shine to you." Shannon smiled and patted the horse's neck. The horse seemed to coo in Shannon's ear. "None of that, you big flirt."

Mia laughed, then heard the whistle. "What was that?"

"That'd be Sean calling Rusty, but it appears his dog is head over heels for you." Shannon roared with laughter. "Makes him crazy."

"Why?"

"Because the dog doesn't do that with anyone except you. He listens to you and won't leave your side when you're here. Drives Sean nuts."

"Oh."

Shannon chuckled and shoulder bumped her. "Don't tell him I said that."

Mia twitched her lips. "Don't worry, I won't."

Sean stepped to the fence on the other side of the paddock and Mia's awareness of him made her spine tingle. She bent low to Rusty's ear. "Go see Sean, Rusty." His mournful eyes begged to stay with her. She patted him and pushed him in Sean's direction. The dog whimpered and every few feet craned his head at her.

Shannon chuckled and whispered. "He'll be like a bear with a thorn in his paw tonight."

Mia could feel the color creeping up her throat and she pulled out her phone. "What days did you have in mind?"

"A sunny day. I'd like outside shots."

After she checked the weather, they coordinated the appointment for the start of the following week. "I'll bring Wendy's proofs with me then."

Mia was conscious of Sean moving away from the fence with Rusty at his side, and noticed new construction in the distance. "What's going on over there?"

Shannon shaded his eyes and pursed his lips. "Sean's building a house. He wants a place of his own for him and Drew. Eventually he'll build an office nearby so he doesn't have to pay rent in town."

"Makes sense."

"Yeah, if he had a wife, it would. What are those two guys going to do over there with just one another for company?"

The look Shannon gave her caused her to wonder what Shannon had in mind for his twin. Mia coughed. "Well, I'm sure he has a plan for himself."

"I sure hope so. Let me walk you to your car."

Mia left with more questions than answers. Sean was

building a home for himself. She wished with all her heart she'd be a part of his life and building a house, but it was a dream she couldn't entertain. Her doctor's appointment wasn't until Wednesday and she had plenty to do. She couldn't worry about Sean or the doctor visit's outcome.

Chapter 22

Mia almost canceled the appointment. Her nerves frayed, but she held onto her fledgling dream of being whole. Thankfully, the doctor wasn't called away to deliver any babies.

Wednesday morning and she sat in a room with every stage of pregnant woman giving her hope that she, too, would one day sit in this very office rubbing her belly like so many of the women.

She froze when the nurse called her name, but Mia arose as if she were a marionette and followed her into the exam room. The routine was the same every time. Strip from the waist down, sit on the edge of the paper-covered table, cover with the thin sheet, and wait for the doctor. The antiseptic smell of the exam room didn't comfort her.

She'd had her annual exam every year, but never asked about children. She fantasized about babies as she stared at the doctor's hall of fame baby montage on the wall opposite her.

A chill traveled down her spine. Maybe she shouldn't have come. She ought to let it go and forget about it. Then a still, small voice reminded her of how much God loved her.

The doctor knocked, entered, and sat at the laptop that held her chart. "What brings you in today, Mia? You're not due for an exam for another three months."

When she explained the situation and the background, the doctor stared at her.

"Your history with this office doesn't show anything like that, Mia. But to be sure, we'll do an ultrasound and have an MRI done along with blood work. Are you considering becoming pregnant?"

Mia tightened her fist around the sheet. "Yes. No. I'm not sure."

The doctor blinked, her voice soft and caring. "Let's just see what the tests reveal and go from there. We have a tech here to do the ultrasound, but the MRI will have to be scheduled at another facility." The doctor patted her hand and her chest ached. She didn't think she had any more tears to shed.

Mia nodded, and the doctor gave her an internal examination. She helped Mia from the table. "I don't see any evidence of what you're describing. Do you have medical records from your previous doctor?"

"No. But I can get them if they're needed."

"We'll submit the form for you, but it'll take time. I sense this is important enough for you to want a quick result."

"Preferably."

When the ultrasound had been completed, Mia filled in the form to request her medical records and scheduled the MRI. The earliest appointment was this Friday, the day before the *Spring Thing*.

She had hoped to get her answer prior to the event, but it didn't matter because she'd fret over the test results, anyway. A sliver of hope filled her heart, and she clung to it.

Maybe she could conceive. Maybe it would work out with Sean. The bitter taste of defeat warred with her hopeful heart.

Sean stopped when he heard Mia's name mentioned, then with purposeful steps, went into his brother's study. "What's happening?"

Wendy pecked at the laptop. "Going over the final details for the *Spring Thing* tomorrow."

Shannon leaned into the well-worn office chair. "How's the house construction?"

"Slow." Sean slumped into the chair across from his twin's desk.

"You know you didn't have to build now. Wendy and I love having you and Drew here."

"Drew and I need to have a home of our own."

"Where is the little guy?"

"Brushing Gingerbell. I swear that poor horse won't have any coat left for as much as he brushes her."

"Don't discourage it, Sean. It's good he's learning to care for the horse. He seems to have settled into life here."

Sean smiled. "He has. His counselor says he's made great progress, although Drew still misses his Nana."

"It's only natural he would," Wendy said.

"But the counselor cautioned me to keep him from becoming attached to the females in the household, if they weren't taking the place of his Nana. No offense, Wendy."

Wendy touched his hand. "None taken. I get it and I try to be kind but to maintain my distance. He needs a mother, Sean."

"And there's a wonderful woman who has already won his heart." Shannon crossed his arms. "Did you forget Drew has a framed picture of the both of you on his dresser? You can't use him as an excuse."

Sean took a deep breath. "Are you two on that again? She can't stand the sight of me." He absently rubbed his beard.

"Not the scar again." Shannon blew out a breath of disgust. "She refused to discuss anything about you when she took the latest batch of proofs for Wendy last Friday."

Dejection filled Sean's soul and his breath whooshed. "Exactly."

"Exactly nothing. I saw the look of want in her eyes when I told her you were building a house for you and Drew."

"You told her?"

"She asked about the construction. I didn't think it was a big secret."

"It's not. You're mistaken, though. She was mad at me at lunch that day."

Wendy perked up and gave him a hard stare. "Why?"

"I asked her what she was doing here."

Wendy drew a breath and shook her head. "If you used that tone, no wonder she got mad. I invited her."

"Doesn't matter. I have no reason to see her again." Sean caught the glance between his twin and Wendy. "What?"

Wendy cocked her head and grinned. "Mia will be here tomorrow taking official event photos."

Drew raced in the door. "Mia's coming to the barbecue? Can I show her what we did with the pictures I took, Da?" Excitement bubbled from him as he hopped from one foot to the other.

Wendy and Shannon chuckled, but Sean groaned and closed his eyes. His son climbed into his lap and put his hands on his father's whiskered cheeks. "Why don't you like Mia, Da? I think you should marry her and make her my mom."

Sean coughed and caught the twinkle in Wendy's eye. His twin winked as they left the room and he hugged his son. "It's not that simple. Mia has a business and she may not have time for a family or a little boy. Isn't it enough I love you and will care for you forever?"

"I love you too, Da. But I want a mom and I like Mia a lot because she taught me to look with my heart eyes."

"Not every lady wants to be a mom and Mia may not either, son." Sean dared not say 'or be a mom to another woman's son'. That would cause irreparable damage and there was no way he'd say anything to hurt his little boy.

"Will you at least try?"

"I can't make you that promise and I don't want you to ask Mia to be your mother either. It's not fair to do that. She has to want to do it on her own or it doesn't count. Understand?"

His solemn son nodded. "I'm hungry."

"Let's get dinner."

Now he was in a pickle. Shannon and Wendy wanted him to pursue Mia and now his son wanted a mother. It was a no-win situation for him. He didn't stand a chance. A woman who he had feelings for, but who couldn't stand him and a family who wanted her in their lives. But what about him? Didn't he merit true love like the love Shannon and Wendy had?

Steve trudged up the stairs to Mia's apartment. She'd been working all hours, running herself ragged, and she'd lost weight. He'd noticed it at church on Wednesday night. He would get her to the doctor if he had to carry her there himself.

His wife noticed the strain in Mia's eyes and called him on it. Something deeper was going on. He sensed it in the odd moment he was alone which wasn't often. Time for him to step up.

Mia opened the door. "Is something wrong?"

He shook his head.

"You scared the daylights out of me. I glanced at the digital clock and thought something happened."

"They're all tucked in and asleep. End of the week. They crash after dinner and Cassie is working. Can I come in?"

"Don't tell me you came to make sure I went to bed?" Mia sighed. "I'd already shut my laptop for the night. I'm the event photographer at the *Spring Thing* out at the ranch tomorrow and need to get to bed."

"That's what I wanted to talk to you about." Steve gazed around the room and the vanilla candle's scent wafted through the room. Tidy as ever, too. "Did you eat dinner?"

"Fiona sent a dish over earlier."

Steve opened the refrigerator and checked the plate. "You haven't touched it." He pinned her with a concerned stare. "I'm worried about you, Mia. You've lost weight."

"Had a granola bar right before Fiona sent the plate over, so I wasn't hungry and I haven't noticed my clothes fit any differently." She crossed her arms. A signal for him to use a soft touch.

"I see it in your face the few times I see you anymore. I want you to come to dinner more often."

"I seem to recall when you were busy with business you didn't eat with us many a night."

He grimaced. "I knew you'd say that."

She reached over and touched his arm. "I'm fine. Really."

"Then tell me about your dead husband." He hadn't

meant to blurt it out like that, but he'd reeled when the detective uncovered her past. And he hadn't mentioned it because he wanted to wait and see if she'd tell him. Seeing her lose weight and knowing she fretted over Sean caused him concern. Her shocked look and white face just about killed him. She didn't want him to know. "Why didn't you tell me?"

"I can tell this will be a difficult conversation. Want a soda?"

"No. And don't sidetrack, Mia."

She released a long breath. "I want one." After she poured herself a soda, she dropped onto the sofa, and flung her fuzzy slippers to the floor. She sipped the cool liquid and hoped it would give her courage.

"I'm waiting, Mia."

"What do you want to know?"

"Everything."

"Everything?" She squeaked.

Steve nodded. "When you disappeared, the detective dug into your life in New York. You also didn't tell me you were a hot-shot fashion photographer. Successful, too. I was and still am proud of you, Mia. Mom and Dad would have been proud, too."

Mia sniffed. "I made a mistake, and I didn't want you to know. You made a mistake of your own and were suffering, too, and I didn't want to burden you with my problems. Besides, the girls needed attention."

"And you gave it to them when I couldn't. You know how grateful I am, but I'm worried about you, Mia." He moved closer to his twin and touched her arm.

"You mean the world to me and Cassie and the kids."

"I know. The business has grown. I think I might need a bigger place." She looked around the living room.

"Don't even think about it!" He turned angry eyes at Mia's chuckle. "I mean it. Unless you plan to get married."

"Whatever gave you that idea?"

The shock registered on her face told him all he needed to know.

"You found Shannon—I mean Sean. I thought perhaps you two hit it off again."

"I did find him. And he's still wonderful, but he has a son."

Steve frowned. "He was married?"

Mia shook her head.

"How long have you known?"

"A while. But that's not important. What matters is even if I wanted a deeper relationship with him, he told me point blank his son's life has to come first because of the circumstances of how Sean came to be a father. I think his journey of faith led him to America."

"Tell me."

Mia explained what she knew about Sean's situation. "What does it matter? He is beyond my reach."

He gave her a sad smile. "You love him."

"And I don't want you to do anything about it, either."

"I wouldn't, but I think you have enough love in your heart to shower a little boy with it. Where's his mother?"

She lifted sad eyes to her twin. "Dead."

"Just like our situation," he whispered. He straightened and smiled. "But look what a wonderful mother my girls have now. You could be that mother for Sean's son and have the family you've always wanted."

"How do you know I've wanted a family?"

Steve smiled. "I'm your twin, remember? When chaos doesn't reign in our house, which is almost never, I have odd moments where I sense what you're going through, but I haven't been able to string them together to make complete sense of them. I'm more in tune with it since I scaled back my time at the office."

Mia leaned into the tufted sofa and hugged accent pillows to her chest. "I'd love to have Drew as my son. And I think he'd like me to be his mother, too. But Sean is adamant."

"Break him of the notion, Mia. I had to forgive Laura long after she died. It's time you forgave your dead husband and Sean and move on."

Mia's eyes grew wide. "That's what I've been doing. Comparing both men and I haven't forgiven either of them, although I told Sean I forgave him."

"You need to or you'll never be free to move on with your life. Now tell me about your dead husband."

He listened as Mia described her rise to fashion photography fame, her whirlwind marriage, her husband's betrayal and subsequent death. What he sensed she hadn't shared was how similar their faith journeys had been. They'd both left their faith behind for a time, and then stumbled back. Their lives ran parallel.

"Before I leave tonight, I want a promise from you that you'll forgive both of them, get some sleep and tell Sean how you feel. It's the only way you'll know for sure."

After they prayed, Steve sensed Mia's burden had been lifted. He and his wife would pray for her and Sean to make a commitment to one another. It amazed him how in such a short time both of them could have fallen in love.

He hoped Sean was man enough to admit he loved her, too.

He could only pray.

Chapter 23

The day of the *Spring Thing* dawned bright with not a cloud in sight, and it was forecasted to be hot. Unseasonably hot. Mia dressed for work, classy and casual, with her most comfortable flats. Since there would be quite a few people at this shindig she might snag new project leads. She ate a late breakfast, packed her equipment in the car, and brought more comfortable clothes for when the party wound down.

Shannon and Wendy would be too busy with the event, and she couldn't even think of being near Sean. The other worry was how to handle the growing affection from Drew.

Disappointed the results of the MRI would not be available until next week, she resolved to have hope, and prayed for a good outcome.

She arrived an hour before as instructed but didn't see Brett's car, so he and Pam weren't there yet. People scurried about moving pots of flowers, setting up tables and chairs under two enormous white tents. Tangy scents of barbecue filled the air and her mouth watered for a taste.

Mia spotted Wendy with a clipboard directing traffic as Shannon positioned the signage. Certain he'd already prepared the horses and could spare a few minutes to give her instructions, she made her way to him.

"Where would you like me stationed?"

Shannon gave her a wide grin. "We have a special small tent for you, so if people want to take pictures of themselves with the horses, you can."

Mia was unaware of this new wrinkle. She hadn't come prepared for this situation, but like her time in the fashion industry, she'd roll with it. Mia followed him to the tent where someone prepared a small table and three chairs. She wished she'd known about this, though.

"You need some help with your equipment?"

"That'd be great."

Shannon's voice rose above the din. "Sean. Get over here and help Mia with her equipment." He smirked at Mia before he trotted off to answer more questions.

Mia's heart sank. The last thing she needed was to spend time with Sean. At least not until she knew the test results.

"Is your car unlocked?" Sean said.

She gave him a single nod. "One more trip for both of us."

"Is your wrist strong enough to carry the load? I can make two trips."

"I'm good." Mia smiled. Sean's thoughtfulness warmed her heart and she remembered his utmost care for her at the cabin.

Brett strode to them. "You ready to take pre-event pictures?"

"Not quite. There's a little wrinkle in the plan," Mia said.

Sean and Brett stopped and gawked.

At their worried frowns, Mia chuckled. "Relax, guys. It's not a big deal. Shannon wants me to take photos of guests who want pictures with the horses."

When Brett's mouth dropped open, she knew it was a last-minute decision he'd been unaware of. "Stay cool, Brett.

We'll adjust. We have time. But I need someone to get me extra SD cards. I brought one that holds over a thousand photos, but I'd rather be safe and not need additional cards than to need them and not have them. I could delete shots, but I don't want to guess which ones Wendy and Shannon would delete. Used my extra and didn't replenish my stash." She flattened her lips. "I won't do it again."

"Tell me what you need and I'll get it. I'll throttle Shannon while I'm at it." Frustration came off of Brett in waves.

Mia put her hand on his arm. "Be cool. Shannon is our best customer and I'm still proving myself. This is not a big deal. Remember my roots. I just have to plan better next time."

Sean crossed his arms and growled. "There won't be a next time."

Both Brett and Mia gaped at him.

"Shannon had no right to drop extra work on you, Mia. I'm very sorry."

She wanted to cry. He was so sweet, and she touched his arm. "It's OK. I would have liked to have been more prepared, but I know these things happen. I'd forgotten I had a shoot checklist. This business is so different, I didn't think I'd need one, but this has taught me a lesson with minimal pain. We can fix this. And I may not even need the extra cards."

"Let me run and get those cards. Pam will be here shortly. Tell her where I went." Brett trotted off to his car.

Sean grabbed the bag from Mia's arms and insisted she carry the lighter items. He placed the equipment on the table. "What else can I help with?"

"If you could get me a glass of water, that'd be great."

By the time Sean returned with two glasses of fresh squeezed lemonade, Mia was ready and made sure she had business cards in her pocket.

"I think Wendy wanted you to take pictures of the preparations," Sean said.

Mia put her half-full glass on the table. "Right."

She took at least a hundred pictures of the servers, tents, and floral arrangements while the caterers worked. Sean accompanied her into the house where she took another hundred shots. "Let me text Brett and tell him to get a half dozen cards. I thought one would be plenty." She fiddled with her camera and grumbled. "Man, am I rusty. I never use more than one card per shoot. I should have known better."

"You couldn't have known Shannon would drop this in your lap. Don't beat yourself up."

"I'm a professional and should be prepared for last-minute changes."

Sean gazed into the eyes of the frazzled woman he loved and couldn't stand it a moment longer. The way that piece of wispy hair dropped across her forehead. The urgency of movements as she fought to make things right for Wendy and Shannon, despite the curveball they'd tossed her. The twitch of her mouth as she tried to get the exact shot she wanted.

He pulled her into his brother's study.

He closed the door and attempted to pull her into his arms. She clung to her camera with one hand and pressed her hand against his chest as he wrapped his arms around her and breathed her hair's fresh lemon scent.

She looked more confused than excited as they gazed at one another. Maybe he'd made a mistake.

He tried to step back. "Sorry, I'm sorry."

"No!" She grabbed his shirt until she had a fistful of fabric in her tiny hand. "You just surprised me, that's all. Took my breath away."

"Aye, is that not a good thing, Lass?"

He knew the very second she'd surrendered and he was going to make the most of it.

Until Wendy burst into the room.

"Oh! Wow. Sorry."

Mia's cheeks pinkened. "No need to be sorry. How can we help?"

"Drew," Wendy said and looked away. "Where's Drew?"

"The foreman is keeping him busy, so he's not underfoot while the caterers work," Sean said. "Then we'll unleash him when the guests arrive."

"Just checking. Hadn't seen him lately. Mia? You OK?"

Mia donned her professional persona and smiled. "Of course. I've already taken a couple hundred. Is there anything else?"

Stress edged Wendy's voice and her hands shook. "Yes. The tables are ready and I'd like photos before the guests arrive and mess them up. I'm sorry I didn't account for a helper for you. Sean, you'll help her with whatever she has to do, won't you?"

Sean watched Mia as she embraced Wendy. "It looks amazing out there. You'll kill this event. The guests will talk about it for weeks, even months."

"You think? It's important everything is perfect. There's so much riding on it."

Sean saw Mia glance at him, but he looked away.

"Yes, I do. Now let me get to work." Mia followed Wendy out the door.

Sean grabbed her arm. "Come on. I'll show you a shortcut to the tents."

He led her through a series of doors and hallways through the kitchen packed with servers and kitchen help dressed in almost formal attire.

"What did Wendy mean by 'so much riding on it'?"

"She's stressed. Poor choice of words."

Mia stopped when they were outside. "I don't think so, but it's really none of my business."

Hesitating, he cocked his head. "It's not a secret. There are a specific number of horses that need to be sold on a regular basis for the ranch to remain profitable. And this is the first big function they've held to attract new business."

She gave a single nod. "Makes sense."

He took her arm again and guided her through outside prep areas where aroma of barbecued meat assailed her nostrils. Spectacular was the only word to describe what the tents looked like now compared to her earlier pictures. With the lights, tables, fine china, chair covers and table arrangements, it didn't look like any barbecue she'd ever been to.

Mia focused her camera. "This is swankier than any wedding I've ever seen."

"Good. If you're impressed then the guests will be bowled over."

She took low and high shots, close ups, and different angles. She took a few shots of him when she thought he wasn't looking. *Progress.*

Mia lowered her camera when Brett and Pam rushed over. "Did you get the cards?"

"I got a dozen. We don't know how many will want photos or multiples. The opportunity for a photo shoot from a professional photographer might be too good for them to pass up."

Grimacing, Mia took the SD cards and shoved them in her bag. "I meant to ask you, what do I say to guests who want copies of the proofs? I don't think Shannon wants to pay for them, does he?"

Brett rubbed the back of his neck and tension filled his face. "Shannon doesn't think. Let me talk to him. We'll devise a plan."

Pam pointed to the parking lot attendees who directed cars. "You'd better hurry on that plan. The guests are here."

Brett hustled away. Mia's trepidation must have shown on her face because Sean pulled her into the corner of the tent. "You don't have to do this, Mia. I'll handle Shannon."

"I can't have you 'handling Shannon' for me." Mia motioned with air quotes. "This is my business, Sean. I'll deal with it." When he opened his mouth, she gave him a hard stare, and he clamped his mouth shut.

She stepped over to Pam. "I know this is asking a lot, Pam, since you're here to have fun, but could you help me with the guests who want photos?"

"Let Pam enjoy the party," Sean said. "I'll help you."

Mia slapped her forehead.

"What?" Worry etched Sean's features.

"I need to coordinate people's names with their photos! A spiral notebook or legal pad will do." She lowered her head as Sean booked to the house to get one.

Mia blew out an exasperated breath. "I didn't sign up for this kind of stress. I want to chew every one of my fingernails down to the quick." She narrowed her gaze at her friend. "And don't say anything to Brett."

Pam took Mia's camera, put it on the table, and enveloped her hands. "Look into my eyes, Mia. Breathe. Slow breaths. You can do this. Just breathe."

Sean came back with the notebook and Mia got it ready and breathed a sigh of relief. "Go have fun, Pam. Sean will help me if I need it."

"Are you sure?" At Mia's single nod, Pam held her palms up and moved away from them.

"Ok. I'm ready to work the event." Mia breathed deep. "Think you can keep up?"

Before he could answer, Drew ran over to them. "Mia! Can I take some pictures?"

Mia inhaled, but Sean was way ahead of her. "Maybe later, son. Mia has to take pictures of the party for Uncle Shannon."

When Drew's face fell, Mia's heart hurt. She crouched to his level and touched his cheek. "I promise, if you're still awake after all the guests have left, we'll take some family shots. And if you're not, we'll schedule a time when just you and I will take photos."

Drew gave her a half grin so like Sean's and glanced at his father. "OK, Da?"

Without expression, Sean gave his son a single nod.

She rose from her position and gave Drew a pat on the shoulder.

Sean crouched to his son's level. "There are some kids your age. Maybe you could show them the horses from the fence. But don't take anyone inside the paddock." Drew puffed out his chest because Sean gave him a job to do.

Guests ate, drank and had conversations in and out of the tent. Mia welcomed the cooler temperatures under the tent but knew she had to take more shots under the warm sun. She captured smiling faces, but the most interesting shots were when the people were unaware of her. They had bored, strained, or exuberant expressions cross their faces.

Sean stood behind her and sometimes beside her. Even though he didn't seem happy, he gave her strength and support. Despite his brooding presence over her promise to his son, she would not cause Drew any hurt. No way.

Before the caterers served the buffet, Shannon announced guided tours around the ranch along with the opportunity of a photo shoot near the horses.

"Can we get a shot of ourselves on the horses?" someone called out.

When Shannon's face paled, she knew he hadn't expected that question. But Shannon did a quick recovery and smiled. "While we'd love to, but unfortunately our insurance providers would have our hides. If you buy a horse today, though, we'll be happy to accommodate you."

The heckler didn't ask another question, and Shannon directed them to his wife who would form groups based on the type of tour the guests wanted and she would help them with the pictures, too.

Sean shook his head and whispered in Mia's ear. "He always comes out smelling like a rose."

She turned. "Quick thinking," she muttered. "That's all it was."

He gave her a heart-melting smile, and goosebumps spread on her arms despite the sun's heat.

Her thoughts turned to their earlier encounter and her heart fluttered. She'd have to keep her wits about her until her doctor gave her the facts she needed to be totally honest with Sean. It wouldn't be easy with Sean acting so different. It was a one-eighty, and she didn't understand it. If she ever needed the Lord's guidance, it was now.

Chapter 24

The last of the guests left after they gushed praise for the ranch. Sean moved to help Mia load the last of her equipment and exhaustion pinched her face. He touched her arm. "Neither of us had anything to eat and I'm starved. Why don't we get some food and you can relax before you head home?"

Mia gave him a tired smile. "I'm afraid if I sit, I'll fall asleep but my grumbling stomach would keep me awake." A brief laugh escaped her lips.

Sean chuckled and grinned. "I remember that grumble."

Her mouth dropped open, but she followed him into the house. Mia tightened her grip on Sean's arm and pointed toward the living room. Drew slept curled on his side and faced away from them. Sean raised his finger to his lips and moved to cover his son with a soft blue afghan. Then he whispered in her ear, "I'll carry him upstairs later."

If they hurried, they could get something before whatever leftovers were taken away or frozen. The caterers scampered around the kitchen and clinked cutlery and glasses. Tantalizing aromas filled the air, and he followed his nose.

Sean viewed the organized chaos in the kitchen and side-stepped servers until he found covered trays of food on the counter. He opened a cabinet, grabbed two plates, and gave one to Mia. "Help yourself."

They loaded their dishes with food, re-covered the trays, and pilfered two bottles of water plus two slices of cheesecake. Sean escorted Mia into the formal dining room.

"I wonder where Shannon and Wendy are?" Mia said.

He swallowed the tasty barbecue. "If I know them, they're probably in the study doing a post-mortem on the event."

"Always a good idea while everything is fresh in your mind." Mia sipped her water and sighed. "I can't keep my promise to Drew, but I'll make time for him as soon as I can."

Sean pressed his shoulders into the chair and sighed. "I don't know if it's a good idea, but a promise is a promise."

Mia pushed her food around on her plate. "I couldn't bear to see him so disappointed."

He jabbed food onto his fork. "He has to accept disappointment, Mia. Life and people can't always give him what he wants when he wants it."

She crossed her arms. "I know, but I upset him the first time I met him and it has bothered me ever since."

He lifted his eyes to hers. "He's forgiven you, Mia. Let it go."

"Easier said than done."

Sean wiped his mouth. "Believe me, I know."

Mia's curious eyes held his.

Sean cleared his throat. "About this afternoon in the study…"

Wendy stepped into the room and held plates of food. "There you two are. Glad to see you raided the kitchen. We're starved."

"Where've you been?" Sean said.

"Going over the success of the event." Shannon forked food into his mouth.

"You did a great job with the guests, Mia." Wendy placed a drink by Shannon's plate.

Sean threw his napkin on the table. "About that—"

"Thanks. It was fun." Mia rose from the table and glared at him. "Let me take this dish to the kitchen and get going."

Wendy waved at her and glanced at Sean. "Leave it. The caterers will get it. You've done enough for today."

Sean took Mia's elbow. "I'll walk you to your car."

He caught the glance from Wendy to Shannon and the smirk on his twin's face. In the best interest to keep the peace, he'd let it go, but this wasn't over. Not by a long shot. His brother's lack of respect for Mia's work dug at him.

The sun had set several hours ago, and the air chilled the evening. He tucked Mia under his arm. "You're shivering."

"I'll text you when I can spend time and take photos with Drew, but it won't be for two weeks."

"He should be out of school by then and you'll fit him in easier. About this afternoon—."

"Don't." Mia pulled away and whirled. "I can't talk about this afternoon. I'm too tired and I may say something I shouldn't."

He leaned closer. "Like what?"

Mia crossed her arms and a mulish look came over her face. "Forget it, Sean. I'm tired."

She opened her car door, and he leaned on it. "Meaning we can talk about it at a later date?"

A fragile smile came over her face. "Maybe. I've got to go."

"Would you go to church with me tomorrow?"

Mia's mouth fell open. "Another time, perhaps. I'm exhausted."

"I'll hold you to it." He backed away from the door and shoved his hands in his pockets. Confusion and hope warred within his heart and mind and marred his features.

The dining room was empty and the house quiet. Sean sighed. He wanted to tackle his brother for his treatment of Mia today, but he, too, was tired and he still had to get Drew into bed.

His son roused for a minute and asked for Mia, but fell asleep again in Sean's arms. His heart wrenched. With his son tucked in bed, he tumbled into his own bed.

Thoughts of Mia swirled around his brain. Maybe? Perhaps? What did those words mean? What about Drew? He couldn't allow their relationship to grow if she dodged him. Was it his scar? He lifted his hand to his face to rub it like he'd done thousands of times since it healed.

But she didn't seem upset, judging by their time together this afternoon. He smiled and closed his eyes and hoped to dream of the exquisite Mia and their future.

Mia groaned when she heard Pam's ringtone. She wanted to let it go to voicemail, but she feared Pam would appear on her doorstep and want to know why she hadn't picked up. A lecture from Betty & Bertha was not her idea of fun.

"How did things go with Sean yesterday?" Pam's voice took on a sing-song quality, and Mia cringed. An inquisition approached.

"Fine. He helped direct traffic. I'm still exhausted. I didn't go to church this morning, but I'll go tonight."

"He couldn't take his eyes off you."

Mia picked at her blueberry muffin. "I was a little busy doing my job. I didn't notice."

"Come on. Brett told me how upset he got when Shannon foisted extra work on you."

"I know. He was sweet." Mia's soft smile turned tough. "But I'm a big girl and he shouldn't protect me from my clients."

"When will you see him again?"

Mia sighed. "I'm holding him at arm's length until I get the results from the MRI, but I promised Drew I'd take pictures with him."

"What MRI?"

Mia knew Pam would hone in on that and she could kick herself for letting it slip. She blamed it on her tiredness. "I went to see my doctor. She couldn't tell by the exam and wanted a full workup including an MRI."

"And if the results are not what you'd hoped for, then what?"

Mia took a deep breath, and inhaled the fresh air wafting through her window. "I go on as I have. I can't do that to him, Pam. I love him too much."

"Listen to me. If he loves you, which I think he does, your ability to have children won't matter."

"Maybe. I don't want to talk about Sean and me. I want to know more about you and Brett."

Pam gave her a dreamy sigh. "He's not what I imagined. He's driven and yet kind. And the entire time we were at the event, he never once flirted with anyone, but me. He invited me to go to church with him."

Laughter burst from Mia's lips.

"What's so funny?" Pam's irritation with Mia came through loud and clear.

"It appears the McDermott men, including Brett, like to take women to church on their first dates."

"How do you know that?"

"Wendy told me Shannon took her to church for their first date. And Sean asked me to go to church with him today."

"And you turned him down?"

"No. I said perhaps."

"Perhaps is no."

"I don't want to get involved in case the results don't look good. Let's get back to you. Are you going to church with Brett?"

Mia could hear Pam's hesitation. "I told him we needed to get to know one another a little better, but I'll go. Just not right now."

"Who is evasive now?" Mia chuckled. "Don't answer. I have two loads of laundry and I want to prepare for next week before church."

As she ended the call, Mia thought of the McDermott men and how they all attended church. How awesome was that? Guys who had faith and went to church warmed her heart.

The muffin she ate turned to cardboard in her mouth as her thoughts turned to her MRI results. She needed answers. Soon.

After church, Sean trekked to the new house to check on its progress. Drew ran ahead while Rusty barked and circled him. Sean sighed and breathed in the scent of late spring wild flowers.

It would be months before the house was completed. His investment in the ranch cost him at least five or more years before he could afford to move his office to the ranch. It couldn't be helped. The ranch and his brother were more important than having his office nearby. Sean longed for the convenience of his office near his home and to make it easier to care for Drew.

His son sat on a pile of lumber in the shade of a large oak tree. His eyes fixed on Sean as he strolled to the construction site. "Da, when do you think Mia will come and take pictures with me?"

Sean frowned. He hadn't heard from Mia since the night of the *Spring Thing* two weeks ago. Brett mentioned there were more than six thousand photos from the event. Shannon and Wendy debated over their selections for the website. He shook his head. "She's been busy working with Uncle Shannon to pick out pictures for the ranch. To make it easier for both of you, we thought we'd wait until after school ended."

Drew gave a deep sigh. "That's not for another week."

Sean dropped next to his son and hugged him. "I know, but think of how much fun you'll have and you can spend more time outside."

"When will the house be done?"

This time it was Sean's turn to sigh. "Not for months and months. We won't finish it until this time next year."

His son's eyes widened. "That's a long time away."

"It is." Sean ruffled his son's hair.

"Is Uncle Shannon and Aunt Wendy coming to live with us?"

"No. It'll just be you and me."

"We need a lady to live with us, Da. To take care of us and sing me to sleep."

Sean laughed. "I'd sing to you, but my voice isn't the best."

"I wish Mia could come and live with us," Drew whispered.

Me too. More than I can say.

"How about we take Gingerbell and Thunder for a ride?" A ride always distracted Drew, but Sean's heart couldn't get a handle on what Mia's feelings for him were. His mind returned to the time he'd spent with her at the cabin, the embrace in Shannon's office, and when he'd followed her around at the event. She amazed and thrilled him. But would he be enough for her? A scarred vet with a son? He grimaced and followed Drew.

Chapter 25

The number of proofs from the event staggered Mia. In all her fashion shoots she'd never shot more than a thousand. Two weeks after the *Spring Thing* and she'd only singled out the vanity guest shots from the actual event photos. It cut the number by half, but she further organized them.

Interrupting her thoughts on how to guide Shannon and Wendy on their choices for the right proofs, Mia's phone chirped. Her heart pounded. The doctor. She said a silent prayer before she answered and stared out the window at the late spring blooms bursting with color.

"We have to reschedule another MRI. The machine had been calibrated, but something happened with your images. No cost to you or your insurance company."

Mia's heart sank and heartburn threatened from her recent snack. "How soon can we reschedule?" She couldn't put Sean off any longer. "What about a faster turnaround? I have some decisions to make and I need the results. I thought I'd know by now."

"I understand. I'll see what I can do. I'll push for a one-day turnaround." From the tension in the doctor's voice, Mia figured the doctor was none too happy with the lab.

"Great. Will I need to come to the office once the results

are in?"

"No. I'll call you."

The doctor told her to be at the lab at nine the next morning.

Focusing on the dilemma with Shannon and Wendy's proofs proved futile, so Mia opted to make herself a cup of tea. The warmth soothed her fractured nerves and the aroma from the fragrant vanilla candle relaxed her.

She settled into her reading chair to think about her approach to the ranch mood boards when Betty & Bertha's ringtone sounded.

"Did you hear anything from the doctor?" Pam said.

"Wouldn't you know it? The equipment failed and I have to re-take the test."

"It's rare for that to happen, Mia. Has the doctor rescheduled it?"

"Tomorrow morning. I'm trying to stay positive, but I need closure."

"Do you want me to come with you? My early appointment for tomorrow canceled."

Mia sat up. "That would be great. I haven't told my family anything."

"Fine. How about we meet at the lab? My later appointment is near there."

"You don't have to do this." Mia's sense of guilt closed in on her. She didn't want to take her friend's time away from something else.

"Forget it. I can hear the stress in your voice and I want to be there for you."

Pam's friendship meant the world to her, and she hoped everything worked out for her and Brett. He had become a great business partner and she didn't have to prod him to get things done. She appreciated his can-do attitude.

After her chat with Pam, Mia's special ringtone for Brett pealed. "What are we going to do with Shannon and Wendy? They're driving me nuts."

"I've narrowed the playing field somewhat and I'll plan a strategy for them to decide."

"Great. Could you speed it up some? I'd like to meet with them tomorrow morning since your schedule is open."

"I have a nine o'clock I can't postpone. Afternoon is open."

"Anything wrong?"

The last thing Mia wanted to talk about with Brett was her medical test. "No. I hadn't had time to enter a personal appointment for Wednesday morning." She hoped he'd be OK with her explanation.

"Fine. Let's make it one. I'll meet you there."

Mia hung up, leaned her head back, thought about the ranch's proofs, and decided. There would be hours of work ahead of her to keep her thoughts from the test and Sean.

She stopped to have dinner with her twin's family and knew the hour and a half would put her work back until midnight. Steve gave her grief about how she worked late hours, so she took her laptop to her room, closed the blinds, and the door, but fell asleep with her laptop on the bed.

Fuzziness filled her brain, and she glanced at the clock. She jumped out of bed and got ready for her appointment.

Mia made the final touches to her presentation when she returned from the lab and determined how to position the best proofs for Wendy and Shannon to choose from.

Brett met her at the ranch and they sat at Shannon's

dining room table and went over the proofs. She hoped she'd see Sean, but she dreaded it and it kept her discussing the various mood boards.

Her approach seemed to impress Wendy and Shannon. With a sidelong glance from Brett, she understood this approach would be used in all future dealings with their clients. It was a good approach and a stab of pride welled within her heart.

"It's about time they made some decisions." The arched doorway framed Sean as he leaned against it.

"Mia is brilliant. She designed a mix of mood boards they can use at different times to give the website a fresh look all the time." Brett said.

She could feel her face heating at his praise. She'd have to hug him later for her confidence boost.

"Fantastic." Sean cast an admiring look at her. "Maybe we could do the same with my website. The number of hits has fallen off."

"No horning in on the ranch's time, Sean." Shannon's voice filled with laughter.

"If your business is completed, I'd like to talk to Mia... privately."

Shannon glanced at Brett and his wife with a slick smile. "Use my study."

Sean grabbed a mug and made himself a coffee. "Grab your coffee and stuff, Mia, and let's go."

A sense of trepidation filled her, and she hoped she could direct their talk to business and her appointment with Drew.

"Have a seat." Sean dropped onto the leather sofa and patted a spot next to him. He placed his mug on the coffee table.

Mia sat a little away from him and opened her laptop to his website. "What did you have in mind for your site?"

"We'll get to that in a moment." Sean touched Mia's hand and her stomach tightened. She wouldn't get away from this conversation. The medical issue notwithstanding, she wasn't prepared.

"I haven't spoken to you since the event but I know you've been grappling with the ranch's work plus your other clients, so I've been reluctant to call you."

"I'm glad you didn't. I've been buried. But we can talk through some of your thoughts on what you'd like to do on your website. Brett should be here for this conversation."

"Brett isn't needed because our conversation will be a little more personal."

Mia placed the open laptop on the table and pulled out her phone. "Good. I want to schedule time for Drew." She scrolled through her appointments then looked up. "Is he out of school yet?"

"Friday is his last day."

"How about one on Saturday?"

"Fine."

When she looked up, his face was so near she could see the stitch marks on his scar and his wonderful masculine scent drew her, but she froze when he lifted his hand to her face. His lips loomed near, a slight smile on his face and he moved in to kiss her. "I've missed you," he whispered before his lips touched hers.

Her heart thumped as he kissed her and his woodsy scent tickled her nose. She adored his kisses, but with reluctance she pulled away. "Sean, we can't do this right now."

Sean rubbed the top of her hand and mesmerized her with his slow touch and low voice. "Seems to me we already did. I couldn't resist. Before that, I meant I wanted to talk... about us."

With jerky movements, Mia removed his hand from hers. "It's not a good idea right now."

Frustration filled Sean's face. "What is it with you Mia? We kiss and you make me believe you have the same feelings I do. Why do you put me off?"

"There are other factors."

"You mean Drew?"

"No, it's personal. I can't talk about it right now."

"Can't or won't?"

"Sean, I—"

The door banged open and Drew ran in with Wendy close on his heels. "Mia. I saw your car. Are you here to take pictures with me?"

Wendy put her hand on his shoulder. "Sorry, I tried to catch him before he barreled in."

"It's ok." Torn from her conversation with Sean, Mia stiffened her spine. "I'm here on business. I've already scheduled our time for Saturday."

"I have to wait two whole days?" Disappointment was clear on Drew's face.

"Son, we talked about your expectations." Sean stood and walked to his son.

"But I waited for a long, long time." He whined as only a child could.

Mia crouched next to the boy and touched his arm. "There is something I want you to do before we meet on Saturday."

"What?" He looked up and wiped his eyes. His sense of excitement returned.

"We don't want to waste time, do we?" She shook her head, so he'd shake his, too. "You need a plan for what you want to do."

"How do I do that?" He looked confused.

Mia smiled. "I want you to get a small notebook."

The looks on Wendy and Sean's faces told her they didn't know where she was going with this. And she had to get them to stand with her so she could leave and avoid any other conversation with Sean.

"I don't have a notebook."

Mia dug through her laptop bag. "Here, I have an extra one, just in case I need it." She thanked God she hadn't removed the notebook from her bag. She seldom used them anymore, and it'd be perfect for what she wanted to do.

"Take this notebook and write the things you want to take pictures of."

"But I already know."

"Maybe there's something you haven't thought of. Take a walk around the ranch and look at everything. Then write what your heart tells you to take a picture of."

He took the notebook with careful hands.

"Go change your clothes. Gingerbell has been waiting for you to ride her." Sean propelled the boy out the door and winked at Mia.

"After I ride, I'll work on the list," Drew called out over his shoulder as he ran up the stairs to his room.

"That was brilliant Mia. You have a natural knack with children." Wendy glanced back and forth between them.

Mia glanced at Sean who gave her a look that said she stalled and he knew it.

"If you don't know what you want for your website, let's table it for now and we can revisit it when I'm here on Saturday." She gave Sean a hard stare and willed him to go along with her plan.

"I'll walk you to your car."

Sean's face closed and his body stiffened with the turn of events, but he took Mia's arm and forced her to look at him. "I expect a conversation on Saturday, Mia. And I'm not talking about the website. We'll deal with that at a later date."

Mia didn't know if there would be a later date for them.

She loved him, but she wouldn't keep him from a full relationship with a woman who could give him more children.

Chapter 26

Saturday started out rainy and overcast, but by the time she left for the ranch, the sun popped in and out of fluffy clouds with cool breezes.

Her heart in her mouth, she spotted Drew and Sean on the steps. Rusty ran to her, and she bent to give him a hug and a pat. His exuberance for her was a bright spot in a dismal future existence.

Tears that dampened her pillow that morning were for a terminal relationship. Never again would she feel Sean's lips on hers. Destined to be alone for the rest of her life, Mia accepted her fate with quiet and lonely dignity.

She gave a single nod to Sean and forced a wide smile for his son and lifted her camera. "Do you have your notebook with your ideas?" She hoped Sean wouldn't hang with them.

"I have a few sick horses in the barn, but I'll see you two later." Sean stepped away and Mia could see he warred over his worry for the horses and his longing to be with her and Drew.

Drew thrust the notebook in her face. The boy never glanced at his father. She marveled at Drew's excitement for photography. She didn't have that kind of liveliness when she was a child. Her passion for the art didn't come until later. Much later.

"You have quite a list here." Mia chuckled. "Let's sit on the porch and see what you have. We'll organize it a little."

"Why?"

"Because we can be more efficient if we organize first and we'll be able to take more pictures faster." When she saw he wanted shots of the lake, her stomach cramped. *How would she function near the water with a little boy who looked to her for direction?*

They prioritized the list, and she made the water shots the last thing on their list so she could work up her courage to be near the lake.

She wondered if Sean remembered her fear of water from their time at the cabin. "Did your dad see your list?"

Drew shook his head. "Can we get started?"

She wouldn't disappoint the darling little boy despite her fear. Mia took a deep breath. *Lord, I need your wisdom in this situation and your almighty strength.*

They took pictures for the rest of the afternoon. The barn, the corral, the trees, the farmhouse, Gingerbell, and other horses Drew loved. Rusty stayed at her side, but he never got in the way. Most of the time it was pleasant and Drew was a quick study for such a little guy. He asked intelligent questions, and she answered them as best she could for a boy his age. Her experience with her nieces gave her confidence she needed.

The lake glistened, and the trees swayed in the late afternoon's much cooler breezes and brought scents of the coming summer. Drew pulled her to the open area by the lake. Sweat pooled at Mia's back and her grip on the camera tightened.

Drew squinted at her hands and he stared at her face which she was sure had turned white. "Are you OK, Mia?"

Mia stumbled over her tongue but gave him the best

smile she could. "I'm fine."

She stared away from the water and allowed Drew to do all the shots. He handed her the camera and ran toward the dock. Her voice stalled in her throat and her heart beat faster as she watched him, as if in slow motion, as he ran on the slick dock. When he slid, she screamed his name as he plunged into the water at the far end of the dock.

Frozen, she watched him struggle to the surface. Rusty barked and pulled her out of her terror. "Rusty! Go get Sean!"

"I can't swim." Drew floundered as his arms and legs thrashed. And he disappeared under the water.

"Drew!" Mia screamed in panic. She dropped the camera and sprinted to the edge of the dock looking for bubbles. He'd drown if she didn't save him.

Her heart pounded as her fear rose from her feet to her brain and she dove in. She grabbed him by his shirt and pulled him to the surface spluttering lake water and resisting her help. He pulled them both under with his struggles. She pushed them both to the surface again and yelled in his ear. "Don't struggle. I have you. If you struggle, we'll both drown."

He quieted and held on to her.

"You can do this," she whispered in his ear. "Move your legs back and forth like little scissors and lay on my chest. I promise I won't let go or let you go under. It'll keep us both afloat and help me get you to shore."

When she looked back at the shore, she didn't realize how far out they had drifted when he struggled. *Lord, give me strength to get us to shore or send someone to help.* She pushed away her fear, tightened her hold around Drew's chest, and moved her body in the shore's direction. Indistinguishable voices at the water's edge pierced her ears and then a splash. She hoped whoever it was wouldn't upset Drew.

Sean dropped to his haunches and checked the horse's fore-leg. "It's a bad sprain. You know the drill."

"I'll have the foreman deal with it. Too many other—" Shannon stopped.

Sean turned to see Rusty barreling toward him at full speed, barking with everything he had.

Rusty jumped and pushed Sean so hard he fell. "What's wrong, boy?"

"He's upsetting Precious." Shannon calmed the horse. "What's his problem?"

When Rusty ran from him, then returned and barked louder than ever, Sean remembered the last time he'd been so vehement. "Something's wrong." When he stood and looked toward the lake, Sean caught a glint of splashing in the water. Mia. She struggled with something in the lake. Drew.

He grabbed Shannon's arm. "They're in the lake. Get blankets."

Rusty ran with Sean to the grassy edge of the lake. "Stay here, Rusty." Sean threw off his shoes and dove into the water, and moved with ease to Mia as fast as he could. How long had they been in the lake?

The tension left her body as he reached her and pulled her into his arms. "I have you."

Sean glanced at the shoreline and saw the grim look on his twin's face. Wendy clutched his arm. When he swam close enough to shore and his feet touched bottom, he whispered in her ear. "You can stand now."

She stood, still clutching Drew who turned in her arms, wrapped himself around her, and buried his head in her neck.

"Don't let go, Mia."

"I won't," she croaked.

Their calm acceptance and silence unnerved Sean.

He lifted both of them in his arms and dragged his feet through the shallow water to the shore where Wendy and Shannon pulled a reluctant Drew from Mia's arms and wrapped him in a towel. The boy shivered and sniffled. Sean set Mia on the grassy banks and wrapped her in a warm blanket.

"I'm fine." Her voice cracked. "See to Drew."

He nodded, lifted the boy in his arms, and struggled to remain calm. "You never told me you couldn't swim."

Wendy helped Mia stand, but her knees buckled and Wendy wrapped her arm around Mia's waist as they started for the house.

Emotion faded from Mia's voice. "Get the camera."

Shannon grabbed the camera, and he paced his steps with Mia and Wendy and opened the farmhouse's kitchen door.

The boy cried as Sean spoke soft words of encouragement in his ear.

Mia. She'd faced her incredible fear to save his son. It made him love her even more. She'd risked her life for Drew. He shook his head. "Let's get them some dry clothes."

Drew didn't relax his grip around Sean's neck and he was certain there'd be bruises in the morning. He set his son on a wooden chair and wrapped him in another dry towel.

Sean stepped into the dining room and called Drew's doctor while Shannon and Wendy settled Mia in the kitchen. The doctor promised he'd get there as fast as he could check on Drew and Mia.

Wendy ushered Mia to another chair and Drew threw himself into Mia's lap. "I'm sorry, Mia." The boy's voice choked. "I didn't know the dock was slippery." Mia's tears fell in hot torrents over her cheeks. She didn't speak, but hugged Drew and he returned the embrace with full force.

Sean stepped into the kitchen to catch a look of worry that passed over Shannon and Wendy's face. He was certain his own face had the same expression.

"Let me get those dry clothes," Wendy said to the silent room.

Sean remained frozen as he watched Mia and Drew hug one another. Shannon stepped over to move Drew from Mia's arms. She didn't seem to want to release the boy. "You need to get out of those wet clothes, buddy." With reluctance, Drew let Shannon move him, but before he did, he turned and kissed her on the cheek. "I love you, Mia."

Her quiet sobs filled the room. Much the same way she cried at the cabin. Sean kneeled beside her and took her frigid hands in his. He feared she'd get sick. He struggled to get her name out. "Lass." Her entire body shook. Shock had replaced the tears.

She squeezed her eyes shut and allowed him to carry her to the guest room down the hall.

Wendy caught them in the hallway, took in Mia's condition, and bolted into action. "We need to get her out of those wet clothes into something warm. You'd better check on Drew and get yourself changed."

Mia stared at the wall and her body continued to shake. He didn't want to leave her, but Wendy was right. With gentleness, he placed her on her feet and Wendy held her. He closed the door with a soft click and his sister-in-law's muffled voice came through the door.

He took the stairs two at a time, stopped by his room, and changed his clothes before he headed to his son's room.

Shannon had Drew out of the tub and into warm clothes by the time Sean made it to the room. "You'll be fine, son."

Backing away, Shannon allowed his twin to deal with his son. "I'll make tea."

"Where's Mia?" His son's voice was unnerving. "I almost drowned."

"But Mia saved you." Sean comforted his son. "We'll make sure you have swimming lessons—."

"I don't want to go near the lake anymore."

Sean knew it was more prudent to stay silent on the topic but he'd make sure Drew learned to swim before the summer was over.

"I want to see Mia." His eyelids drooped as Sean held him and he fell asleep.

Sean wasn't sure if it was wise for him to sleep after the trauma he'd had, but he couldn't let him upset Mia. He covered his son, kissed his brow and left the room.

By the time he reached the hallway to the guest room, Wendy sobbed in Shannon's arms.

Sean's heart dropped. "What happened?"

Wendy turned toward Sean, sorrow filled her face. "I've never seen anything like it. I dressed her in warm pajamas. Her quiet sobs undid me. She stopped sobbing and turned into a complete zombie. I talked, but she wouldn't look at me or answer. That's not our Mia."

Sean swallowed as visions of her when he rescued her surfaced in his brain. He reached for the door handle. "You left her alone?"

Wendy grabbed his arm. "She's asleep. I told her to lie on the bed and I'd get her a cup of hot tea. But when I turned, she was out, and I didn't want to wake her."

The doorbell rang and Drew's doctor listened to the

231

day's events. He checked both Drew and Mia. "Sleep is the best thing for them. It'll restore their body's ability to keep a good perspective on the trauma they've suffered."

"Should we wake them at some point?" Sean's voice cracked.

"They might sleep for a few hours or they could sleep until morning. However long their bodies need for restoration." The doctor shook Sean's hand. "Call me if you notice any strange behavior."

When the doctor left, Sean went to the kitchen and poured tea for himself. His nose twitched when he caught a whiff of the earthy lake water on his skin. No one spoke.

Wendy cupped the mug and appeared to be deep in thought. Sean worried more for Mia than Drew because of her past and her fear of water.

Through the dinette's bay window, Sean stared at the darkening shadows cast over the lake. He'd never asked Drew if he could swim. The boy had been more than happy to hang out in the barn with the horses. He'd never ventured near the lake. His lips pursed, and he vowed to make sure his son was trained to swim. What kind of a father was he that he didn't even know his son couldn't swim?

His thoughts scattered and moved from his son to Mia. He had never asked her about her fear of water. Never had a chance. He wished she would awaken so he could ask her.

Sean sipped his tea. "History repeated itself, today."

Shannon squinted at him, glanced at his wife and then at him. "What do you mean?'

Sean looked over at his twin. "What?"

Wendy touched his hand. "How did history repeat itself?"

"Mia sobbed the same way when she couldn't remember her name." Her sobs haunted him. "Did you know she's afraid of water?"

"And she jumped in and saved Drew from drowning," Wendy whispered.

Shannon turned a thoughtful gaze on his wife. "Explains her zombie-like state."

Sean took a deep breath and blurted. "I love her. Not just because she saved Drew, but because of who she is. Strong, beautiful, and feisty. I can't deny it any longer. I need her. Drew needs her."

The surprise on his twin's face sent heat to his cheeks. "I'll admit, I pushed my feelings away because of my fears and insecurities, but now it doesn't matter." He nodded toward the lake and gripped his mug. "She could have drowned out there today, and I wouldn't have told her." He downed the bitter tea and slammed the mug on the table. "No more."

Shannon played with the handle of his mug. "Are you going to tell her?"

"As soon as she wakes up." Determination set Sean's features. "She won't leave this house until she knows it."

Wendy stared into her cup. "And then what?" She raised sad eyes to his. "It's not enough to tell her you love her. Are you asking her to marry you?"

He frowned and his face went slack. "That's a given."

"If you only tell her you love her, she won't know." Wendy gripped the table. "She needs to know it's for the long haul."

Shannon peeled his wife's hand from the table and kissed her fingertips. "Are you speaking from experience?"

She touched his twin's cheeks. "You know I am."

Sean wanted what they had. A loving marriage. If Mia loved him half as much as he loved her, he'd be a happy man. He'd spend the rest of his life proving his love to her.

A strangled scream shattered the silence. Sean jumped out of the chair and raced to the guest room with Shannon and Wendy right behind him.

Mia was in a nightmare, but this time from today's trauma and not from a forgotten situation. Sean gathered her in his arms and cooed in her ear.

"Sean." Mia gulped air, but she struggled. She pulled at him and he nodded to his family to leave. The door's quiet click roused Mia.

She turned tear-filled eyes on him and he kissed her brow. "You're OK. I won't let anything happen to you."

He allowed her to sob while he rocked her in his arms.

When she had calmed, Sean took her hands in his and stared into her striking blue eyes. "I love you, Lass." At his declaration, Mia hid her face in her arms and cried. "It's not fair. You can't love me."

"Mia, honey, you're not making any sense. What's not fair? And I do love you. I fought it for so long, but today scared me." Sean tightened his hold on her and choked. "If something had happened to you today—"

"You don't understand. I'm not whole." Mia sobbed a loud, heart-wrenching sob so different from her sobbing earlier and in the past.

"What?" Sean pulled away from her. "I'm not getting it, Mia. Please explain."

"I can't have children, Sean, so I can't be involved with anyone. I've had tests done. That's why I pushed you away. I didn't get the results until yesterday."

Sean shook his head. "And yet you came to make a little boy happy despite your own pain. Doesn't matter, Lass. I want you, not your womb." Sean smiled and kissed her forehead. "I have a son. And we both love you so much and want you in our life. Permanently."

She turned wide eyes on him. "Are you saying—"

"I love you and I want you to be my wife. Drew is desperate for you to be his mother, but I've needed you since I left you at the hospital. I need you more than I can say."

"Pam told me you wouldn't care."

"She knew?"

Mia nodded and hugged him to her.

"Wise woman. I hope Brett doesn't mess it up."

"I don't think he will."

Sean gave a single nod and hugged Mia. "I promise I'll make you happy, Mia."

Mia sighed. "You already have." She turned in his arms and put her hands on his cheeks. "I've been in love with you since the first kiss at the cabin, but I fought it then because I didn't know who I was. And I fought it afterward because of this condition."

Sean toyed with her hair as he looked deep into her eyes. "If you want a child, Mia, we can adopt. I'm open to anything you want."

Mia kissed him until he couldn't breathe.

"You never told me why you're afraid of water."

"Oh, Sean, it has to do with what happened five years ago, and I promise I'll tell you everything you ever want to know about me, but I don't want to visit that and not enjoy this moment with you. And I'm going to get past it, I don't want to live with this fear.

He squeezed her tight. "Fair enough. We'll deal with it all as it comes. The important thing is, you overcame your fear today to save a little boy."

"And I'd do it again." She shivered. "I'm still afraid. But I know now it won't defeat me."

She settled into Sean's arms, but when her stomach grumbled, Sean chuckled. "Let's get you food and share the good news with my family.

Sean helped Mia to her feet. "Now will you go to church with me, Lass?"

Mia grinned and kissed him again with the promise of a beautiful life.

Chapter 27

Mia fussed with her hair and stared in the mirror at Pam and her sister-in-law Cassie as they rushed around the ranch's guest room. "Will you two stop? You're making me nervous."

Pam sighed and took Mia's dress off the bed. "I love a fall wedding. So romantic you wanted to be married on the same day Sean found you."

A soft smile graced Mia's lips. "We thought so." Pam crossed her arms. "Betty & Bertha want it to be perfect."

Cassie stopped mid-stride and cast a confused gaze at Pam. "Who's Betty & Bertha?

Both Pam and Mia burst into peals of laughter. "Tell her, Pam."

Pam had lost weight, but Betty & Bertha were still a prominent part of her anatomy. She turned around, gave a wiggle and pointed to her behind.

Cassie coughed. "You named your…"

Pam chuckled. "Yep."

"That's hilarious." Cassie shook her head.

Fiona knocked and opened the door. "You're not ready yet, Lass? Your man is pacing on the porch. Nervous as a hen with a fox prowling outside the door."

Mia frowned. *He's nervous? I'm not nervous.*

The three women helped Mia into the cream dress that hugged her subtle curves and fell with a graceful swish to mid-calf. Her something new. Mia adjusted Wendy's wedding hat on her head. Her something borrowed. Mia's engagement ring glistened in the mid-morning sunlight. Not a cloud marred the sky. Muted sounds of guests arriving came through the open window.

Mia had always wanted an outdoor wedding. It reminded her of her brother's first wedding. And although she hadn't liked Laura, the wedding had been enchanting, and she dreamed of something like it for herself. She could never have imagined the wonderful man or the beautiful wedding venue the Lord would have in store for her.

Her something old was her mother's delicate diamond earrings. Her brother had saved them for her and she cried when he had given them to her as an engagement present.

Fiona sniffed when Mia placed the earrings in her ears. "Your mother smiles in heaven. She prayed for her children's happiness."

Cassie handed her the bouquet and Mia drew it to her nose to inhale the fragrance. Her something blue was the various shades of blue pansies that were mixed among the cream roses of her bouquet.

She hugged Fiona. "We're both happy. Happier than we could have ever imagined. God has blessed our family despite every heartache. We have overcome and have been strengthened because of it."

Fiona pulled away, sniffed, and wiped her eyes. "Get on with you. Your man has probably run out of patience by now."

Cassie and Pam strode down the hallway. Wendy met them in the living room "It's time." She walked ahead of them out to the lawn which had been transformed into a beautiful chapel.

Mia took a deep breath and walked onto the porch decorated with potted fall flowers and white swaths of netting. Steve offered her his arm and winked at her. She gazed at the gazebo that had been built for the occasion. Her future husband stared at her with loving eyes.

She grinned and leaned into her brother. "We'd better hurry. Drew's necktie won't be there for long judging by the way he tugs at it."

Steve chuckled and escorted her over the wedding aisle runner to the gazebo where he handed her off to Sean. Her twin struggled with his emotion when he left her side.

Sean whispered in her ear. "You're stunning."

Mia blushed and turned to the pastor and they said their vows. When Sean gave her a tender kiss, her heart soared.

The rest of the day passed in a blur with everyone wishing them well. A small dance floor had been erected at the far end of the tent and a DJ played tunes for their guests. She had given Brett a crash course in photography the day before, and he served as the official photographer.

With Sean's hand in hers, they stepped off the dance floor. Becka and Robbie Marino, her sister-in-law Cassie's brother and sister-in-law walked toward them.

Robbie shook Sean's hands. "Thank you for inviting us to your wedding,"

Sean grinned. "No problem. We're practically related."

Becka stared at Sean then her breath whooshed. "I can't get over the feeling that I've met you, but that's crazy because I know we haven't met until today."

When Sean turned toward her, his eyes widened. "No. We've never met. But I look forward to getting to know both of you."

"And we will. But right now you have guests to see to. Thank you, again," Robbie said.

"I've met Becka before and I've never seen her look like that. Like she'd seen a ghost or something," she whispered.

Sean's face took on a thoughtful frown. "It was strange. I had an unusual feeling when we were introduced. I can't explain it." He shook his head. "I'll think on it later. I want to enjoy our wedding day." And he planted a kiss on her upturned face as they watched their family enjoy the day.

Drew played with her nieces and showed them Gingerbell, who Drew said had to stay in the corral so he could watch Sean and Mia get married.

Before they even had gotten married, Drew had called her Mama. And Mia grabbed every chance to hug and cuddle him. No longer did she fret over her inability to have children. She had a son who'd love her forever.

When the time came for Mia and Sean to leave the wedding, Drew hugged them tight. "I wish you weren't going away."

Sean squatted to his level. "We talked about this. Mia and I will return on Friday. Uncle Shannon and Aunt Wendy will take good care of you. And you'll be able to ride Gingerbell every day. Rusty will keep you company, too."

Drew pulled away and frowned. "You'll come back, won't you?"

His insecurity squeezed Mia's heart, and she hugged him tight. "Of course, we will."

She begged Sean with her eyes. *Maybe we shouldn't go to the cabin and just forgo our short honeymoon.* Sean gave her a slight shake of his head. She understood. He wanted alone time with his bride, but this wrenched her heart.

"You promise," Drew said.

"Absolutely. And when we return, the three of us will do something together."

Drew brightened. "Like go riding and take pictures?"

Mia and Sean laughed, ruffled his hair, and nodded. "Your two favorite things."

When they returned from their honeymoon, they settled into married life. They would live with Shannon and Wendy until their house was completed.

Sean slipped under the covers and embraced Mia. "I'm so glad we married before any of the interior decisions on the new house had to be made because now, we can make them together."

Mia peered at him and laughed. "Are you sure you want to travel that path?"

Confusion etched his features. "Why wouldn't I?"

"Because marriages go through rocky times when husbands and wives deal with house construction issues."

"I trust you, Mia. And above all, I trust God will see us through every aspect of our marriage, if we put Him first."

Mia snuggled deeper into his arms.

A month later, Mia's face paled when she lowered her phone to the table.

Sean jumped to her side. "What is it?"

"Steve's stopping over. He wants to talk to us."

"He didn't say what it was?"

Mia shook her head. "His secretary called." Worry pinched her face and her mid-morning snack had a gritty taste in her mouth.

Sean hugged her. "Don't jump to conclusions, Lass."

"In the middle of a weekday afternoon? Steve never came home at lunch time."

"Stop fretting. Doesn't have to be bad news."

When the bell rang an hour later, Sean whispered in her ear. "He's here."

They both went to the door to see Steve's smiling face.

"What's wrong with you two? You look like you lost your best friends." Steve gathered Mia into a hug, shook Sean's hand, and frowned. "Everything OK?"

"She was worried." Sean motioned Steve to the living room where the fire burned and gave off a pleasant woodsy scent.

Steve followed his brother-in-law. "Why?"

"Never mind. You're smiling so it can't be bad, right?"

Mia sat on the sofa with her hands clasped.

Mrs. O'Neill brought in a tray with coffee and cookies. When they had fixed their mugs and sipped the fragrant brew, Steve pulled an envelope from his pocket and handed it to Mia. "I wanted to give you this on your wedding day, but Cassie convinced me to wait until we could have a conversation about it and you returned and settled into your life here."

She placed the mug on the table. "What is it?"

Steve motioned to the envelope and smiled. "Open it."

Mia's eyes widened. "I can't accept this."

Sean looked over Mia's shoulder at the check in her hand, gasped, and shook his head.

"Cassie said you'd say that. It's yours, Mia." Steve stood and paced. "Mom and Dad put money away for both of our weddings from the time we were little. I didn't know until after they died. They kept my wedding money to give us a down payment on a home. After Laura died, I used my portion to make improvements on the house and put the pool in." He shoved his hands in his pockets.

"Why didn't you ever tell me?"

"You left for New York by the time I figured out what the money was for. When you came home, I was so busy trying to keep the business afloat it slipped my mind, then later, I thought it best to just let it accumulate so you'd have a nice nest egg to start married life. And now you're married, and it's time to give it to you."

"I know how much the both of you want to build an office that houses both of your respective businesses." He pointed to the check. "That'll go far to fulfill your dream. But to be honest, I don't know how a photography studio will work with a vet practice but that's your problem." Steve laughed and sipped his coffee.

"Sean?" Mia gazed at her husband.

"It's your money. I can't tell you what to do with it."

"But can we use it for the offices and get started on them while the house is being built? I'd love it if we could do this sooner rather than waiting years for it to happen."

"I couldn't agree more." Steve got up. "I need to return to work."

Mia hugged her twin. "Thank you."

"Don't thank me. Mom and Dad had foresight. They'd be pleased about how our lives turned out, despite our rocky beginnings. With God in our corner, how can we fail?"

Sean smiled. "We can't."

After Steve left, Mia wrapped her arms around Sean's neck. "I love that we can get started on the building. I have some design ideas, but we need to make sure we think of everything before we call in an architect."

"We'll pray for wisdom."

"Right." She looked up into her husband's warm eyes.

"And I love that you take things to the Lord for his guidance." Sean smiled and gave her a tender kiss. "And I'm thankful he answered my prayers with a wonderful woman like you."

The End.

FREE BONUS STORY FOR YOU!!

Interested in knowing what happens to Mia & Sean after the story ends? To read on about their happily ever after key in this URL into a browser. https://dl.bookfunnel.com/36c4m3pfrt

OTHER BOOKS BY SERALYNN LEWIS

Women of Worthy Series:
Cassie's Secrets – Book 1

Sneak peek of book 3 in the Women of Worthy series…

Kate's Quest

Kate Callahan's entire life had been one colossal lie.

Her head pounded as she pulled her car into the driveway of the magnificent bed & breakfast after passing through the small town's charming and quaint business district.

The change in climate from the icy cold in her hometown of Steamboat Springs, Colorado to the somewhat milder temperatures of Worthy, Ohio wreaked havoc on her sinuses even though spring hovered just around the corner.

She hoped the over-the-counter medicine she'd bought earlier would kick in and allow her to rest that afternoon, then she'd figure out what to do next.

The need to find a job surged to the top of her to-do list before she tackled the search for her biological mother. She rolled her neck and leaned into the headrest. Tiredness made her eyes blur. She needed closure. But she'd have to get out of her old SUV, check in, and get some much-needed sleep. First things first.

The drive had taken much longer than she'd expected. Her anxiety rocketed and she worried over more disappointment. She'd followed so many clues in the search for her mother the past year that giving up became a distinct possibility. The answer pointed to settling somewhere peaceful and new. Worthy seemed as good a place as any.

And bonus—no one knew her.

"Well, no one knows me… yet," she muttered to herself.

The letters she'd found after her mama died shocked her

and made her do the most irrational thing she'd ever done. She quit her job. Her colleagues and former boss called and stopped by her house at odd times. The fussing and worrying over her drove her crazy.

Even her long-time pastor had cautioned her that what she sought might cause more heartache than not knowing. He led her to scripture verses, prayed for her, and reminded her that her parents were there to kiss every scuffed knee and praise her every achievement in life. He showed her how much love her parents had had for her and told her how much God loved her in the here and now. In her heart, she knew he spoke truth.

But they lied to her. The abandonment and anger at her mama went bone deep. And where was God in her time of need? So, she fled her hometown and her friends. Away from everything she once held dear.

Now her quest to find her birth mother captured her thoughts. If the final clue lead nowhere, the pursuit for truth ended. She couldn't put herself through another failure.

She dragged her heavy bag behind her, climbed the four steps to the wide front porch, and entered through the beveled glass door. The foyer of the historic building enchanted her with its soft lighting and polished wood paneling. The pictures on the B&B's website drew her to stay there instead of a well-known chain in Columbus, and it lifted her spirits. The old-world elegance stunned her and the smell of fresh baked goods reminded her she had eaten nothing since early morning.

She stepped to the registration desk, rolled the bag next to her feet, and hit the buzzer. While she waited, she scanned the dining room to her right with its deep blue damask drapes and matching upholstered chairs.

She pressed the buzzer again and craned her neck to

the open doorway behind the counter, but no one appeared. Maybe she'd contact Amy, the owner, to get her key. With her phone in hand, ready to shoot off a text, a young guy in a flannel shirt and jeans strode through the front door.

He walked with purposeful steps to stand behind the counter. "Sorry. You must be Kate. Amy said to expect you. I'm her brother, Bryan."

She extended her hand. "Glad to meet you. Whew! I didn't know what to do. I've never stayed in a B&B."

Bryan pushed the registration book in her direction and smiled. "Well, we hope you enjoy your stay. Breakfast is between seven and nine every weekday morning with brunch on Saturday and Sunday from ten to noon."

"Will Amy be here in the morning?"

He took the register, placed his hands on the counter, and gave her a lopsided grin. "Of course. Amy comes in early to bake fresh muffins and scones. They melt in your mouth." He kissed his fingertips like a practiced French chef. "It's best to come to breakfast early because they go fast." He pointed to the dining room. "We meet in there and Amy serves tea in the living room at four p.m. during the week."

"Great."

He moved around the counter to reach for her bag. "I'll get your luggage."

"I can manage." She chuckled and held her hand out. "Just need the key."

He slapped his forehead with a theatrical flair and went behind the counter and rummaged through a drawer. "Here you go." He handed her an old-fashioned skeleton key.

She must have looked at it as if a snake slithered toward her, and she could tell he tried not to laugh.

"Yeah, Amy ordered new locks for the doors, but she loves

these old-fashioned keys. It's the one thing guests don't like."

"It's fine. Just surprised, that's all." She took the key and pocketed it.

She trudged up the stairs with her heavy bag in tow and wished she'd grabbed her smaller case, but she hadn't wanted to dig it out from under all her worldly possessions.

She opened the door and her mouth dropped open. The room shrieked history with its deep red Persian carpets and highly-polished wood floors. And if the antique canopy bed's fluffy white comforter engulfed her with its softness, she'd be asleep in no time.

The thumping in her head faded as she tugged off her shoes and climbed under the covers, not wanting to change, but just sleep. Then the terrible whirring noise next door started. Her eyes flew open. *What in the world?*

Her hunger and exhaustion made her cranky, and it didn't bode well for the person in the next room. She dragged herself out of bed and groused over discourteous guests, slipping her frigid feet into flats. The droning sound stopped just as she lifted her hand to pummel the door, then it started again.

She brought her palm up and smacked the hard wood several times until it opened and a rugged guy in army fatigues and boots came into view. "Do you mind?"

He lifted a single brow that made her breath whoosh out. Of all the nerve. He couldn't care less that he made a ruckus.

"Do I mind what?" His dark, chocolate-brown eyes brightened as he scanned her face.

Was he flirting with her? Annoyed, she waved her hand to the shared wall. "Stop whatever you're doing over there. I need to sleep."

He frowned and looked thoughtful. "No one was supposed to be here this afternoon." Opening the door wider, he pointed an electrical tool to the gaping hole in the wall where wires exploded in every direction and the smell of construction dust permeated the room.

"Can't whatever it is you're doing wait until tomorrow? I need to rest." She crossed her arms, scrunched her lips, and stood at her full height. At five foot, six inches, it disconcerted her he didn't tower over her even in her flats. Tall skiers and ranchers were the norm for her. *They must not grow them overly tall in Ohio.*

He seemed to take in her appearance from head to toe. "No, it can't. The owner needs this room ready for guests."

"I'm a guest and I need quiet."

"It's not that loud. Wear ear plugs," he said.

Her blood pressure rocketed. "Wear ear plugs? Are you kidding me?"

"I'm not kidding." His face had an aren't-you-being-a-little ridiculous look.

She lifted her chin. "I'll speak to the owner about the noise."

He narrowed his gaze and turned away. "You do that," he said over his shoulder.

She couldn't believe he'd dismissed her concerns and went back to work. Her anger got the best of her as she stomped down the stairs. The headache that had nearly disappeared now returned with a vengeance.

When she reached the bottom of the steps, she didn't know which way to go. At the top of the stairs, the army guy stood and held his drill aloft with that annoying grin again. But in her tiredness, it seemed more like a smirk and only incensed her.

She slammed her hand on the buzzer at the front desk and seethed. Her day kept getting better and better. Not. So much for a nice afternoon nap to bring her mind back in focus. Maybe small towns differed from resort towns. She didn't know. She'd only known her hometown.

Bryan appeared in the doorway with a smile. "What can I do for you, Kate?"

"I've been driving for hours and I have a headache." Even to her own ears, she sounded like a whiny child. "A guy in the room next to mine is making noise and I can't sleep."

His brow furrowed. "Oh. I didn't think you'd be sleeping this afternoon. I'll have him stop."

She gave him a tiny smile. "Thank you. That'd be great."

Bryan climbed the stairs behind her as she disappeared into her room. She hadn't made a fabulous first impression, and she didn't know how long she'd be here. Her nature gravitated toward kindness, not nastiness, but her anxiety over the search for her mother had taken its toll.

When she snuggled into the down comforter, a door slammed, and then blessed silence. Her eyelids drooped, and she fell into a deep sleep fractured with images of finding the letters that almost destroyed her.

James Woodford fumed and his upper arms tingled—a sure sign his PTSD had kicked in. He practiced the deep breathing techniques his counselor suggested, closed his eyes, and envisioned big puffy clouds drifting in the sky and imagined the smell of freshly cut grass. It helped in situations where it hadn't gone to full-blown anxiety. The first time in weeks he suffered a hint of it. Of all the arrogant…*forget it.* Thinking about the crabby guest next door only made it worse.

Bryan barged through the door and his chest heaved. "James, you can't work in here now." He stared at the hole in the wall.

"What do you mean?" His voice lowered and his speech slowed. A trick he learned as an army officer to make his men pay close attention. "Your sister wanted this job done quickly because her busy season starts next month. It'll take time to get the Wi-Fi installed in all the guest rooms."

Amy had begged him to finish that room today so Bryan could use the Wi-Fi for work and not have to use his hotspot. And now he had given in to the striking woman next door.

"I know, but Kate, the guest next door, needs to rest. And Amy will have my hide if she doesn't stay the full two weeks she booked."

Kate, huh? She looked like a Kate. All fiery, but soft. Thoughts like that got him into trouble.

He stared at the wall and breathed deep. "I'm sorry."

Bryan's face brightened. "The room at the other end of the hall is vacant and next on the list. Why don't you work there for the rest of the day and then finish in here tomorrow?"

"Leave it to a redhead to mess up a good day's work," he muttered. Probably an entitled rich girl, although her clothes didn't look it. He remembered her flashing gray eyes, but her attitude left a lot to be desired. The military taught him to scrutinize everyone and everything. "I told her to wear ear plugs."

He wouldn't even be in Worthy if his mother hadn't insisted his cousin needed his help at the diner. He could stay with her, help her at the diner, and look for work in Columbus. It's what he needed. A fresh start. But his cousin's trip out of town for a few days caused him to look for other accommodations. His army buddy told him about the B&B, so he bartered for a bed by wiring the rooms until his cousin returned.

Bryan blinked and his voice rose. "You did what?"

He shrugged and swatted the air. "She banged on the door and demanded I stop working. I offered a solution.

Simple as that."

"No wonder she was upset. Amy's going to go ballistic."

"Relax." He sighed. "It wasn't that loud. She overreacted. I'll talk to your sister."

"No way. I'll tell Amy."

"Maybe the woman was hung over. Who sleeps in the middle of the afternoon?" His lip curled as he fought the attraction.

"She said she'd been driving for hours,"

Bryan worked as a contractor for the military. They had a mutual friend who introduced them. With that connection, he felt comfortable having the conversation.

"Why are you defending her?"

"I'm not. Amy needs guests to keep this place afloat."

"I understand, but people who complain to get their own way frost me." He blew out a long breath. "I'll move to the other room, but I want to finish this room tomorrow." He had only a few days to get all the connections running before his cousin returned.

"Thanks, man." Bryan jabbed him in the arm. "I'll grab you a cup of coffee and bring you two of Amy's lemon scones you salivate over."

"Deal." He smiled and grabbed the tools he had laid on the floor in a precise manner and shoved them in his tool belt while Bryan swept the debris and dropped them into the construction bucket. A fine layer of dust covered everything, but the exposed wires caught James's eye.

"There's nothing we can do about the wires, since sleeping beauty needs her rest."

Bryan turned a watchful eye on him. "Wow. That cutie must have gotten on your one good nerve."

He ignored his new friend. The fiery redhead hadn't gotten on any nerve. The military trained him to complete tasks.

And it had been ingrained. "I'll finish this room tomorrow. That is, if the princess next door doesn't object."

He hoped his cousin returned soon because interacting with that spitfire wasn't on his agenda, even though he had a thing for redheads.

Kate's Quest will be available winter 2021

THANK YOU!

Thank you so much for reading Mia's Irishman. As a voracious reader myself, I know there are tons of books available for you to read so I'm honored you selected my book. I look forward to providing you with more reading pleasure as time goes by.

Building a relationship with you is the very best and most important thing about writing. I occasionally send newsletters with details on new releases, special offers and other bits of news relating to the Women of Worthy series or writing in general.

And I love to hear from readers…what and who they loved, what and who they didn't love…and why. Feel free to contact me at info@seralynnlewis.com or at my website at www.seralynnlewis. com. While you're there, take a peek at my blog *A Woman's Heart.*

If you have a book club or bible study, download the *free* book club and/or bible study questions located under *more* in the menu.

If you enjoyed Mia's Irishman, I hope you'll consider leaving a review on Amazon or Goodreads which would be helpful to me as an author. I would so appreciate it.

You can also find and connect with me on:
FACEBOOK, TWITTER, AND INSTAGRAM: SeralynnAuthor
PINTEREST: seralynnlewis | **LINKED IN:** seralynn-lewis

And, thank you for your support!

Seralynn Lewis
AUTHOR

Dear Reader...

Within the pages of this book, you read about the character's spiritual life. If you were wondering how you could have the same confidence, it's as easy as A-B-C.

Admit that you are a sinner: **Lord, I am a sinner.**
Romans 3:23 For all have sinned and come up short of the glory of God.

Believe that Jesus is Lord, died for your sins and rose from the dead: **Lord, in my heart I believe you died for my sins and rose from the dead.**
Romans 6:23 For the wages of sin is death, but the gift of God is eternal life through Jesus Christ.

Call upon His name: **Lord, come into my life and be the Lord of my life.**
Romans 10:13 For whoever calls upon the name of the Lord Jesus Chris will be saved.

Your salvation does not depend on your good works, or how good of a person you are. You are saved by grace and grace alone!

No one is guaranteed another day. Please don't wait. Follow the ABCs and call upon the name of Jesus today and be saved. And please, contact me at info@seralynnlewis.com so I can pray for you and welcome you into the family of God!

Many blessings,

 Seralynn Lewis

ABOUT THE AUTHOR

Seralynn Lewis was born and raised in a small historical town in northern Ohio. After having lived in various parts of the United States and for a short time in Germany, she and her husband have found their forever home in the Raleigh-Durham area of North Carolina.

She has two grown daughters, two lovely grandchildren, and a husband who supports everything she does no matter what it is.

But it wasn't always like that. A single mom for many years, she put herself through school, but couldn't find a job. Her brother's wife mentioned there were women who met to pray, and would she be interested? It couldn't hurt, and it might help. That meeting changed her life forever.

When the woman asked her, "Where will you spend eternity?" She didn't have an answer and really needed one. That's when her life changed.

In those days, romances were mostly sweet romances, but they got increasingly graphic. She stopped reading them because she felt they were a hindrance to my walk with Jesus and learning His word.

Fast forward almost nineteen years later, after many years of prayer, she met a man who loved Jesus and loved her. He is her biggest cheerleader and holds her heart in the palm of his hand. Together they know that without Jesus in their lives they cannot do anything. He is the glue that keeps them strong.

As she dialed back on her formal career, she had more time on her hands and went back to reading romances for pleasure. As she looked for books, there were wonderful inspirational romances that she enjoyed.

Considering those new romances, and the many scenes that floated around in her head, there was a yearning in her heart to share the truths she learned in her life's journey through romance. And that's where she is today. Writing sweet, inspirational romances.

When she's not writing, thinking about writing, or plotting her next novel, she's busy preparing a telephone Bible Study that's she's been doing for years. A long-time lover of romance novels, she would like nothing more than to sit on a deserted beach somewhere sipping iced tea and reading to her heart's content. She and her husband travel to visit family and friends in her hometown where she browses and delights in her favorite library.

Made in the USA
Las Vegas, NV
09 February 2022